THE POWER OF LOVE

THE POWER OF LOVE

. . .

Lori Foster
Erin McCarthy

Toni Blake · Dianne Castell
Karen Kelley · Rosemary Laurey
Janice Maynard · LuAnn McLane
Lucy Monroe · Patricia Sargeant
Kay Stockham · J. C. Wilder

BERKLEY SENSATION, NEW YORK

THE BERKLEY PUBLISHING GROUP
Published by the Penguin Group
Penguin Group (USA) Inc.
375 Hudson Street, New York, New York 10014, USA
Penguin Group (Canada), 90 Eglinton Avenue East, Suite 700, Toronto, Ontario M4P 2Y3, Canada
(a division of Pearson Penguin Canada Inc.)
Penguin Books Ltd., 80 Strand, London WC2R 0RL, England
Penguin Group Ireland, 25 St. Stephen's Green, Dublin 2, Ireland (a division of Penguin Books Ltd.)
Penguin Group (Australia), 250 Camberwell Road, Camberwell, Victoria 3124, Australia
(a division of Pearson Australia Group Pty. Ltd.)
Penguin Books India Pvt. Ltd., 11 Community Centre, Panchsheel Park, New Delhi—110 017, India
Penguin Group (NZ), 67 Apollo Drive, Rosedale, North Shore 0632, New Zealand
(a division of Pearson New Zealand Ltd.)
Penguin Books (South Africa) (Pty.) Ltd., 24 Sturdee Avenue, Rosebank, Johannesburg 2196,
South Africa

Penguin Books Ltd., Registered Offices: 80 Strand, London WC2R 0RL, England

PRINTING HISTORY
Berkley trade paperback edition / June 2008

Library of Congress Cataloging-in-Publication Data

The power of love / Lori Foster . . . [et al.].—1st ed.
    p.   cm.
  ISBN 978-0-425-22148-8
  1. Love stories, American.   2. Short stories, American—21st century.   3. Women—United
States—Fiction.   I. Foster, Lori, 1958–

  PS648.L6P69   2008
  813'.08508—dc22   2008003408

PRINTED IN THE UNITED STATES OF AMERICA

10   9   8   7   6   5   4   3   2   1

SWEET DREAMS

LORI FOSTER

·1·

CARA COMPTON WOKE FROM A DEEP SLEEP, BOLTING upright in her bed, her eyes wide in the dark room.

Holy smokes.

She ran her hands over her face and realized she was damp with sweat. And no wonder, given that vivid, purely sexual dream . . .

Appalled at herself, needing to dissipate the effects of the dream, she threw back the sheet and sat up to turn on a lamp. The June weather had turned stifling hot, and no air stirred in her room. Trying to obliterate the tingling in her stomach and on her skin, she strode to the window to open it wider. It slid up easily, letting in a warm, restless breeze, and . . .

Her heart froze in her throat.

Across the way, in the same apartment complex but in the building adjacent to hers, the object of her hotter-than-hot dream stood at his own window. A soft light limned his body.

Jamison Lawton. Bare-chested. His hair mussed. Knowing he looked right at her, Cara lifted a limp hand to wave.

He braced his arms on the window frame above his head and stood there. Seconds ticked by.

She felt his intense scrutiny.

Ha. Silently mocking herself, she shook her head. Jamison couldn't see her clearly enough for scrutiny, Cara assured herself. Not in the dark hours of the night. Not across such a distance. He could only see her outline, as she could see his. And being friends, he knew where she lived, so he knew which window was hers.

Suddenly he moved away and seconds later, her phone rang. The sound was so jarring in the silence of the night that she jumped and then dove on the bed to answer it.

"Hello?"

"You couldn't sleep either?"

His voice sounded deep and rich, and oh so sexy. Why had she never before thought of him in terms of sexy?

Because she'd been too busy carving her niche in the business world. Getting ahead. Forging her independence.

"No, I couldn't." She hadn't had time for men, not even an outstanding man like Jamison. "It's . . . hot."

"Too hot to sleep," he agreed.

"Yeah."

"Wanna take a swim?"

Take a . . . Cara looked around her room as if seeking the perfect reply. Nothing came to her. How could that be? She'd made her mark by knowing what to say and how to say it. She had one of the most successful advertising businesses in the area. She'd started from ground zero and built things her way, on her schedule.

And now her brain was totally blank.

"Cara?"

"It's late . . ."

"But neither of us is sleeping anyway. I figured you were awake because of your anniversary."

"My anniversary?"

"Five years since you started the Sweet Dreams advertising company, right? Tomorrow is the day."

"You remember that?"

A stretch of silence left her uneasy, until he said with a smile in his voice, "You'd be amazed what I remember, Cara."

What did *that* mean? She licked her dry lips. "You're good, Jamison. I had it marked on my calendar to help remind me." She sat comfortably in the bed, stretched out her legs and crossed her ankles. Not that she'd really needed a reminder. She had so many things she'd sworn to accomplish in that time frame.

"You've reached all your business goals and then some. You should be very proud of yourself."

"Thanks." So why did she feel so hollow tonight? Probably because she'd never thought of personal goals, and yet suddenly they were in the forefront of her brain.

With Jamison.

"Dreams woke me up," he continued. "And then I couldn't go back to sleep."

Her heart started tripping again. "Dreams?"

"X-rated stuff." His voice lowered and went gruff. "Sweaty stuff."

Sweaty!

"Explicit sexual stuff." He paused with significance. "Cara, are you wearing a blue T-shirt by any chance? Just that? Well, and panties." Another pause. "I assume you're wearing panties?" Curiosity added a purr to his tone.

Cara couldn't get out a single word, but that didn't stop Jamison.

"Since I've never slept with you . . ."

He let that hang just long enough to send her into palpitations.

". . . I can't be sure, but I assume you're not a naked sleeper."

"Are you?" She slapped a hand over her mouth. What was she saying?

"Yeah. I am."

She heard his amusement and recognized the provocation. And still she said, "Really?" New heat built inside her. "You sleep naked?"

"Really. And I'm willing to bet you're in a blue T-shirt."

Caught between confusion and excitement, Cara looked down at her oversize blue T-shirt. "You could see that all the way from your apartment window?"

"Of course I couldn't. I just . . . knew."

"How?"

"I'll tell you at the pool."

Looking toward the open window, Cara saw the endless black sky and the blanket of stars. She felt that stirring breeze and the thick humidity. In desperation, she asked, "Isn't the pool locked?"

"Doesn't matter. We can get over the fence. Bring a towel. I'll meet you by the gate in five minutes." He hung up, cutting off her opportunity for more hesitation.

Feeling wicked, uncertain, and anxious, Cara considered going. What could it hurt? She and Jamison were friends. They always had been. She'd met him in college and although he'd asked her out, she had other plans and he'd accepted that. Being three years older than her, he'd graduated first, but still, when time allowed, they'd hung out.

And talked.

And shared.

In most ways, he was her best friend. They had many things in common: keen business instincts, motivation, sense of humor. They liked the same movies and bands, the same type of ice cream, and they both adored being near or in the water.

They were very much alike—except that Jamison dated and she didn't. Somehow he'd managed to have it all—a growing business and an enviable social life.

But . . . he hadn't dated anyone lately. Like . . . in months.

Had a dry spell spurred his sexual dreams?

And how did he know what she wore?

Her advertising business was five years mature, thriving,

getting better by the day. Physically small enough for her to handle, but with an incredible forecast for continued financial growth. What would it hurt if she did something off-the-wall—like take a night swim with a gorgeous man whom she liked and respected?

She'd earned the right, hadn't she?

At this point, it couldn't interfere with any of her plans.

Her mind made up, Cara put the phone on the bed and bounded into her bathroom. One look in the mirror and she faltered. Summer humidity and damp dreams had left her short dark hair curlier than ever. Well, she'd just have to get to the pool before Jamison and dip into the water.

She brushed her teeth in record time, exchanged her T-shirt for a two-piece swimsuit, and slid her feet into flip-flops. Thoughts churning, she made no noise as she snuck out her apartment door and dashed down the stairs and outside.

Moon shadows followed her as she hurried along the grassy walkway and then across the blacktop lot to the locked swimming pool.

Tingling with anticipation, she put her hands on the chain-link fence and pondered how to scale the thing. A warm hand settled on her shoulder and she jerked around in startled surprise.

"Shhh."

So close that she breathed in the warm scent of his body, Jamison Lawton stood in front of her. She didn't have to see him clearly to know how he looked. Familiarity had burned his appearance into her mind: tall, dark, and sinfully handsome.

In a rough whisper, she said, "You got here fast."

"I've been waiting at least two minutes for you." His white teeth gave away his smile. "You smell good." He tousled her curly hair. "All sleepy and warm."

Cara stared up at him. She stared some more. Finally, she cleared her throat. "Thank you. I'm a mess though."

"Mmm. How come?"

She'd had her own charged dreams, but she said only, "I'm a restless sleeper, I guess." Turning away, she gestured at the fence. "How are we getting over this—hey!"

Jamison scooped her up and easily lifted her to the other side of the fence. He bounded over right behind her. "That's how." Taking her arm, he led her toward the water. "Let's keep it down so we don't get busted."

She wouldn't have yelped if he hadn't taken her by surprise. Again.

Without a word, he went to the pool and levered himself into the water, then held his arms up to her. "Come on." He took a slow breath. "It'll feel good. I promise."

Why did those words seem to have dual connotations? Was it just her, or did Jamison use the innuendo on purpose? It didn't really matter, because she wouldn't chicken out now.

It seemed very risqué to slip into his embrace, but then, this entire night seemed like an extension of her dream. When her body settled against his, he didn't release her, but instead pushed them both farther toward the center of the large pool. His legs brushed hers, and his hands held her waist.

She braced her hands on his hard shoulders. "Jamison?"

Voice hushed, he said, "Admit it. I was right."

"About what?"

"It feeling good."

Did he mean the water, or being together? She didn't dare ask. Not yet. "So how did you know I was wearing a blue T-shirt?"

"I didn't. Not for sure. But in my dream you were."

In his dream. Meaning *she* was in his dream?

Cara was adjusting to that when his hands moved from her waist, one going to her back, the other going to her nape.

"You were in that T-shirt, and we were sexually . . . involved."

She stiffened in surprise, but he tugged her closer and their bodies meshed from chests to knees. He could still stand, but she couldn't.

"In fact," he continued, "I was just about to take it off you when I woke up."

"But . . ." That was *her* dream. Had they awakened at the same time? "I don't understand this."

"You will. I promise."

It had been so long since she'd let anyone get this close to her. Her body was starving and her heart ached. She thought he'd kiss her and she wanted him to, but instead he urged her head to his shoulder.

"Cara? Are you wondering what brought on that dream?"

"Yes."

Gently, he rocked her from side to side. "I was in my bed, not quite ready to go to sleep, and I was thinking of you. Not sexual stuff." He smiled against her temple. "That came a few hours later, after I nodded off."

Disappointment stirred. So he hadn't been thinking of her in intimate ways. "What were you thinking?"

"All kinds of things. About us, our history together." He tipped her back. "Do you remember when I first met you?"

She'd never forget. "I'd taken a job at the bookstore on campus, and you came in to get some things."

"You worked at the pizza place off campus, too. From what I remember, you put in a lot of hours. That was your first excuse for not dating me. Between classes, work, and studying, you didn't have any spare time."

She shrugged. "I had to pay for the education somehow."

"I know." He released her and fell back to dunk himself in the cool water. When he emerged a second later, he came back to her. "School loans weren't part of your long-term plan."

"No. Paying back loans would have slowed me down when I wanted to get ahead as fast as I could."

"Mach speed." His smile came and went. "I remember. You were like a laser zeroed in on the big goal. That's part of what I was thinking about tonight."

"It bothered you? That I wouldn't date you, I mean?"

His laugh echoed over the water in the pool. "Of course it did. You wounded my ego."

"Yeah, right." Her smile came easily, as it always did with Jamison. "You didn't act wounded."

He took her hand and led her over to the pool ledge so they could both stand. "It wouldn't have been macho."

With his face turned up to look at the moon, Cara could study the strong lines of his straight nose, his rugged chin, his long dark lashes.

He turned toward her. "So I became your friend instead."

"I'm glad. You've been a very good friend."

"I hope so."

He went silent after that, leaving Cara unsettled. The water was so refreshing that she went to her back to float.

She couldn't see Jamison now, but she knew he was there, close by.

As he'd always been.

"Jamison?" He still stood at the ledge. "What else?"

"Hmm?"

"What else were you thinking about?"

His body cut through the water in a silent approach. Cupping the back of her head, he said, "Spread out your arms. Relax for a change."

She did. It was nice. And stirring.

"I thought about how hard you studied, your grade point average. How important it's always been to you to do your best."

"That was a long time ago."

"Five years. But remember that night we took a long walk after the rain? It was early May. Still kind of cool outside. You'd just gotten off work and I came by to walk you to your dorm."

Memories swelled inside her, making her throat tight. "We walked right past my dorm."

"Because we were talking."

She half laughed. "Because I was bitching."

"You were tired, and with good reason. I asked you why you pushed yourself so hard and you told me. At least some of it."

Cara turned and swam away. She didn't want to talk about her past. Not ever again. It was in the past, and there it'd stay.

Jamison caught her before she reached the steps. He turned her, and Cara expected . . . well, something other than a kiss. But that's what she got.

His mouth touched hers. Lightly. He breathed deeper. "Cara," he growled.

On impulse, she put her arms around his neck and deepened the kiss. It proved a revelation, the taste of him, the feel of him touching her, his scent and the warmth inside her.

How *right* it felt.

His tongue touched her lips, then licked into her mouth. He tilted his head, groaned, pulled her more tightly to him.

And then suddenly he was gone. She almost went under, but he brought her upright again.

"I'm not doing that, Cara."

"That? What?"

"Getting distracted."

She had no idea what he meant. "You didn't want to kiss me?"

His face came close to hers. "Damn right I want to kiss you. Everywhere. A hundred times."

"Oh." Sounded like a plan to her. At least, tonight, right now, in the dark and silence, it did.

"But I want to talk, too. It's been five years. Don't you think it's time?"

Confused, she shook her head. "Time for what?"

He stood there before her, tall and proud. Moonlight reflected off the water, off his shoulders and wet hair. Cara sensed his determination and his arousal.

And more.

Finally, he said, "For us."

·2·

"Us?"

"That's right. Me and you. Not just as friends, but as a couple."

That threw her for a loop. "But . . . you've never . . . I didn't think . . ."

"You made it clear that you had plans, and they couldn't include me. So I've been patient."

Temper brought her closer to him. Five years demonstrated more than mere patience. "You're saying you've carried a torch for me all this time?"

"Carried a torch?" He laughed at her. "No one talks like that, honey. I've wanted you from day one. I still do. I stayed out of the way of your plans. I encouraged you where I could. But it's been *five years*."

So he wanted her. He had other women if all he needed was sex. "Five years that you've been dating everything in a skirt."

"Ha! And that's a complaint? Jealousy? You never let on that you cared." His face was very close to hers. "I knew that you did, but I wanted you to know it, too."

Her eyes narrowed. "What do you mean, you know I did?"

"I'm not an idiot, Cara. And I know you almost as well, in some ways better, than you know yourself. You would have denied it until you convinced yourself it was true, but you feel the same about me."

"What makes you think so?"

"How many close friends do you have? Male or female?"

That stymied her. "I don't know."

"Let me help you. None."

An edgy panic strengthened her voice. "I have friends."

"Charlie the delivery guy? Karen, your personal secretary? Your accountant? Your financial advisor?"

"Yes!"

"How many times have you ever had dinner with them, other than to discuss business?"

She went silent. What could she say? They both knew she didn't do personal dinners.

Except with Jamison.

"When do you even see any of them other than for work?"

Feeling small and ridiculous, she shrugged. "I don't know."

His tone softened. "You see me. When you're happy about something, when you're pissed. When you're bored or tired or busy. You *always* make time for me."

Cara wrapped her arms around herself. Had she really

been so transparent? Apparently. And now he wanted to take advantage of her feelings.

But that wasn't like Jamison, not the Jamison she knew and . . . No. She wouldn't even think it.

"We spend more time together than most married people. That says it all, Cara, whether you want to admit it or not." Drawing her nearer, Jamison caressed her shoulders. "And I'm glad. I love being with you."

Hearing that "L" word set loose a million butterflies in her stomach.

Using the edge of his fist, he lifted her face. "Now I just want to be with you in other ways."

He wanted sex, she thought.

He said, "I want you to trust me enough to talk about anything. Everything. And that includes the past you're always burying."

Talk? "No."

He shook her lightly. "So your parents were shit. Not everyone is born into the perfect family."

Sex would be easier to deal with than a baring of her soul. "I said *no.*"

He held her there when she would have turned away. "Your folks were selfish hippies. Druggies. It's nothing to be ashamed of."

Cara rounded on him. "I hated them. And that is reason for shame."

"Honey." His voice, his attitude, softened. "You can't lie to me. Haven't you figured that out yet?"

Was she lying?

"If you hated them, you wouldn't have gone home and missed classes for two days when they needed you. I know better than most how serious you were about your grades. You needed to set yourself apart from them, and you've succeeded."

Feeling exposed, Cara whispered, "I'm sorry I ever said anything to you."

"I'm sorry you haven't said more." He released her and stepped back. "We share our dreams, Cara. And I'm not just talking our dreams for the future where we both want solid careers and a secure lifestyle."

Already she missed his touch.

"I've known you so well for so long. I know what you're thinking and why, when you're hurt and hiding it. I know when you're frustrated and when you're excited. And now, thanks to our dreams, I know how much you want me, too." He reached out a hand and cupped her face. "Knowing you so well, I guess it was bound to happen."

He couldn't be serious. "Jamison . . . that's not possible."

"Let's compare dreams." He moved closer, eased her against his body. His voice dropped as he said, "Right before I woke up, I was doing this." He settled his hand over her breast, gently cuddling her, seeking out her nipple with his thumb.

She closed her eyes at the deliciousness of it.

"You wore only that thin T-shirt and I could feel your nipple puckered tight, just as it is now." Still teasing her, he whispered, "Am I right so far?"

She nodded.

"I didn't stop there, though, did I, Cara?"

"No."

He left her breast and smoothed a hand over her waist, lower on her belly. Slowly, he insinuated his hand into the front of her bathing suit bottom.

Cara held her breath.

"It was just as I got a finger inside you . . ." He matched action to words, searching over her until he could slowly press his middle finger deep. ". . . Feeling you soft and wet and hot, and then . . ." He pulled away. "I woke up."

The suddenness of his retreat left her cold.

"And so did you."

Her heart pounded. "Yes."

"I could take you now," he whispered. "We both know it. We both want it."

"Yes." She did want him now, tonight.

"But I want more," he explained gently. "I want everything."

He wanted her to dig up the most painful parts of her life. Cara rubbed her head and hoped to reason with him. "Jamison, if there was anyone I'd tell, it'd be you. But it's not something that's pleasant to talk about."

"You've shared with me before."

That was so long ago. When she'd still been young and vulnerable. "That night we walked around the block . . . I was too upset to think straight."

"Too upset to keep up the barriers, you mean."

She lifted her chin. "Maybe."

"It's time to let down the barriers. It's time to let me in."

The very idea left her frightened. "I don't know."

"I'll help you to get started. You already told me that your mother overdosed."

Pain sliced into Cara. "She almost died."

Jamison drew her close and let her clutch at him. "Bad as that is, it wasn't the worst you'd ever seen, was it, honey?"

The disturbing memories flooded her brain, ready to be shared, instead of staying hidden. She made up her mind, and she wouldn't be a coward about it.

Cara straightened away from Jamison and looked up into his eyes. "I've seen them near death a dozen times. Dad died a few years back in a drug-related deal that went bad, and eventually drugs will kill my mother, too."

"And when you were young?"

"They used to shoot up in front of me. The older I got, the

more I had to hide from them and who they were, the things they did."

As if he already knew the answer, he said, "The people they brought around?"

She shrugged and it felt as if she'd shrugged off a very heavy burden. A lifelong tension eased away from her. "Last I heard, Mom had remarried and was attending a state treatment facility for substance abuse. But I don't see her anymore. And I'm glad."

Jamison considered that. "Tonight, I was thinking of you when you started your business. I kept wondering if you missed having your parents there to share in the accomplishment."

She was shaking her head before he'd finished. "No. I didn't want them there."

"Are you sure of that?"

"Positive." She went over to sit on the pool steps, half in the water, half out. "You come from a great home, so you can't understand how it was. I never liked my parents, and I never wanted to be around them. When I was, they embarrassed me. Or tried to use me. I was so afraid they'd taint my life, that somehow people would find out about them and assume the worst of me."

"That's understandable. I'm just surprised you never cut them completely out of your life."

"I wanted to, believe me. But before Dad died and Mom remarried, I felt a sense of responsibility toward them."

Jamison came to sit beside her. "That speaks more of the type person you are than of any natural way of things. A lot of people would have turned out just like them."

She couldn't believe that.

As if he'd read her mind, he said, "I'm afraid so. People either see the bad and emulate it, or they learn from it. It's easier to emulate, but you, Cara, never take the easy route."

He took her hand. "Unfortunately, in the process of making yourself such a wonderful person, you cut out everyone."

He made her sound cold and unapproachable. "I had more important things on my mind than parties or dating."

"More important things than me. I know."

Her heart twisted. Damn it. She'd been so unfair to him without even meaning to. "Jamison . . ."

A light came on and the apartment manager showed up in his robe and slippers. More than a little disgruntled, he demanded, "What are you two doing in there?"

·3·

WITHOUT MISSING A BEAT, JAMISON SAID, "WE'RE leaving right now," and only Cara heard the underlying laughter in his tone.

She couldn't look at the manager, but Jamison had no such problem. He hoisted himself out of the pool, then helped her out. "Where's your towel?"

"I forgot it." It suddenly dawned on her that in her haste to join him in the pool, she'd forgotten everything . . . including her key to get back into her own apartment.

One quick peek at the manager, and there was no way she'd ask him to let her in.

"Use mine." Jamison put his towel around her shoulders. After picking up his wallet and keys, he took her hand and walked with her over to the gate.

The manager grumbled, "I don't know how you got in there, but I didn't bring my keys."

"No problem." And again, Jamison lifted her over.

They left with a promise that they'd never transgress again and the manager was too tired to debate the issue. As they hurried across the grassy lawn, Jamison started snickering.

Cara poked him in the side. "You're a bad influence."

He swung her around in front of him and kissed her hard. "I can be a great influence if you'll give me half a chance."

"How?"

"Come to my apartment with me?"

A perfect opening. "Well . . ." She touched his chest, smoothing her fingers through the damp hair there. "The thing is, I forgot my apartment key anyway. I was going to ask if you'd mind putting up with me till morning."

An expectant pause thrummed in the air. "You were in a hurry to join me tonight?"

"Lying wouldn't do me any good, would it?"

"No." His hands held her face up to him. He put his forehead to hers. Voice rough and deep, he said, "But I'd love to hear it anyway."

"I was very anxious to see you."

His breath sucked in. He kissed her hard again, then took her hand and hurried her along the way to his apartment. Feeling lighthearted and free, Cara laughed as they practically ran over the lush grass and then the warmed blacktop, through the front door and up the stairs.

Jamison cursed as he fumbled with his keys, and finally the door swung open. He stepped back for her to enter, and in the next second the door closed and he was against her, kissing her, touching her. "I want to finish that dream, Cara."

She did, too. Even if she'd only have a brief sexual relationship with Jamison, she wanted it. "Me, too."

Breathing hard, he forced himself to step back and take her hand again. "Come on." He led her down the hall to his bedroom and flipped on a low light. "Let's get out of these wet suits."

Because this was all so new to her, Cara knew she should have been embarrassed. But instead, she was anxious. She removed her top with no help from Jamison, but paused when he turned to her, fully naked, and put his thumbs in her bikini bottoms.

"You're beautiful."

"Not really, but okay."

He laughed. "Trust me, I think you're gorgeous, inside and out." The bottoms went down her legs and he took only a few seconds to look at her with heated appreciation before urging her to the bed. "Will you take my word for it that I'm usually good in the sack, but tonight my control is shot?"

Cool sheets touched her back, and Jamison's warm weight settled on her front. "You're good at everything you do. I know that."

He groaned. "You're forcing me to muster up some finesse so I can be worthy of your faith." His smile tickled as he kissed her, but in no time at all, they were both too busy touching each other to talk, or to smile.

His damp mouth moved over her throat, her shoulder, and settled on her breast. Cara held her breath, waiting, and then he gently sucked at her nipple.

She sank her fingers into his hair. "Jamison?"

"Hmmm?"

"Enough finesse already. I've been waiting five years."

That was all the encouragement he needed. Watching her face, he pressed a hand between her legs and touched her, making her more than ready, almost frantic. His fingers moved in her, over her. When she started trembling he rolled on a condom, settled between her legs, and entered her with determination and great care.

"Perfect," he whispered harshly.

Cara couldn't reply. He filled her, not just her body, but her mind and her soul. Putting one hand beneath her bottom, he tilted her up and thrust even deeper, setting a rhythm that was both maddening and acutely pleasurable.

When Cara felt the first tremors of release, she whispered his name, and Jamison let himself go.

Her heartbeat still thundering, Cara held on as Jamison started to move away from her. Everywhere, all over, she tingled with residual pleasure. "Wait."

He settled back, and the weight of his body was so comforting. Smoothing his hand over her damp, tangled hair, he asked, "What is it, honey?"

She was pathetically awkward at after-sex chitchat, and she knew it. "I know asking for promises right after sex is probably taboo—"

"You can ask me anything."

She gave a small nod. "Will you please promise me that . . . even though we've had sex and everything . . . we'll always be friends?" The idea of possibly losing him brought tears to her eyes and clogged her throat. "I don't think I could keep up with my goals, or my life, without you."

Jamison stayed very still, saying nothing, not even moving. Cara's heart broke, especially when he sat up away from her and turned on a light.

Feeling horribly exposed, she tried to curl to her side, but he caught her shoulder and kept her flat on her back in the bed. Naked, vulnerable.

"I think you've misunderstood, honey."

Oh God. "I'm sorry."

The corners of his mouth tilted in a small smile. His thumbs brushed the tears from her temples. "Cara, you love me."

"I really do," she agreed. How would she go on without him if sex ruined it all, if it made their friendship awkward?

His smile became ironic. "Not just as a friend, Cara, though I cherish our friendship. You *love* me." He leaned closer. "As a man." He kissed her. "As your partner."

Her eyes widened. She knew it was true, but she didn't know what to do about it.

Until he said, "And I love you, too."

Her breath left her. "You do?"

His laughter made her smile. "What did you think was going on? That I just wanted a fling?" He waggled her head and kissed her again. "Woman, I love you. I always have. I've waited for you for five long years. I've shown the patience of a saint. I've kept my hands, and my feelings, to myself, because you're more than worth waiting for. But I figured now that even our dreams are meshing, it's past time to—"

Cara pushed him to his back and kissed him silly. "Jamison, I love you. I do."

"Thank God."

Because she was an organized woman who needed things in order, she said, "Marry me?"

He laughed again. "That was my question, but yes." He held her back. "On one condition."

"What?"

"That you don't make our wedding a long-term goal. No way in hell can I wait another five years. Not even one year."

It was the sweetest dream ever, coming true. Cara softened. "I don't want to wait five days."

He turned to put her back beneath him. "You see. We agree on everything."

Cara laughed as he tried to kiss her, and more. Marrying Jamison hadn't been the goal, but it'd be her most wonderful accomplishment ever.

UNPREDICTABLE

Erin McCarthy

ANNAH SAW IT COMING. A MAN DRENCHED IN sweat wearing a knit cap came barreling toward her and she sidestepped him, reaching out her hand to catch the purse she knew he would drop.

What she didn't anticipate was the police dog.

Until she was pinned against the wall being held hostage by yellowed fangs and a vicious snarl.

"Good doggie. You're not going to bite me or drool on my rayon skirt, are you?" Clutching the purse, she tried not to move, annoyed that yet again her mild psychic ability had provided her with thoroughly useless information—like when to catch the purse—but failed to warn her she was the next episode of *When Animals Attack*.

"I didn't steal the purse," she pleaded with Lieutenant Lease, who growled again, showing no sign of easing up. "This has all been a mistake, really. Haven't you ever found yourself in a situation and thought, 'how did I get here?'"

"He can't understand you, you know."

Hannah looked past the toffee-colored fur into the amused eyes of one very good looking cop, uniform straining across his broad chest.

"Recall, Ralph."

The dog sat down and his tongue lolled out.

Hannah's bladder relaxed. "His name is Ralph?" Then she knew the answer before he spoke. "Oh, you named him after your old sergeant?"

The cop tilted his head a little and frowned at her. "How'd you know?"

Because she'd been born a genetic freak, who on an annoying and random basis heard people's thoughts before they spoke them.

"Lucky guess." She thought to elaborate, but instead found herself rendered speechless when her eyes drifted down the muscular length of the police officer. Hello. Cincinnati's finest was just that.

Then Ralph stuck his head in her crotch and barked, vibrating her thighs and whining like he'd struck gold.

Hannah backed into the wall of the storefront and yelled, "Recall, Ralph." Instinctively she locked her knees together to trap his head and prevent him from going deep.

The cop bit his lip, but not before a snort of laughter flew out first. "Jesus, I'm sorry."

The apology was nice, the chortle she could have done without. She fought the urge to assure him that she had showered that morning. "Just get him off of me."

He touched Ralph and gave him a hand signal, but Ralph wasn't backing off. "He wants the purse," the cop explained, running a finger over the leather bag she was clutching between her hips like a bull's-eye. "It's his target and he feels like he's failed if he doesn't return to me with it."

Without hesitation, she dropped the purse onto the sidewalk. "Go for it, Ralph. I don't want you to feel like a failure." She felt that about herself often enough, no need to project onto a German shepherd. Of course, the dog had a job, which was more than she could claim.

The morning's interview at the library hadn't gone well. She'd flunked the typing test, but had known the minute she'd met the librarian in charge of hiring that her future didn't lie among the stacks. The woman had instantly hated her because she was a blonde, and *That bitch whore Ron had run off with was blonde.* Sometimes it was a curse to hear other people's thoughts. Actually, make that all the time.

While Ralph retrieved the purse, his owner smiled at her. "Thanks. I'm . . ."

"Luke. Luke Warner. Nice to meet you. I'm Hannah." Hannah who had spoken too soon. "Hannah Godwin."

Luke tilted his head. "Did I tell you my name already?"

"Probably." Hannah was confusing herself, there was no way she could expect him to keep up. With gorgeous Luke standing a foot in front of her, distracting her with that fabulous bod, not only was she confused, she was starting to sweat a little under her rayon skirt.

Then without thought, she ran her fingers through Ralph's thick fur and gave him a hand signal. Luke looked at her in shock. Ralph backed up and whined.

Hannah said, "Um . . ."

"How . . . ?"

"Did I do that? I don't know."

"Because . . ."

"No one knows those signals but handlers? I know."

"And how . . . ?"

"Can I keep finishing your sentences?" Hannah tugged her blouse forward to get some air down there, and tossed back her hair, which was corkscrewing in the humidity. "I can do that because I'm just a little bit, well, psychic. Just a little."

Luke took a page from Ralph's book and backed up a step. "But that's . . ."

"Impossible? I know, but there it is." She'd return it if she could, but nobody had asked her. It could be worse, she supposed. She could have a big nose. But at least people with big noses had careers. Unlike her, who was going back to college for her third bachelor's degree in I Don't Know What The Hell To Do With Myself.

"Stop . . ."

"Saying what you're going to say?" She clapped her hand over her mouth. "I'll try, but when I get nervous it just happens."

Luke frowned. "So you know what I'm thinking? And what's going to happen next? Can you control my thoughts?"

Yeah, right. She wished. That would make her alleged gift actually *useful*. "No, of course not. And I don't know what you're thinking, not really, things just pop into my head. Like I knew that guy was going to run by and drop the purse he stole, so I caught it."

Beyond that, she could honestly say she didn't know a thing.

Luke thought the woman in front of him, blinking her wide blue eyes, was too cute to be a psychic. He had no opinion one way or the other on that see-all crap, but he had always pictured psychics as old women with strawlike gray hair, gnarled hands, and thick glasses. Definitely not bouncy and blonde like Hannah.

But she had known what he was thinking every time. It was weird as hell the way she'd said his own thoughts before he'd even spoken them, but maybe it was just good people skills, that's all. She was perceptive, a good guesser. Used her gut instincts, just like a cop did.

Yet he still found himself wondering if she knew exactly what was going through his head, which was that her shirt looked really damn good stuck to her in the July heat. That he thought she had nice breasts. Full breasts.

And what the hell was he doing thinking any of that when he was on duty and a purse snatcher was escaping down the street? Luke glanced down Vine Street. Escaping? Make that long gone. Damn.

"At least you got the purse back before he stole anything

out of it." Hannah gestured to the bag he'd taken from Ralph.

Annoyed that he'd been so easily distracted, he raised an eyebrow. "Your psychic ability tell you that, too?"

Her nose wrinkled. "No. But he obviously grabbed it and ran with it, so there couldn't have been time to dig through it. And it was heavy, so her wallet's probably still in it. It was just common sense."

Common sense. Funny, he seemed to have lost his. He could have caught that thief in less than half a block if he hadn't been going ga-ga over Hannah, the little bit psychic, with the cute curls and wide smile. Not to mention the throaty voice that brought to mind whispering in the dark. And he still didn't want to leave.

"Well, thanks for your help, Hannah." Luke took a small, might-as-well-not-have-moved step backward, dredging through his mind for a reason to extend the conversation. It wasn't every day a good-looking woman got pinned by Ralph, and Luke's social life had been sketchy at best since his ex-girlfriend had given up on him nine months earlier.

He didn't regret their breakup, since he had been straight with her from the start that he worked strange hours, and that his dog was with him twenty-four/seven. But nine months was a long time and he had the hard-on to prove it.

"Glad I could help." Hannah tucked a wayward curl behind her ear and moistened her plump bottom lip with the tip of her tongue.

Damn. No way could he let her walk away. Hannah was the kind of woman who just reeked of femininity. Everything about her was soft and pretty, her hair free and flowing, her clothes floral and silky. Luke had never dated women like Hannah because they were the mothering type who liked to pack his lunch and wash his shirts, and his own mother had forever cured him of wanting to be taken care of.

He'd always gone out with strong, independent career women. But there was something about Hannah, a sensitivity, her acute sense of awareness, that had him very interested in appreciating all her feminine softness.

To prolong the conversation, he said, "We had a psychic come in to the station once to work on a child abduction case. You ever do anything like that?" Luke had thought the woman was strange, but she had directed the detectives straight to the body, and he had learned a long time ago there were some things in life that were unexplainable.

Her expression fell. "No. No, I can't do anything useful with it. Like I said, I'm just a little bit psychic. It's lame."

Now what the hell was he supposed to say? He'd obviously made her uncomfortable. He commanded his eyes not to drop to her chest as he searched for reassuring words. "I'm sure you could be useful."

Oh, hell, that sounded suggestive.

But she smiled back and he felt another stirring below the belt that was not Ralph rubbing against him. Jesus, he had to be careful. He had the funniest feeling he could fall for Hannah, despite the mind-reading thing she had going on.

"I know what you mean." Hannah leaned forward. "I could fall for . . ."

While Luke tried to retrieve his gut from his mouth, Hannah said, "Walk, Ralph."

She and his dog started off down the sidewalk.

Luke followed. "Do you think . . . ?"

Hannah glanced over her shoulder. "Yes."

Whoa. Hold on. "Yes, what?" Luke scrambled after her, completely unnerved by the sight of her leading his dog off. His trained dog, who wasn't supposed to respond to anyone but him. His dog, who knew commands in English and German, and had just reacted to the German hand signal given by Hannah, who couldn't possibly know that unless she was . . .

Shit. She might think her ability was lame, but it was blowing his mind.

"Yes, the woman who owns this purse is inside that record store right there."

Oh, right. His job as a cop, he remembered that. "How do you know?"

He maneuvered between her and Ralph and clamped Ralph's leash on his collar. Just so she was clear on whose dog this was. His dog. His leash.

Hannah's eyebrows rose under her tumbling bangs. "I just know."

Luke exchanged a look with Ralph as Hannah pulled open the door to the record store and strolled in. The floral skirt she was wearing swirled around her ankles and clung to her backside.

"She's really damn cute," he murmured to Ralph.

His dog gave a bark of agreement before licking his black nose.

"Obviously you agree since you just walked off with her like you'd never seen me before in your life." He gave Ralph a stern look of reprimand.

Ralph didn't look at all worried about his gaffe.

He and Ralph followed Hannah into the store and were immediately rushed by a fresh-faced woman in her early twenties.

"My purse! You brought it back. Oh, geez, thank you. I just cashed my check and have all that money in my wallet. I thought it was gone for good."

Putting Hannah out of his head, or trying to anyway, Luke forced himself to deal with the task at hand. It took less than ten minutes to wrap things up, during which Hannah hadn't left the record store. She was picking through a row of classic rock CDs. Damn, she had the Doors in her hand and was studying the Rolling Stones. Her being gorgeous first, and having good taste in music second, was not helping him stay rational.

Though rational was overrated when he just wanted to lift those curls off the back of her neck and kiss her warm skin.

Hannah turned and clutched the CD to her chest. "Don't."

"Don't what?" He stopped in front of her and commanded Ralph to sit.

"Kiss me."

The warm blood that had been pumping through him, heading south at a rapid rate, iced over. "What makes you think I was going to kiss you?" Even if he had been thinking it, he hadn't planned on doing it.

"You were. Don't deny it." She tapped the back of her neck. "Right here."

Damn. Good thing he hadn't asked her out when the urge had struck him. Who the hell was crazy enough to date a woman who knew what he was thinking?

Not Luke.

Neither confirming nor denying, he said, "I just came over to say thanks for your help. We didn't catch the guy, but that girl is happy to have her money back."

Hannah lowered the CD, pursed her lips. "You're welcome."

Luke took one last long look at her, kind of sorry that he hadn't asked her out. He would have liked to have seen what she was hiding under that blouse and flowing skirt. And she seemed very sweet, very sincere . . .

"Hannah?"

"Yes?" Her fingers trailed absently over Ralph's fur, and his dog, who wasn't supposed to respond to anyone but him, who was a working dog and not allowed to enjoy petting, just about rolled his black eyes back in his furry head in ecstasy at her touch.

Luke pictured himself doing the same thing.

"Are you sure you aren't more psychic than you think you are?"

She cocked her head and smiled a little. "I'm positive."

"Do you want to go out for a drink sometime?" It was out of his mouth before he could question the wisdom of it.

But Hannah shook her head. "Thanks, that's very flattering, but I'm not dating right now."

What the hell did that mean? "Anyone?"

"Anyone."

He hoped she could read his mind and hear his loud and clear disappointment.

"I can hear it. And thank you for that." She smiled again and walked out of the store.

Luke glanced down at Ralph. "What the hell just happened?"

·2·

"IF YOU WEREN'T MY SISTER, I'D HATE YOU." HANNAH licked raisin cookie dough off of a spoon and watched her sister, Julie.

"That's really flattering, Hannah." Julie started expertly transferring cookies from the sheet to the cooling rack.

"Well, I can't help it." Hannah fished a raisin out of the bowl of dough and chewed it. "I'm jealous of you. You have this perfect, absolutely wonderful life, with your fabulous husband, your great house, your stellar career, and your precious children."

Her six-year-old niece screamed from the other room. "Get off of me, Bryce!"

"Precious, that's them." Julie glanced toward the family room ruefully.

"Okay, so every moment of your life isn't perfect, but pretty darn close." It was exactly the life Hannah wanted, but she was missing a few pieces to make it complete. Like all of them. No job, no husband, no house, no children.

"You're feeling sorry for yourself, Hannah Banana." Julie shook her spatula at her.

"So? I'm entitled. I bombed the library interview today." Hannah gave up on the spoon and just stuck her finger right into the dough and pulled out a baseball-size glob. She bit a piece off of it. "The whole guy thing and the kids, if that doesn't happen for me, I'm okay with that. There are definitely pluses to being on my own, not having to be responsible for anyone but myself, and I freak men out. I understand that. I accept it."

But Officer Luke had certainly been cute.

"What really happened with Robert? You're obviously really hurting and I wish you'd talk about it."

Hannah grimaced and dropped her dough ball. "Well, let's just say it sort of kills the mood when you're in bed with your boyfriend, getting ready to have an orgasm, and you hear him thinking about what a complete and total freak you are, but that at least you're a good lay."

Julie's mouth fell open and her pin-straight blond hair slid over her face. "No!"

"Oh, yes." Needless to stay, the orgasm had eluded her. "I'm telling you, I'm cursed. Absolutely and completely cursed."

Hannah swore she could smell Julie's pity over the fresh-baked cookies. "Oh, Hannah, it can't be that bad. You have your health."

It was such an old lady thing to say that Hannah burst out laughing. "Okay, I'm not completely jealous of you. You're such a dork sometimes. But it's still not fair that I got this pseudo-psychic thing and you didn't. Not to mention that you got the straight hair and I got this mop. Where's the genetic justice in that?"

"But you get to just stand there and eat dough while I bust my behind making six dozen cookies for my daughter's day camp bake sale."

"Well, you have a point." Hannah wiped her sticky fingers on a dish towel featuring a rooster. "But I just wish I could figure out what to do with myself. I'm twenty-six, Julie, and I want a career. I want to be successful, make a difference. Yet I bomb out at everything I try, and nine times out of ten it's because I weird people out with my cursed sixth sense. While it hurt, Robert was right—I am a freak. And I can't ever keep my mouth shut or be discreet about it. I have the social skills of a baboon."

"Actually, baboons have a highly developed social structure."

Hannah rolled her eyes. "Is that before or after they eat their own vomit?"

Julie grimaced. "Don't be disgusting. Grown women shouldn't bring up vomit in a conversation."

"See? No social skills." Even her own sister thought she was gross. That didn't bode well for her future.

"I didn't mean it like that. And maybe there's a field where your ability would actually come in handy. Like the medical field, or maybe law enforcement."

"Funny you should mention law enforcement." Hannah told Julie what had happened with Luke and Ralph that afternoon, editing out the excavating the police dog had done in her floral skirt.

She expected more pity. But Julie actually looked excited, strange woman. "That's it—you should join the police force! You would have great instincts."

Hannah almost laughed but could only manage incredulous. "Are you joking? Would you really trust me with a firearm? And I couldn't run a lap around this kitchen, let alone pass some kind of cop boot camp." Just the thought made her lungs strain and her side cramp. "I understand it's very competitive to join the force, and all the equal-opportunity laws in the world couldn't get me hired."

No matter that for a split second that afternoon, when Luke had asked if she had ever done police consulting, she had been intrigued. Hannah found the idea of solving crimes very appealing. Not that she had any burning desire to pick up a killer's thoughts, but it would be very satisfying to be a factor in convicting a brutal criminal.

Except that she couldn't. Plain and simple.

"As for being a police psychic, you know as well as I do it doesn't work that way. I can't turn it on and off. Sometimes I hear things and sometimes I don't." If Hannah actually had control of it, she wouldn't be whining. She'd be married to Brad Pitt.

"What am I thinking now?" Julie stared hard at her.

"Julie." Hannah rolled her eyes back in her head with vehemence. They had tried this about a million times when they were young and it was apparent Hannah was a little different from other kids. A lot different. "It won't work."

"So what was unusual today? How could you know everything that guy was thinking?" Julie grinned. "Maybe he's your soul mate."

"I don't think that would make sense . . . it seems like I should know everyone else's thoughts *but* my soul mate's." And Luke was good looking, but she wasn't willing to leap ahead to mind-meld stage.

"Maybe your ability is growing. Maybe age is allowing you to harness it."

"You mean aging could actually have a positive outcome? That's a happy thought." And if she could actually learn to control her irritating and random verbal vomiting, and do something useful with her sixth sense, she really wanted to find out.

It was the need to be useful in some capacity that had her sitting in front of one Sergeant Kelso two days later, trying to convince him that she could be of assistance to him in solving otherwise unsolvable crimes.

It wasn't working.

It didn't take a mind reader to see that Sergeant Kelso thought she was a few bananas short of a bunch. His eyebrow had shot up so high it threatened to slip over the backside of his head.

"We don't usually take on outside consultants, especially since we're under a budget crunch," he said with more diplomacy than Hannah would have given him credit for considering the frown on his face. He was middle age, with short graying hair and a fine-looking physique behind the uniform. No beer gut on this guy.

It wasn't shocking that he didn't believe she could help, given that she didn't really believe it herself. She needed to work on her confidence. She was never going to get anywhere in life—personal or career—if she didn't accept and embrace who she was and try to push forward.

That was what had brought her to the station. She wanted to own her future and stop feeling sorry for herself.

"I don't want any money or anything. I'm volunteering." Of course, maybe she could join the circus or a carnival as Hannah the Dame of Destiny, instead of squirming in front of Sergeant "You're on crack" Kelso.

"Have you worked with any other PDs? Solved any cases? Missing kids, maybe?" Kelso leaned back in his chair and watched her politely. *Another nut job.*

Hannah stopped wiggling like a toddler and straightened

her shoulders. "I'm not a nut job. I'm trying to help." She may be different, but psychics are people, too.

Kelso looked instantly alarmed. "Did I say that out loud?"

"No." Hannah shot him a smug look. "I heard you say it in your head." Which was damn satisfying.

He gave her a cop stare, the one that suggested if there had to be a winner and a loser, he planned to be the winner. "No way. That was a lucky guess."

While she hated the unreliability of her mind reading, it was never a guess. She always knew, and there was no way she was backing down now. "Was not."

"Alright, so what am I thinking now? Snow . . ."

He was quizzing her? Bring it on. "Bunny."

"Apple . . ."

"Strudel."

"Hair . . ."

"Net."

"Mud . . ."

"Hens." Hannah wrinkled her nose. "What's a mud hen?"

But Kelso had blanched, shoving his chair back several inches like she had a contagious skin rash. "That's incredible. Bizarre."

"True. But potentially helpful?" she asked, crossing her fingers behind the desk. "Luke Warner can vouch for me. I helped him recover stolen property two days ago."

"Really? I don't think he mentioned that."

Whoops. Hannah also thought maybe he'd never told her his last name. But he had asked her out, and she almost regretted saying no.

Given that her social skills had never been all that great, Hannah's dating experience had been sporadic, and consisted almost entirely of men wearing glasses who had smaller waist sizes than she did, which had made Robert's freak comment sting all the more. She may be a freak, but he was a geek. So while she had no intention of subjecting herself to that kind of humiliation again, she admittedly had spent a huge portion of the night before lying in bed fantasizing about Luke's body and a personal encounter with the long arm of the law.

Kelso picked up the phone on his desk and punched a button. "Come on down to my office," he said into the receiver. "I need to ask you about something."

Hannah bit her lip and figured this could be a good thing. Maybe. Kelso was either considering using her skills or he was going to have her escorted off the premises by the SWAT team. Either way it sounded more fun than going to another library interview.

Especially since Luke Warner strolled into the room, Ralph at his side. He was one fine-looking man, and Hannah was determined to ignore the curse she heard ringing in his head when he spotted her.

·3·

"YOU WANT HER TO RIDE WITH ME?" LUKE WAS horrified at what his boss was suggesting. A whole day with Hannah, in his squad car? Smelling her, listening to her low, throaty voice? Just take away her clothes and throw them together in the Garden of Eden with an apple while you were at it. Christ.

How much could he be expected to handle? Hannah was so goddamn cute, and she had turned him down. Just flat out said no when he'd asked her out. She was like a tempting

donut next to a pot of coffee at ten a.m. and he wasn't allowed to take a bite.

Yet Hannah's eyes lit up. She stood, nudging Ralph to the
side so she could leave the chair. Ralph moved, but stayed
glued to her leg. "That would be great."

Kelso just shrugged. "Sure, why not? Citizens ride with
officers from time to time for news stories, for career shadowing, for curiosity. And while I'm skeptical on the whole psychic thing, who knows? Maybe she can be helpful in some
way."

Hannah beamed. Kelso looked determined. Luke felt rail-
roaded.

But on the flip side, he didn't want her riding out with
anyone else. She was wearing a really short skirt and sandals
that added several inches to her height, and her legs looked
twelve miles long, all creamy flesh and smooth skin. Once
she sat down in the car, that skirt was going to edge up into
dangerous territory and there wasn't one guy on the force he
trusted to not at least take a peek.

Last donut in the box, that's totally what she was. He
knew he shouldn't take it but the thought of someone else
coming along and snagging it had him reaching for the donut every time. It *really* sucked that she had turned him
down.

Hannah cocked an eyebrow. "Are you hungry? I keep
seeing donuts when I look at you."

"Yeah. I'm hungry." For her. Which he wasn't about to
admit out loud. Let her read his mind and figure it out.

"We can stop at the bakery," Hannah told Luke with a
smile as they headed for the parking lot, determined to pre-
tend nothing was wrong. "Get you a jelly-filled. And then
after the bakery, what are we doing first?" Hannah pictured
high-speed car chases, frisking street punks, and rescuing
tied-up bank tellers.

"We drive around, looking for suspicious activity, and wait for a call to come in."

"Oh." What a letdown. Hannah reached for the passenger door of his squad car.

Ralph erupted in wild and vicious barking, inserting himself between her and the car. Startled, Hannah stumbled back three feet and grabbed her chest. Yeesh, he'd about given her a heart attack. "What? What's the matter?"

Luke rested his muscular forearms on the roof of the driver's side of the car, twin tattoos of barbed wire wrapping around both impressive biceps. He grinned. "Ralph's been trained to own the car. He doesn't let anyone in until I give them permission."

While Hannah tried to swallow her heart back down her throat, Luke slapped his thigh. "Recall, Ralph."

Ralph sat down.

"Good boy."

She wrinkled her nose at the German shepherd. "I thought you liked me."

The dog gave a bark.

"Let her in the car, Ralph."

Luke walked around to her side and put his hand on the small of her back, where it burned and turned her on way more than any random finger touch through a cotton shirt ever should. Ralph hopped into the middle of the front seat, and Hannah figured it was a good thing. She needed a chaperone.

The denim skirt she'd put on had been impulsive, a semiconscious need to look attractive when she saw Luke again. But she didn't wear anything above the knee very often—okay, *ever*—and when she slid into the seat the skirt shot up to her panty line.

No hope that Luke hadn't noticed. He was bent over, head in the passenger door, like he was going to say something, but had completely forgotten how to speak. His eyes were pinned on her thighs and a strangled gasp filled the car.

Wet drool landed on her leg, and Hannah hoped like hell it was Ralph's, not hers or Luke's.

Her nipples popped up in her tight-fitting cotton shirt. The car filled with heavy breathing. Mortified, she was about to lift her butt off the seat and yank the skirt down as far as it would go without baring her pelvis from the north, when Ralph solved her problem.

He draped himself across her like a fur throw and rested his snout in the depression between her thighs. Hannah relaxed a little until she heard Luke's parting comment as he ducked out of the car and started around the front.

"Lucky dog," he said as he trailed his fingers along the hood of the car.

Hello. Hannah wasn't even sure if he'd said it out loud or if he'd just thought it, but either way, it seemed Luke was fighting the same attraction she was.

Of course, she knew that. He'd asked her out. But she wasn't up for the eventual distaste and recoil she would get from Luke once he realized the true nature of her freakiness.

Then again . . .

He already knew she was a freak and it didn't seem to bother him.

The question was, did she have the guts to take a chance on him? Hell, take a chance on herself?

She thought maybe she did.

Luke was jealous of his dog.

He couldn't believe it, but it just seemed cruel to him that he had to stay restrained and professional, while Ralph got to slather himself all over Hannah's thighs and tuck his nose down into the warmth between her legs. Not to mention that

Ralph and Hannah had seemed to develop an instant connection, an elemental bond that the dog had shared only with him until this point.

"So how long have you and Ralph worked together?" she asked, fingers trailing over Ralph's fur.

"Almost two years. He's a real pro and has about seven or eight years left in him before retirement if the suits don't cut the program."

"He lives with you?"

"Yep. Since we started his training."

Luke turned on his radio and pulled out of the parking lot, intending to cruise down Vine Street to show police presence. With quirky retail shops, college students, and low-income housing all crashing together on Vine, it was usually a hotbed of activity. Nothing major, just the usual shoplifting, underage drinking, and the occasional overzealous panhandler. He hoped that at ten in the morning tempers wouldn't be as hot as the day already promised to be.

The humidity was stifling and the AC on his car not up for the job. Hannah's already curly hair was migrating up and out, in fuzzy little curlicues, a few damp tendrils plastered to her forehead. Her cotton shirt clung to her breasts, giving him an enticing display of those lush curves.

He scanned the area, which was quiet, and tried to be casual. No problem. He had a semi-erection, but he'd had those before. It would go away eventually if he ignored it. Maybe.

"Ralph seems so sweet when he's like this. I can't believe the way he can turn it on and off. He's got a heck of a bark when he means business."

Luke took in Ralph lolling about in Hannah's lap and shook his head. "This isn't standard procedure. He's usually not so relaxed in the car or on duty. He knows when his police collar goes on he's working, and he's always serious and professional. But you have a strange effect on him."

On both of them.

"I like him," she said simply, stroking behind Ralph's ears in a sensual rub. "He feels good."

Luke took the corner and decided never to look at Hannah again. It would be safer that way. "At home, when his badge is off, he's just a regular German shepherd. He sleeps, he plays, he eats too much dog food. But he loves to come to work. On my days off he's up at the crack of dawn, hauling his collar over to me."

Most of the women Luke had dated didn't understand the relationship he had with his dog. Ralph wasn't a pet during the day, he was a partner. Someone Luke could trust with his life and know that he would always watch his back. Ralph might not be able to talk, but he was a hell of a lot smarter than a number of humans Luke had run across.

"You have the perfect partnership. It would be a shame to lose that," Hannah said.

He broke his vow not to look, disturbed by the way she could take his thoughts and force them into coherent sentences, as if he'd spoken them that way. Hannah just watched him, unblinking, blue eyes wise and understanding.

"Yeah, it would be." And he wanted a perfect partnership with a woman, too. For the first time, he really felt the lack of that. Easy companionship with someone who could read his very thoughts . . .

Good God. Where had that come from?

Disturbed, Luke scrambled for conversation. "So what about you, Hannah? What do you do when you're not busting up purse snatchings?"

A little sigh emerged. "Well . . . I'm in college."

"To be . . . ?" It was hard to visualize her as a doctor or a lawyer or a CPA.

"I'm not sure. I've tried a few things and haven't been good at them. Sometimes I can't control what I'm saying and the most inappropriate or irrelevant things come out of my mouth. When I was a kid, my parents said I would outgrow it, but I'm still waiting. And waiting."

"It's tough to be different when you're a kid." Luke clenched his hands on the steering wheel. "I had allergies and asthma when I was a kid and it was always a big deal. I was always ruining snack time because there couldn't be anything with peanuts or dairy products, and I had to sit out during gym class. It was hard as hell to be singled out like that." And why in the hell had he just told her that? He'd never been one to spill about his childhood.

Hannah raised her eyebrows. "You don't look like a kid who sat out during gym class."

He hoped there was a compliment in that. "Turns out physical activity is good for asthma." He'd moved out of his mom's and immersed himself in a healthy lifestyle, with good nutrition and a lot of exercise. Part of his reason for joining the force had been to prove that he could. That he was no longer that sickly little kid who'd been picked on.

"You look in top form to me." And then some. Hannah wanted to see all of his form, and was wondering exactly why she had thought she couldn't. All she had to do was tell him she'd changed her mind. That she wanted to go out with him. The only thing preventing her was her own insecurities. The radio crackled to life, spewing out a bunch of codes and car numbers that meant nothing to Hannah.

Luke stopped to listen, idling the squad car at the corner and picking up his radio. "Seventeen responding. I'm on McMillan and Calhoon." Luke turned on the lights but not the siren and they drove at a fast clip without speeding.

"What is it?"

"A domestic dispute on Probasco. You'll have to stay in the car." His hand stretched over to Ralph and gave him a hand signal.

The dog leapt off her lap immediately and stood at soldierlike attention, nails digging into the upholstery when they took a corner hard.

Hannah lost her balance and cracked her head on the window.

Damn it. She had not seen that coming.

·4·

DOMESTIC CALLS WERE USUALLY TIME-CONSUMING and tested every ounce of patience in Luke's body. Nine times out of ten no charges were ever pressed and the parties involved just spent a lot of time swearing at each other.

It was worse if there were kids around, clinging to the mom's leg and watching Luke with big eyes that saw too much. Luke ached to help those kids, to reassure them that everything was all right and the world was a safe place, but it didn't always work that way. This call didn't involve any children, nor was there any swearing. Just a hysterical woman convinced that her boyfriend was stalking her.

"He's here," she insisted, taking a hit on her cigarette. "Up in the bathroom."

Luke studied the hand that shook, her scattered expression, and tried to make sense of what she was saying. "He's not allowed to be in the bathroom?"

They were standing on the front porch and Ralph was next to him, at the ready to go in if Luke gave the word. Out of the corner of his eye he could see Hannah sitting in the front seat of his car, staring at them.

"No! I told him yesterday I don't want nothing to do with

him anymore, and then I get up from napping on the couch and the bathroom door is closed."

"So why do you think it's your boyfriend in there, ma'am? Did he talk to you? Is the door locked?"

"He didn't say nothing. But I know it's him."

Or the wind. Luke felt a little more confident that this call could be resolved quickly. All he needed to do was open the bathroom door and show her the room was empty. Then suggest she change her locks.

"Let me go up with my dog and check it out for you. Which way is the bathroom?"

"I'll show you." The woman stepped into the crowded foyer and started up narrow steps, losing her balance and hitting the wall. Ashes from her cigarette trailed past her leg in a flutter.

She had the vacant half-aware stare of a drug addict. Luke figured this was paranoia brought about by her chemical dependency, but it was his duty to investigate. Set her mind at ease.

He knocked on the bathroom door. "Is anyone in there? This is the police. Open up, or I'm coming in with my dog."

Ralph growled low in his throat, like he sensed danger. Luke sensed the same thing, something in the air changing around him, shifting from relaxed to wary. There was someone behind that door. The woman jerked away down the hall with uneven footsteps and an excited, weird little laugh that set the hairs on Luke's neck on end.

He drew his gun.

Hannah drummed her fingers on the window and watched her breath create a little cloud of moisture on the glass. Luke had left the car running for her with the air-conditioning on and she was actually getting cold. Rolling her window down, she turned her face toward the hot wave of steamy air. Luke had left the porch and gone into the house with the woman. He looked so cool, so confident in his uniform, so sure of himself and his role. It would be nice to feel that level of security, to trust your instincts and to know you were doing the right thing.

Hannah never felt confident unless she was taking an exam in a college class. That was easy. She listened to the professor, read the material, studied, took mock exams at home, then usually went in and aced the tests. But what good had that done her? Last time she checked there were no jobs available for professional test takers.

She was mulling that over when suddenly she jerked upright. It was there, in her head. Clearer than anything she'd ever seen. Danger. A gun.

Luke was in trouble.

Without hesitation, Hannah threw open the car door and ran toward the house, cursing the sandals she was wearing for holding her back from a dead run. God, oh, God, she needed to warn Luke, to let him know he was in danger.

"Luke!" she screamed as she crossed the porch and ran through the open front door.

The house was dark and gloomy, a stale smell lingering in the air. She stopped to look around wildly, sure she had only seconds before something terrible happened. There was no movement on the first floor that she could see or hear, so without thought Hannah charged up the narrow stairs.

Halfway up she spotted Luke in front of a closed door, hand out to open it.

"No! Stop! He has a gun, he has a gun!" she screamed, reaching the top step.

Hannah threw herself onto Luke's back to knock him to the ground and out of bullet range.

Only he was in such good shape that he didn't fall to the ground.

Huh. She hadn't predicted that.

Luke knew the minute Hannah entered the house. He could hear her sandals clomping on the wood floor and her agitated voice shouting. His first thought was to turn around and escort her back out of the house. But that would leave his back turned to the bathroom door. Beyond which he suspected was a crazed junkie.

His other option was to subdue and cuff the guy before Hannah could climb the stairs and put herself at risk. Luke was already reaching for the doorknob to do that when Hannah started screaming.

She'd taken the steps much quicker than he'd given her credit for and he was about to abort and get her out of the house when she landed right smack on his back. All of her. Christ Almighty. Careening off balance, they slammed into the wall right as the door opened.

With Hannah dangling from around his neck, Luke raised his weapon. And lost his hearing when Hannah let out a violent shriek in his ear. Fortunately, she seemed to stun the man in the bathroom, too, who paused in the doorway and looked at Hannah incredulously.

Long enough for Luke to aim his gun and give the signal for Ralph to be at the ready. The man, who was in his early twenties, skin pasty and eyes watery, had a gun in his hand, but pointing toward the floor.

"Drop your weapon." Luke's words came out with a hell of a lot less authority than he would have liked, since Hannah's arms were cutting off his windpipe.

Her legs were wrapped around his waist and she gave

little hurried breaths of distress in his ear. It didn't seem to occur to her to get off him, and he didn't have the time to address the issue.

Ralph growled and showed his teeth, which had a greater effect than Luke's wheezy command. The man dropped his gun to the floor with a clatter. Luke glanced down the hall quickly, making sure the woman hadn't reappeared.

The guy wiped his nose and edged back into the bathroom, away from Ralph. "Man, you, uh, you got a girl hanging off your back."

No shit.

"Oh!" Hannah said, and slid down the length of Luke, breasts and ankles and everything in between molding his back and thighs.

"Hands on your head." Luke reached for his cuffs and stepped away from Hannah, dragging air into his throat.

As he quickly cuffed the guy and retrieved the gun, he shot Hannah a look. "Go downstairs. And don't move this time."

Hannah opened her mouth, closed it, and went down the stairs, holding on to the railing for support as her noisy sandals clunked on the wood steps.

With Ralph still on alert and Hannah out of the way, Luke tried to figure out what was going on. "What are you doing in the bathroom with a gun? Your girlfriend says you're not allowed to be here."

"It's registered," he insisted. "You can check it out. Jim Clark's my name. And Leslie's just pissed at me because I wouldn't give her any more money to buy drugs."

Luke wasn't sure he believed the guy or not, but if there were narcotics in the house, Ralph would find them. He gave Ralph the command to sniff for drugs, starting in the bathroom. "Why was your gun in your hand?"

"I heard all this noise, thought someone was breaking in."

"Your girlfriend called us."

Ralph came back quickly, which indicated to Luke there were no illegal substances present. Luke left the guy cuffed in the hall under Ralph's guard and went in the direction the woman had gone. He found her passed out cold in the bedroom. Great.

"You might want to think about checking your girlfriend into rehab."

Jim Clark shrugged. "She won't go."

Which meant the only thing left to do was to verify that Jim's gun was registered and run his license. Luke would take him down to the car and do that while Ralph kept an eye on him.

Hannah was waiting for him at the bottom of the stairs.

"I'm sorry . . ." she started. "But I thought you were in danger, and, and . . . God, I'm such a lame psychic. But even I can predict that you're mad at me."

Her cheeks were pink, and while he was thoroughly annoyed, it wasn't for the reasons she seemed to think. He believed in her sixth sense. Had seen and heard enough evidence of it to know it was there. He thought there was something really damn cool about it, actually. But the fact that she had put herself in danger made his blood pressure do seriously dangerous things.

"I'm a cop. I'm always in danger. I can handle it. I told you to stay in the car."

"You're a psychic?" Jim Clark asked, hands cuffed behind his back. "Can you tell my fortune?"

Hannah stopped Luke at the bottom of the stairs by putting her hand on his chest. She didn't even look at Jim Clark. "Luke, um, I think that someone stole your car."

"What?" He moved past her and found the driveway empty. The squad car that he had left running with Hannah in the passenger seat was gone. A twitch started in his left eye. "Where the hell is my car, Hannah?"

"That's a good question," she said. "And I'm somewhat sure that maybe possibly if I hone in on it, I might be able to ascertain where it went. Maybe."

·5·

THIS HAD TO BE A CLEAR INDICATOR THAT FALLING for a woman made you lose your mind.

Luke was driving around the steep, narrow steeps of the Mt. Adams neighborhood at dusk scanning left and right for his squad car on nothing more than Hannah's psychic ability, which wasn't exactly fine-tuned.

He wasn't sure which grated on him worse—the fact that this was clearly a fool's mission, or that Hannah was wearing clothes. All day long he'd been fantasizing how they could spend the evening, and this wasn't it. He'd been reamed for the squad car back at the station and he was feeling like he could use a little comfort in the form of cuddling. Naked. Under the sheets. With Hannah.

Not driving around in friggin' circles.

Ralph panted in Luke's ear, his rump resting on Hannah's lap. She was absently petting the dog's back as she scanned out the window, and once again Luke found it odd that Ralph was so easily subdued by Hannah and so quick to answer her signals.

Apparently French fries talked. Luke had seen Hannah

slip one to Ralph from the extra-value meal they'd grabbed at the drive-thru.

"I could see the city behind the house, and sort of a big empty space to the left . . ." Hannah repeated for the fourth time.

Luke figured it was a sign that he really liked her that he wasn't tempted to scream. He did believe her, he just wasn't sure that any of it mattered anymore. Except that he knew it did. That was why he was driving in circles. Hannah needed to understand and appreciate the gift or talent that she had. It was suddenly intensely important to him that this sweet and caring and generous woman understand how special she was.

Seeing a rare parking spot on the street, Luke pulled his truck in as Hannah pointed to the right.

"See that monastery?" she said. "And this church across from it? It's got the greatest view of the city. Let's go check it out."

A few streets over, people were dining and hitting the bars and art galleries, but here it was quiet. Luke opened Hannah's door and took her by the hand to help her out, and as an excuse to touch her. Her skin was soft and warm, her hand small in his. Ralph padded along next to them as they crossed the street and went through the church's parking lot. There was a flimsy sort of railing behind the church, and beyond that was the Ohio River and the city, both spread out in the hot hazy summer night. Luke stood there and watched the barges sluggishly move up the river.

As Ralph started sniffing around the dry dusty grass, Hannah leaned on the railing and took in the world in front of her. "I've always loved it here," she said, almost forgetting that she was getting a little desperate to find Luke's car.

She had dragged him out here, and so far the only thing they'd seen out of the ordinary was a tabby cat with a chipmunk hanging out of its mouth. And that was more disgusting than unusual. But Luke seemed to be all right. He leaned next to her, his forearms on the railing. His hip brushed hers.

"Hannah, it doesn't matter about the car. Really."

She drew a deep breath and tried not to feel like a miserable failure, to let it go and accept it for what it was. "Okay. Thanks." Chewing on the tip of her fingernail, she heard a truck honk somewhere below her on the interstate. "You know, I've realized something. I'm not perfect. But no one is. And I like who I am, psychic-ness and all."

It was true. When she wasn't expending energy making herself miserable, she was happy. She would find her place sooner or later. She had a lot to offer, and she could be successful if she just stopped doubting herself.

"I like you, too, psychic-ness and all."

She turned, and in the dusky, silent night, with solemnity and confidence, he kissed her. A perfect kiss, slow and easy, that spoke of admiration and respect and lots of possibilities. Hannah's mouth was falling open, ready to take it deeper, arms clinging to Luke, when Ralph barked.

Not a cheerful, *Yay, my people like each other* kind of bark, but a serious, *Don't do that* kind of growl.

Hannah bent over and rested her hand on his snout. "Are you jealous? Silly Ralph."

Luke snorted. But Ralph immediately calmed down and rubbed his head into her skin.

"You know, a trained dog is only subordinate to his handler. And to anyone his handler is submissive to." Luke turned to her in amusement. "I think Ralph has known the score since the second I met you."

"You're submissive to me?" Hannah asked stupidly. Hello.

"Well, not submissive in *that* sense, but he knows I like

you." Luke brushed her hair off her cheek. "I know you said no when I asked you out, and usually no really does mean no, but are you sure we can't try?"

"Yes." How could she be stupid enough to say no to him twice? She couldn't.

"Oh. Okay." His face fell and he started to pull back.

Hannah realized that he was taking her agreement as confirmation that she didn't want to try. She grabbed his hand so he wouldn't leave. "No! Luke, I mean, yes, I want to go out with you." She needed to trust him and to trust herself.

A grin split his face. "Cool."

He was leaning forward, clearly to kiss her again, when Ralph interrupted with another bark.

Distracted, Hannah looked just beyond Luke's shoulder. "Hey, isn't that your squad car?" She pointed absently.

"Huh?" Luke snapped his head up and turned around. "Holy crap, it is. Parked behind that house next door. Hannah, you found it!"

Well, what could she say? She was psychic.

Somehow what had started out as a celebratory kiss over Luke's found squad car had landed Hannah naked in her living room.

She wasn't complaining.

When Luke's mouth closed around her nipple as she lay spread out beneath him on her floral couch, she gave up a low moan. "Oh, yes."

Luke nipped at her taut skin with his teeth, then flicked his tongue over her. She clutched his forearms, feeling the force of that lick all the way to her toes.

It seemed like she should be doing something, making some sort of effort to participate, but it took all her strength to not have an orgasm. Anything more was too much to expect from her.

"Hannah, Hannah." Luke skimmed his lips across her skin to her other breast. He had stripped off his shirt but was still wearing his jeans. Denim scraped along her bare thighs, the button on his fly pressing into her hot flesh. She wasn't sure what had happened to her clothes.

One minute they'd been kissing, the next he'd had her naked and flat on her back. A man of action, clearly. Most men she'd dated had been hesitant, fumbling, more confident taking a pawn in a chess game than unzipping her shorts. Luke wasn't hesitating at all, and if she could speak, she'd express her gratitude.

"You really are the prettiest woman I've ever seen." Luke pulled back, ran his eyes up and down over her face, her chest, her stomach. "So feminine, so sexy."

Hannah could hear his thoughts floating out over her, but she would have believed him anyway. His face was open, honest. Which was why she was doing this, going from a kiss to wherever this might lead—okay, where it clearly was leading—but she knew as sure as she'd seen that gun in her head that Luke was different. That he accepted her.

"Thank you," she whispered, her heart swelling, her brain scrambling, her body incinerating like dry kindling. "Now stop talking and take me."

Luke gave a wicked grin. "No hurry, Hannah. We've got all night to get to know each other." He slid her knee up and dropped her thigh open. "Every inch."

Then the man bent his head and kissed her. On the lips she didn't use for talking.

She gave a squeak of surprise that trailed off into a heartfelt groan that dissolved into a desperate pant when his tongue lapped over her hot, swollen flesh. "Ohmigod," she whimpered. "I can't believe you're doing that."

Shocked, but glad. Even as she spoke, her thighs were relaxing, spreading farther for him, her body growing slicker, her fingers pinching into his shoulders.

He pulled away to murmur, "I can still keep you guessing? That's good to know."

And Hannah decided to shut up. If she talked, he might feel obligated to answer, like he just had, which meant he couldn't be doing those very delicious things with his mouth that he had been doing. She lifted her legs in a desperate attempt to encourage him to continue.

He laughed softly, breath teasing across her thighs. "Liked that, huh?"

"Like isn't a strong enough word." Adored it, reveled in it, ached from it, wanted to beg him for it. That was more like it.

Luke used his thumbs to massage her curls, and spread her folds apart. Her mouth went hot, her legs trembled, her eyes drifted closed. Hannah sank into the lumpy cushion of her hand-me-down couch and relaxed her body. Arms and legs dangled like spaghetti, slack and helpless. She wasn't going to move. Ever. She was just going to lie there for the rest of her natural life.

Then when Luke's tongue dipped deep inside her, she broke that vow and almost levitated to the ceiling. "Oh, Luke!"

Followed by a curse that would cause her mother to drop dead of a stroke.

Fortunately, her mother was nowhere in the vicinity, because that would have been awkward. Hannah was starting to think she was losing her mind, all while her body burned and pulsed and shattered through an overwhelming orgasm.

Luke's whiskers pressed into the smooth shallow of her flesh, his mouth still working—slower, languid, confident. When she pried her eyelids open, he glanced up at her and moved back, finger wiping his bottom lip. The tips of the hair above his forehead were damp with sweat, and his eyes were dark, sensual. The corner of his mouth lifted into an arrogant grin.

And she didn't even care. He deserved to feel pride after what he'd done to her. She swallowed hard, still supine on the couch like a satiated cat in a sunspot.

"Is it okay . . . are you ready for . . . ?" The snap on his jeans popped loud, ominous, and anticipatory, in the room. The traffic on the street was loud and persistent, her air-conditioning gave a determined *whoosh*, and her upstairs neighbor had rap music blaring. Yet it all faded behind the sound of Luke's heightened breathing, her shallow *pant, pant*, and the blissful tinny sound of his zipper heading down.

"Ready," she said, like they were preparing to race through a burning fire to safety, not have sex.

Though there were definite similarities. Intense heat being one of them.

Luke stood up. Hannah dropped her thighs closed instinctively. Not that he hadn't already seen everything she had to offer and then some, but she wanted to be artfully arranged, like a sensual sculpture, not splayed like a Thanksgiving turkey.

Up on her elbows, Hannah eagerly watched Luke shove down his jeans.

Luke paused while taking his pants off, his gut clenching. Damn. Hannah was licking her lip like she was anticipating a really tasty treat. He had meant to take things slow, but instead he'd come on like a weapon of mass seduction.

Not that she seemed to mind, and everything on him ached with want. His muscles were bunched in tension, his fingertips tingling with the need to touch her, his mouth dry with the memory of being buried between her thighs. Even his teeth hurt from clenching them.

There had never been a woman, not even when he was awash in teen testosterone, who had done this to him. He shoved down his pants. Stepped on one leg with the opposite foot and yanked out of them, then repeated the effort until he was standing on his jeans instead of wearing them.

Ninety-nine percent sure he had a condom in his wallet, Luke bent over and begged for mercy. "Let it be there."

"A condom?" Hannah leaned over the couch, her hair spilling over his shoulder.

He could smell her. The fresh, fruity smell of her hair. The melon-fragrant lotion she rubbed on her hands. The tangy scent of her desire clouding his nostrils and making his hand shake as he dug in his wallet.

"Yes."

Her breath was hot on the side of his face, her warm flesh brushing against him, her breast teasingly close to his mouth. The nipple was puckered, deep pink, topping off a breast that was full and round, and fit just perfectly in his hand. He wanted to bite it. Bite and suck her everywhere.

"Do it," she said.

Luke fisted his hand in front of his mouth and cleared his throat, afraid that if he spoke he'd sound like Bart Simpson. "Do what?"

"What you're thinking of doing." Hannah ran her fingers through her hair at the shoulder.

"Do you know what I'm thinking?" In some parts of the world he could get arrested for the thoughts he was having.

She smiled at him, her soft fingers strolling over his cheek, down to his lips, something sweet and deep and pleasing dancing across her face. "I can hear your thoughts loud and clear. Does that bother you?"

Reflecting on that, he decided it didn't. "No. Hell, you'll

always know what I want, right? And if I'm about to completely screw up and say or do something stupid, or get you a
crap gift, you can fix it before it happens."

She laughed. "True. Though most men don't take it this
lightly."

"I'm not most men. I work with a dog. I understand the
value of that sixth sense. The question is, do you see its
value?"

Hannah's smile fell off her face and she nodded, her expression serious. "Actually, I do. Maybe for the first time."

Sucking on her flesh, he rolled on the condom, then sat on
the couch next to her. "Come sit in my lap." He patted his
thighs and raised his eyebrows suggestively.

Hannah laughed. "Is that what bad boys say to good
girls?"

"Only if it works." Luke wanted Hannah to feel in control
of their lovemaking, comfortable with the rhythm. And he
wanted her face in front of his, so he could touch her lips,
study her expression, watch her pleasure.

Not to mention the narrowness of the couch would probably have him pitching to the floor if they tried this any
other way.

He watched her deliberate, half sitting up, half lying
down. Her feet tickled the hair on his calves and he couldn't
resist reaching over and stroking the smooth curve of her
backside. Her skin was a deep golden color, but her behind
was several shades lighter, a clear indicator that Hannah
didn't sunbathe in the nude.

His thumb worked between her legs, stroking its way
back to her moist center, and Hannah groaned.

"Okay, it works."

She struggled to sit up, and Luke reached out and grabbed
her elbow to pull her into his lap. After a minute of wiggling
adjustment, where her breasts knocked his chest, and her

backside bounced on his hips and her hot inner thighs collided with his erection, she gripped his shoulders.

And slid down on the length of him.

They groaned together as she rested there for a long, erotic second. Then Luke nipped at her swollen bottom lip, wrapped his arms around her dewy body, and thrust up into her, wanting to feel all of Hannah, taste her, touch her.

Her chin jerked up, her eyes drifted close. Her teeth dug into her lip as a little sigh rushed out. She met his thrust with one of her own, and Luke was lost. He moved harder, faster, sweat rolling down into his eye, gripping her waist and pouring himself into every push of his body into hers.

"Hannah." He wasn't sure what he meant to say. Wasn't sure how to put into words that something was very different about how he felt about her. That he wanted to return the pleasure that she was giving him.

Her eyes locked with his, burning with awareness, and then she shuddered, fingers convulsing on his shoulders. Seeing her shatter, Luke couldn't hold back any longer. With one last thrust, he exploded.

It careened on and on, pulses of pleasure that echoed throughout his whole body, and Luke found himself kissing Hannah's neck, her ear, lifting her damp curls and tracing his lips along her jaw. Pressing his mouth to the little dimple she had.

"You're amazing," he said.

"I think your company brings out the amazing in me," she whispered, before giving a husky laugh that sent shivers of desire back up his spine.

"I think that together, we're pretty amazing." Luke shifted until he was lying down, Hannah draped across him. He kissed the tip of her nose. "Tell me tonight isn't it, Hannah. That we're going to see where this thing between us goes. Tell me you see that."

Hannah didn't see, feel, or hear anything except her own conviction that Luke was a good man who respected her and didn't mind her unusual talents. She definitely wanted to see where it could go between them, but she needed to be sure that he knew what he was getting into. "You know, since I met you, my little bit psychic-ness has been growing, for whatever reason."

"Maybe . . . maybe we bring out the best in each other."

It sounded almost normal and sweet when he said it like that. But she still warned him, "Life with me will be unpredictable, you know."

He squeezed her hand. "Are you kidding? I'm counting on it. Remember, I'm a risk taker. With an inhaler."

Then she saw his teeth flash as he grinned. "Think of the advantages of you knowing what's in my head. You'll never have to doubt my feelings or get jealous, and I can make crude suggestions in my mind to you in public and no one will know."

Hannah laughed and snuggled up against Luke's chest. "I do see us having a lot of fun."

"And Ralph getting fat on French fries."

Oops. Busted by a cop. "Hey, you can predict the future, too! Cool."

Hannah kissed Luke softly.

And Ralph gave a *knew-it-all-along* bark.

AFTER HOURS

Toni Blake

MARLA SHEPHERD GLANCED UP AS HER BOSS, Michael Gates, strolled past her desk, all tall and broad and handsome in his dark Armani suit.

Then she imagined him naked.

Of course, it wasn't the *first* time she'd imagined him that way. In fact, a little quick math told her it was quite possibly around the seven-hundredth time, since she'd been his administrative assistant for two years now and probably thought of him naked at least once a day, starting with the very moment she'd met him.

Although on some days—okay, a lot of them—she'd envisioned him naked more than once, so that probably upped the total to a thousand, minimum.

She let her head droop with a sigh. A thousand fantasies and not one reality.

And now it would *never* be a reality.

Which maybe wouldn't feel quite so devastating if she wasn't in love with the guy. Yep, what had started out as pure, unadulterated lust had, over time, transformed into love. That gut-wrenching want/need/just-adore-being-around-him sort of love that she recalled from her first such affliction in high school, when she'd fallen desperately for Tommy Jamison, quarterback and student council president. One *more* fantasy that had never become a reality. She sighed again, then tried to focus on her last few tasks of the work day: sending a couple of e-mails and going through her inbox to prioritize items for tomorrow.

She and Michael had both stayed late, wrapping up a large mailing to his clients. At thirty-three, he was the youngest investment advisor at Keating & Company and she was his veritable Girl Friday, always ready to lend a hand, work overtime, or move heaven and earth if necessary. Whatever he needed, she gave him. Both because she was a hard worker and because she was just so darn gaga over him.

The love part had happened not at work, though, but when professional lunches had turned personal. The two of them had simply clicked, become friends. So she knew a lot about him—how he'd grown up locally in Cincinnati, a hometown boy who loved being near his family. And how he loved to travel, and that he placed a high value on friends, and that his secret fantasy was to be a relief pitcher for the Reds. She also knew about Dahlia, the one big love of his life, whom he'd wanted to marry but had lost due to a long-distance relationship that just didn't work out when she took a job in another city. Marla had shared just as much of herself with Michael—and along with everything *else* she knew about him, she knew they'd be a perfect match if only he ever started seeing her as a woman and not just a coworker and friend.

But now . . . well, now that would never happen. Because her life was changing.

Through no effort of her own, she'd been offered a great job in Pittsburgh, a five-hour drive away. She'd been born and raised in the Cincinnati area, too, so the idea of packing up and leaving her whole life behind was terrifying—but she had to do it, she just had to. The job was perfect and would fulfill her in a way administrative work never could. And despite how difficult it was to be so brave, the hardest part, she knew, would be leaving Michael—her unrequited love.

Oh Lord, how stupid that made her feel—to be so wrapped up in a guy who had no romantic interest in her whatsoever.

It was Tommy Jamison and high school all over again. But maybe that aspect of the situation provided some of the impetus helping her to leave. A girl had to know when to lick her wounds and move on, had to hang on to her self-respect. After all, she was thirty years old. If she didn't take control of her life now, when would she?

So, as much as she'd been dreading this moment, she drew in a deep breath, rose from her chair, and took the few steps to Michael's office.

Peeking through the door to see him shutting his briefcase, she tapped on the door frame.

He looked up with his usual winning smile, his blue eyes owning her. Even after ten hours at the office, every dark hair on his head was in place, and the only hint of a long day was the sexy stubble shadowing his chin. "Ready to take off?" he asked, acknowledging that they were both probably exhausted. The rest of the office sat quiet, dark, and indeed her stomach was starting to growl for dinner.

"Almost," she said, then bit her lip. God, this was even harder than she'd expected. It wasn't just about quitting a job, it was about quitting her love for him. "But first, I need to tell you something."

"Come in," he said, eyebrows knitting with concern. Clearly, her tone had informed him something big was coming. Although he'd been half out of his seat, preparing to leave, now he settled back into it.

Taking another deep, fortifying, you-can-do-this breath, Marla walked around his desk and perched on the edge, near his chair. They were comfortable enough together, good enough friends, that she could do that. And she would miss that comfort. Along with his very nearness—the musky, manly scent of him, the warmth his eyes emitted, the sense of almost knowing what it was like to be wrapped in his strong arms just from being so close to him.

But you can't think about that right now. And you also can't think about the way the crux of your thighs is tingling so madly, how heavy your breasts feel, how easy it would be to just grab him and kiss him.

Another deep breath. In, out. *Okay, you can do this.*

"What's wrong, Marla?"

She pursed her lips, wishing she knew where to begin. *You'd think you'd have a plan, you'd have rehearsed this*—but she hadn't. She'd been more wrapped up in the emotion of it than the execution.

"This is really difficult for me," she started. She'd crossed her ankles and now casually swung her pointy black pumps to and fro, but the way she gripped the edge of the desk with both hands surely belied her nervousness.

"What is it, honey? Whatever it is, you can tell me."

Whoa. He'd just called her *honey. That* was new. And possibly inappropriate given their positions—but she loved it.

She swallowed back the lump in her throat and tried to go on, tried to spit this out. "I've . . . I've been thinking about this a long time, Michael, and . . . and yet, I still don't know how to tell you. Maybe I shouldn't make such a big deal out of it, people do this all the time, but . . . I guess I'm not most people. So it's . . . harder for me than it probably *should* be."

His voice came warm, soft, reassuring. "I'm *glad* you're not most people." And he reached out a hand to cover one of hers.

As the small shock of pleasure rippled up her arm and straight down into her panties, she forgot her nervousness long enough to look up at him. "Huh?"

His eyes narrowed on her with a sexy determination she'd never witnessed in them before and it made her surge with moisture. "Marla, if you're trying to say what I *think* you're trying to say . . . well, I've been feeling the same way for a long time, too. And I haven't known what to do about it, because we work together, and because you know the company policy about that—but hell . . . maybe I don't care anymore."

Before Marla could even think, Michael slid his hand onto her knee, just below the hem of her skirt. She gasped involuntarily as the sensation ricocheted through her body like a pinball.

"Michael." She heard herself whisper his name without planning it.

The next thing she knew, he was on his feet, leaning in close to her. Her whole body felt sensitized, electrified, as he lifted a palm to her face. She thought he would kiss her then, but instead he only moved nearer, nearer, until his forehead touched hers. She could feel his breath on her skin, shockingly intimate. "I don't want to freak you out or anything, Marla, but . . ."

It was all she could do to speak as her heart hammered against her chest. "But what?"

"But I'm pretty sure I'm in love with you."

Oh boy. Oh God. She didn't answer, couldn't summon words, but she supposed her dreamy sigh said it all.

And *he* answered with—*finally*—a kiss.

At first, his mouth barely grazed her lips, yet the pleasure it released inside her was immeasurable. When the kiss grew firmer, more demanding, it moved through her like warm liquid, slow but potent. By the time it ended, they were both breathing heavy, the only sound in the room.

Their eyes met, and despite being in a high-rise office building that bustled with hundreds of people each day, Marla felt completely isolated, like nothing existed but the two of them—and desire. Even the vague sounds of downtown traffic on the streets below had faded to silence.

And something in his eyes, in her heart, in the passion

that now stretched so tautly between them, urged Marla to make the boldest move of her life.

She parted her thighs.

He glanced down, then back to her face, but his gaze had changed—his look deepening from mere want to something more needful, feral. His palms skimmed up her thigh-high stockings, under her skirt, to the lacy edges. "God, these are sexy as hell," he murmured near her neck.

"Glad you like," she barely managed, but what she was really thinking was: *Now you know nothing stands between us; no pesky, awkward pantyhose, just a little slip of silk.*

"I want to make you feel good," he breathed in her ear, and as his hands eased higher, up to her hips, her ass, she knew he was thinking the same thing.

She drew back just enough to meet his eyes, suddenly a wanton—because that fast, she knew, with Michael, it was okay. He would know she didn't do this just every day. He would know this was just for him. "I'll let you," she said.

He pulled in a ragged breath, then kissed her again, harder now, pushing his tongue into her mouth with a firm pressure she felt everywhere. His hands left her hips and rose to warm her breasts, the hot sensation forcing a gentle sob from her throat. Her arms fell around his neck, drawing him closer, closer, until his erection met the juncture of her thighs. Oh God, he was so hard. She'd dreamed of this. Well, not exactly *this*—here, in his office. But somehow, that made it even better. The wild abandon of it was intoxicating. She locked her legs around his to force him even nearer.

When he unbuttoned her pale blouse, they both glanced down to see her breasts heaving within the cups of her bra.

"So pretty," he murmured, then reached for the center clasp, deftly unhooking it.

He pushed the white lace aside, cupping the undersides of the bared mounds in his palms, studying them. She'd never felt more prettily on display, her own gaze drifting from her taut pink nipples to the glazed look in Michael's beautiful eyes. "Please," she said.

Please kiss them, she meant.

He understood.

Glancing softly at her face, he bent to rake his tongue over the peak of her breast even as he closed his mouth over it. The moist pull stretched all through her, making her moan. She ran her fingers through his thick hair and relished watching his ministrations.

He didn't linger there long, though, soon whispering, "Need to taste more of you," against her skin as he dropped to his knees before her.

She bit her lip as his hands glided once again up her outer thighs, under her skirt, raising the fabric sinfully high. "Lift," he said, and she did, without hesitation, just long enough for him to pull her panties down. She watched as he carefully drew them across her knees, then lower, easing them over her shoes.

Letting them fall to the carpet, he peered up into her eyes as he used strong hands to spread her legs once more. She sucked in her breath, hard, at the stark intimacy of revealing herself to him that way. But when he leaned in, stroking his tongue deep into her moisture, she forgot everything but sensation.

Michael could scarcely believe this was happening. Two years of working with her, and at least a year of wanting her—and now, finally, he was *having* her. She was so wet, warm, gently pushing herself against his mouth. Her eagerness made him harder every second, because while he'd known Marla was sweet and kind and responsible and beautiful, he *hadn't* quite imagined she was the sort of woman who would have sex in the office, let alone doing it two minutes after he admitted how he felt about her. It was like the perfect, luscious cherry on top of the sundae of his dreams.

Above him, her breath grew thready and he licked her deeper, wanting to take her to heaven. *Come for me, honey. Come,* he willed her. It wasn't that he wanted to rush things—it was that he wanted more and more of her, all he could get, and he also wanted to *give* her all he had to give. He used his whole mouth, soaking up her moisture, the sweet scent of her, everything. *Come, baby.* If she didn't soon, he feared *he* would come, in his *pants.* He'd never had anything like that happen before, but he'd probably never been as deeply excited by a woman as he was right now.

"Oh!" she cried out. "Oh God!" And then she bucked gently against him, her soft, pretty sobs echoing down over him, thrilling him still more.

Only when she went completely still did he ease back to peer up at her. "You're so beautiful," he heard himself say. He wasn't usually one for spouting romantic sentiments during sex—but damn, apparently Marla had more power over him than he'd realized.

"In me now," she said, voice soft, breathy, sexy. "I need you in me."

A low groan left him at the words and he reached in his back pocket for his wallet as Marla started undoing his belt.

The next few moments were rushed, urgent. He hurried to open the condom as she freed him from his pants. And then his hands were back up under her skirt again, curling over her round flesh just before he entered her with one firm thrust. *Awww* . . .

They both cried out at the connection. She appeared both impassioned and weak, which only fueled his heat.

"I . . . I can't believe you're really in me," she said, looping her arms around his neck.

He tried to catch his breath enough to answer. "I know. And I . . ." A stab of worry struck him. And again, with any other woman, any other sex, it wouldn't have, but Marla was different. "Tell me you wanted this. Tell me I'm not a jerk who made this happen too fast."

"Oh, I wanted it all right," she assured him, her tone laying any doubt to rest. "And I want more of it. *Please.*"

Damn, he liked that she asked for more. Liked that her need ran as thick as his. And though he still thought about going slow, the hunger in her eyes said he didn't have to, so he didn't hold back—at all. He drove into her deep, hard, making both their bodies jolt with the sheer force of it. They both cried out at each stroke, and it was hot, and it was wild, and it was every suit-and-tie guy's office fantasy come true, but it was also sweet, and good, and deeply binding.

"I love you," he heard himself tell her again, even as he thrust into her warm, accepting body. This wasn't like him, to be so open, so "lovely dovey" with a woman—but being with Marla made him that way.

"Me, too," she said on a moan. "I love you, too."

A fresh pleasure saturated him from head to toe. She loved him, too. Twenty minutes ago, she'd been his employee whom he secretly lusted after and cared for. But now he was inside her and she loved him, too. "Oh God," he said, because that was all it took to push him over the edge of ecstasy. *"Oh God!"*

He came inside her with a driving power, plunging deep, deep, deep, and only as his body finally went still, emptied, did he think to whisper, "Did I hurt you at all?"

She shook her head, their faces close. "No. You were perfect." Then she touched his face, his cheek, and bit her lip. "I can't believe this."

He drew back slightly, giving her a small grin. "I know. But it's good, right?"

She nodded, her soft blond hair falling around her shoulders. "*Really* good."

"I've wanted to tell you how I felt for a long time, but I just kept resisting, worried it was the wrong thing to do."

Another gentle nod from the woman he loved. Then a sheepish smile. "Want to know a secret?"

He gave her his best wolfish grin. "I *love* secrets."

She bit her lip, then admitted, "I've wanted you since the first day we met. The first interview."

Michael's skin warmed with surprise and his eyebrows shot up as he forgot all about being a wolf with her. "Really? That long?"

She nodded. And he kissed her.

He couldn't *not* kiss her.

He didn't know how any of this was going to affect their jobs, their working relationship, but at the moment, he didn't care. "Want to get something to eat? Or maybe come back to my place and order pizza or something?" He just wanted to be with her, in normal ways, but also with the brand-new knowledge that they were in love and had just had mind-blowing sex.

With a coy bite to her lower lip, she grinned. "Yeah, that sounds nice."

Marla walked down Fourth Street holding Michael's hand, the late-setting summer sun turning the light between the downtown buildings shadowy and romantic. The soft breeze of a warm June night wafted over them—and even blew up her skirt a bit, reminding her that she remained bare there. She hadn't put her panties back on, just letting him stuff them in his jacket pocket, leaving her to feel wonderfully naughty. She'd never had occasion to go pantyless before, but sex with Michael had just inspired her.

Deciding they were too hungry to wait for pizza delivery, they stopped into a chili parlor just a block away from their building. She knew some people thought of chili strictly as a cold-weather dish, but Cincinnati chili was a delicacy the locals ate all year round, for any and every occasion, and she liked the casual ease of celebrating what had just happened in such a simple, carefree way.

As they sat across from each other in a booth, his knees touched hers, and they exchanged intimate smiles. As soon as the waitress departed with their orders, Marla found herself slipping one foot from her shoe to slide it up his leg beneath the table. His small, responsive groan rushed all through her, and she found herself shaking her head in wonder. She still couldn't believe she'd just had wild office sex with the man of her fantasies. She leaned over the table, glad the place was mostly empty, and spoke quietly. "I can't believe I'm sitting in Skyline Chili with no panties on."

He replied with a hot, seductive grin. "You just made me hard again."

She bit her lip, since *that* made her wet again.

Strange how natural this felt, along with how amazing. They'd slipped so easily from being friends and coworkers into being full-blown lovers, with all the intimate flirtations that came with it. If anyone had told her she and Michael were going to have sex in his office—well, first, she wouldn't have believed it. But once she got over *that* part, she would have certainly expected to feel shy and awkward about it after. Yet just the opposite had occurred.

The effortlessness of the moment spurred her to blurt out another one of her most private secrets. "I've spent the last two years imagining what you look like naked."

His eyes locked on her with reckless heat—just as their gray-haired waitress arrived bearing two plates of spaghetti, chili, and cheese. "Two threeways, one wet," she said, lowering them to the table, and Marla and Michael simply exchanged secret smiles, trying not to laugh.

"Are you thinking what I'm thinking?" he asked when the waitress walked away.

"That you never realized how dirty the Skyline menu sounds?"

He grinned. "Close. But I kind of moved right past that part to . . . that kind of talk makes me want to take you to bed."

She tried to look playfully coquettish as she forked her first bite of chili and spaghetti into her mouth. "You *might* just be able to talk me into it. Nothing against the desk, but the bed sounds cozy."

"It will be. And we should hurry, because it'll have to last us for a week."

Damn. She'd forgotten. They'd stayed late to finish the mailing because he was leaving on vacation tomorrow. What timing. She couldn't resist a little playful sarcasm. "Great, now I get to spend a week wondering exactly *what* you're doing with *whom* on the beach." He was headed to Jamaica with some old college buddies.

He tilted his head and gave her a grin. "A shame *you* can't come."

She let out a laugh. "Yeah, I'm sure your friends would love you bringing a chick along on a guy trip. I might cramp your style just a little."

His eyes sparkled beneath the restaurant's lights. "Nah—as of right now, I'm officially not looking to party with any beach bunnies. The guys probably won't like that, but hey, they'll just have to understand I have a girl waiting for me at home. An . . . office bunny."

Fifteen minutes later, they'd finished eating and were back out on Fourth Street, hand in hand, exchanging kisses as they walked, and talking more about the reasons they'd both kept their affections to themselves.

"The way I see it," Michael concluded, "we only have one problem now. What to do about work. I mean, we can try to keep this a secret for a while, but to be honest, it's not really a secret I want to keep. I don't want this to be a sneaky, illicit thing."

The sentiment warmed her heart. And then she remembered.

The reason she originally went into his office.

To tell him she was quitting her job. Moving to Pittsburgh.

Her stomach dropped.

Oh God.

The realization set her mind spinning.

And in an instant, she was tempted to forget the whole thing, the whole move. Tempted to just stay here with him. Work out the interoffice dating problem. Be with the man she loved and who—*oh God!*—actually loved her back.

After all, how could she leave this behind? Every aspect of it, from the passion she'd felt on his desk to the simplicity of this moment, holding his hand as they strolled the city streets, was too perfect. He was the man of her dreams and he wanted her, and nothing else should matter.

Only it *did* matter.

She *wanted* the job in Pittsburgh. She wanted to be more than his administrative assistant; she wanted to pursue her goals.

In college, she'd gotten a degree in education, focusing her studies on teaching the deaf. She had a deaf cousin with whom she was close, and good education for people with special needs was a cause dear to her heart. She'd fallen into the investment business entirely by accident, simply because she couldn't find a local job in her field after graduating. But the moment she'd been contacted about the job at the Pittsburgh school, well—it was as if her *heart* had moved there already.

Her inner turmoil must have been written all over her face, since Michael squeezed her hand and said, "Honey, don't worry—we'll figure out the job issues." Then he grinned—his sexy, gorgeous grin. "Nichols is always saying he wants to steal you away from me." Nichols was another investment advisor, whose office sat just down the hall from Michael's. "If Pam ever quits like she keeps threatening, maybe you could work for him instead. Maybe if we weren't working *closely* together, the powers that be would let us slide on the interoffice dating rule. But whatever the case, don't fret—it'll work out. I'll make sure of it."

Like not long ago, Marla could barely breathe. But for entirely different reasons now.

Tell him. Just tell him.

And this time, be sure you actually get the words out of your mouth!

She took a deep breath, then let it back out. Then forged ahead. "Well, the good news is—I don't think the interoffice dating policy is going to be a problem for us. But the bad news is . . . when I came into your office, I wasn't trying to tell you I was crazy about you, even though I am. I was trying to tell you . . . I'm moving to Pittsburgh."

Michael stopped walking, pulling up short. "What?"

She felt the blood drain from her face. This was so hard. Hard to say, and it would be even harder to actually *do*, but she had to. "Michael, I was offered a job by the Western Pennsylvania School for the Deaf. I didn't go looking for the job—*it* came to *me*. And you know I studied to teach deaf children." She'd told him about it many times over their lunches together. "It's what I've always wanted to do—I just haven't been able to do it yet. And now I can."

His eyebrows knit, his expression looking troubled. "So . . . you've already accepted this job?"

She nodded, lips pursed, muscles tensed. "There were a series of phone interviews, and then I drove up to check out the school and meet the staff one weekend last month. It's a really wonderful place, steeped in tradition, but also very cutting edge. It's exactly the sort of place I've always seen myself teaching."

He stayed quiet for a long moment, during which the shadows between the tall buildings seem to grow longer, darker, twilight descending with full force. When he spoke, his voice came stilted and stiff. "Well. That's great."

She couldn't ignore the obvious. "You don't *sound* like it's great."

He no longer met her gaze, his eyes flitting toward the sidewalk as he spoke. "I guess I'm just surprised. And . . . hell, I'll just say it. After what we just did, and the things we just said to each other—you expect me to be jumping for joy here?"

She swallowed, suddenly put on the defensive. "I wasn't expecting this—me and you. I was just trying to take hold of my life, not let it pass me by without pursuing my goals."

"That I get. What I'm sketchy on is . . ." He let out a heavy sigh. "Not an hour ago, you told me you loved me, that you've loved me since we met. But at the same time, you're getting ready to take off for Pittsburgh?" He narrowed his eyes on her. "When you're in love, Marla, you don't just pack your bags and get as far away from the other person as you can."

Now it was her turn to let out a long, hard breath. She'd expected him to be disappointed, but he sounded almost angry. "Michael, I never expected you to love me back. I felt like a high school girl who mooned over you but thought you'd never notice me. When the teaching opportunity came up, it would have seemed foolish not to take it. And Pittsburgh isn't the other side of the globe or anything."

"It's a freaking five-hour drive."

"I know. And that's tearing me up right now."

"Then stay."

Her heart pounded at the request. Without even trying,

she could see herself sharing a home with him, years down the road, as his wife, the mother of his children. A vision of them all at the beach, and just as quickly, another, this one around a Thanksgiving table, entered her head. It was a pretty great vision. And suddenly it didn't seem even remotely out of reach.

But then she realized. This was simple. So simple. When she'd started the interviewing process, the idea of moving had seemed huge and frightening and almost impossible, but somewhere along the way, it had also become *real*, a thing she was going to do, the path her life was supposed to take. There was no other answer.

"I have to do something for *me*, Michael," she told him. "And this is my chance. The only chance I may ever have to pursue what I want to do, something that will fulfill me and make me happy."

"So tonight didn't mean anything."

She blinked in disbelief that he was making this feel so "all or nothing." "It meant *everything*. And I don't see why this has to be over."

He looked her in the eye, letting her see the frank honesty in his gaze. "You know how my last long-distance relationship worked out."

Yeah, she did. He and Dahlia had grown apart and Dahlia had cheated on him. "I'm not her," Marla said.

"And *I'm* not up for a relationship that can't go anywhere because we're not in the same place." He stopped, sighed. "I love you, Marla, I really do. And so I'm asking you again. Stay. For me."

One more time, she considered it, envisioned the perfect life she could have with him. Perfect in every way except one. Which was that she'd never forgive herself if she didn't go to Pittsburgh. "I can't. I'm sorry. I have to do this. I have to follow my dream."

"Which clearly doesn't include *me*."

With that, Michael turned and walked away, leaving her to stand alone on the darkening street, unable to believe any of this had even happened.

"Morning, Carol," Michael said as he passed his new administrative assistant's desk, briefcase in hand.

"Good morning, Mr. Gates," she answered. Carol was a bright woman in her midfifties, happily married to a guy named Howard, and about to become a grandmother for the first time. She was competent, and learning Marla's job quickly, but kind of old school in some ways. She kept bringing him coffee when he was perfectly capable of getting it himself, and she insisted on calling him Mr. Gates.

"Michael," he reminded her.

She nodded, but he knew he'd still be Mr. Gates the next time she addressed him.

It had been a month since he'd seen Marla, that night on the street. She'd packed up and left the office during the week he'd been on that hellish vacation, drinking too much and lamenting how things had ended with her—he'd be lucky if his college buddies ever wanted to travel with him again. He'd quickly hired Carol and was thankful that nothing about his new assistant said "love interest."

As he powered up his computer and thumbed through the phone messages Carol had placed on his desk, he thought of what he'd done on that *same* desk with Marla.

Damn, he missed her.

Not just because he wished they'd gotten to do more of what they'd done on the desk, but he missed her voice, her smile, her intelligent conversation, her sense of humor— everything.

He knew it had been asking a lot to suggest she stay, but

it wasn't as if he'd been asking her to *really* give something up—was it? She hadn't even started the job yet when they'd talked that night—how important could it have been to her?

Of course, he firmly regretted the way he'd reacted. Everything had happened so fast, he'd been scheduled to leave on vacation the next morning, and old emotions from finding out Dahlia had been unfaithful to him had crept in quick. He worked pretty hard in life not to be a jerk, but he knew he *had* been—that night of *all* nights, with that woman of *all* women. He shook his head, sorry for his behavior.

Yet each time he thought through it, he still felt the same. He wished he'd taken the time to express it differently, more patiently, clearly—but he still didn't want a long-distance relationship. And he still found it difficult to believe she was really *that* crazy about him if she could just pack her bags and drive away without blinking.

"Mr. Gates?"

Carol's voice from the doorway made him realize he was sitting at his desk, elbows propped on his blotter, his head in his hands. He probably looked like he was about to self-destruct. He sat up straighter, tried to smile. "Yes, Carol? And remember, call me—"

"Michael," she finished for him. "Is everything all right . . . Michael? Is there anything I can do to help?"

He smiled softly at her use of his given name, the first time she'd actually called him by it. And because he had a habit—for the good or the bad—of developing personal relationships with coworkers, and because he really respected Carol, he said, "Let me run something by you, if you don't mind."

"Certainly," she said, and likely expecting him to share something of a professional nature, she took a seat across from his desk.

He told her the whole story about Marla, from start to finish. Well, he left out the part about sex on the desk—but he left *in* the part about the *I love you*s, concluding with, "So what do you think about that? That she would leave, just like that." He snapped his fingers for effect. "That's a woman I should try to forget about, don't you think?"

Carol didn't answer for a long moment, but he waited patiently, until finally she said, "Michael, I can tell you love your job and worked hard to get where you are. So take a moment to think about if the situation were reversed—if you'd been the one leaving, going to some other city, for *this* job. Would you have given it up? Or would you have expected her to understand?

"Love is important. So is passion. But there *are* other things in life that matter—a lot. And having something for one's self, be it great or small—well, that's what makes a person complete."

Marla sat on her sofa in her new high-ceilinged living room, trying to concentrate on the latest reality TV show, hoping to get wrapped up in other people's silly emotions instead of her own.

She'd rented an apartment that was actually part of a grand old home built in the early 1800s, and the architecture was fabulous. She'd mostly unpacked and even gotten a start on decorating. And although it was summer and she wouldn't be teaching until the fall session, she'd been getting acclimated at school, working with other instructors on designing her curriculum for the elementary-aged students who would be in her charge. She'd been in Pittsburgh for just over a month now, and it was wonderful and new and exciting and . . . well, okay, also a little bit sad.

She loved her new life, but she missed her man. Yet she

simply tried her damnedest not to think about him too much, because she still knew she'd done the right thing. She just wished she could stop fantasizing about him naked on a daily basis, the instances of which had increased considerably since her departure from Cincinnati. It had only been a month, but she was betting the number topped twelve hundred by now.

When a knock came on her door, she flinched. Who the hell could be out there? It was after dark on a Friday night and the only people she knew in the whole city were her new co-workers, who would surely call first if they needed something.

As she walked to the door, ready to peek through the peephole, she saw that it . . . didn't have a peephole. Damn. The things you don't miss until you need them.

The knock came again, so despite everything she'd ever learned about not opening the door if you don't know who's there, she threw caution to the wind and undid the lock, pulling on the knob.

Michael stood on the other side.

He wore blue jeans and a T-shirt and hadn't shaved and looked good enough to eat. Her stomach flip-flopped, and when she met his eyes, that quickly, she was lost in them.

She said nothing because she hadn't a clue what to say.

A sheepish smile made its way onto his face as he fished in the front pocket of his jeans, pulling out a scrap of white lace. "I forgot to give you back your panties."

She simply blinked, her heart beating a mile a minute, the crux of her thighs tingling madly. Fierce hope flirted around the edges of her heart, but she had to be cautious here. "That's it? That's why you drove five hours?"

"No." He paused, took a deep breath. "I also came to tell you that I was wrong. And that I acted like an asshole. And that I hope you can forgive me. And that I'm willing to try the long-distance thing if you are."

Oh God, was this real? He'd really come to Pittsburgh for her? To make up? To make things right? "So you finally figured out I'm really not Dahlia?"

"*Oh* yeah," he said. "You're *nothing* like her. Not by a long shot. You are . . . your own woman, Marla. And I *love* that about you. It just took me a little while to get over my selfishness and figure it out."

She took a calming breath, trying to get hold of herself and not look as wildly happy as she was on the inside. "So how will we do this?"

"Well, there's a weekend after every five days of work," he said with a hopeful grin. "And there are vacations and holidays. So I'm thinking I'll come here sometimes, you'll come home to Cincinnati sometimes. And in between all that, there are good cell phone plans with lots of monthly minutes. And, if all goes well, then maybe one of us will eventually decide to give up our job and move to where the other one is."

She let out a sigh as disappointment set in. "You mean *me*. You mean maybe *I'll* decide to move home."

But Michael just shook his head. "No—I mean *one* of us. Maybe you. Maybe me. Because if any woman could make me want her more than I want my job, it's you, honey. That simple."

And suddenly everything changed. All the tension that had filled Marla's body for the past month—tension she'd attributed to the move and the new job—faded to nothing, and she understood that was just how badly she'd missed him and how much she loved him. Everything was going to be all right now, as it *should* be.

"Can I kiss you?" he asked. "Because it's been a hell of a long month after just getting those first little tastes of you and not being able to have any more."

A flood of desire rushed Marla's body and she answered by

lifting her palms to his chest and pressing her body flush against his.

"I'll take that as a yes," he said, peering warmly down into her eyes, then brushing the most gentle kiss she could imagine across her lips.

"Mmm," she said, overwhelmed, like once before, at how powerful such a tiny little meeting of mouths could be.

But also like before, Michael didn't stop there, bringing his mouth down on hers more firmly until she was consumed by his kiss, and thoroughly turned on by the hardness now pressing so sexily against her thigh. "Is that a cell phone in your pocket or are you just glad to see me?" she whispered in his ear.

"Definitely the latter."

She sighed her pleasure and said, "I'm so glad you came."

"Forgive me for being a jerk?"

She nodded. "Forgive me for leaving?"

He nodded in return.

And that's when it hit her. Despite their hot, reckless office sex, she'd *still* never fulfilled any of her twelve-hundred-plus fantasies. "I've still never seen you naked," she announced without weighing the words.

First he grinned at her bluntness. But then his eyes darkened with a heat she felt all the way to her core. "That's about to change," he told her.

She didn't want to wait a minute more, so she took his hand and said, "Come inside."

And by the next morning, when Marla thought of Michael naked, instead of being a fantasy, it was a memory. One which she planned to refresh often.

LAST
OF THE RED-HOT
MAMMAS

Dianne Castell

"HONEY, THIS HAS NOTHING TO DO WITH FALLING madly in love or happily ever after or a meaningful relationship. This is about you needing to feel a man's weight on top of you, strong arms around you and getting yourself in a better state of being before someone locks you in a closet and throws away the key!"

Gloria listened to Sue Ellen—sister, best friend, and business partner—sitting on the other side of the marble counter in the back room of Scrumptious Savannah. "Your point being?"

"You need to get yourself laid!" Sue Ellen's eyes rounded and she slapped her hand to her mouth. "Heavenly days, I can't believe I blurted that out. At least the tearoom's closed for the day and no one heard, but it's true enough all the same. We're starting to lose customers." She leaned across the counter. "It's because two years is a mighty long time to go without and I'm guessing you probably can't recall the last time you were with a man."

"Excuse me?"

"Honey, you need therapy. Man therapy."

Gloria assumed a beady-eyed, older-sibling to younger-sibling stare and growled, "I'm forty, Sue Ellen. My chances of finding Mr. Right are less than getting struck dead on the street by a meteor, and one-night stands mean I'm a barfly over at the Blue Note. Yuck!"

Sue Ellen folded her hands beside a stack of cooling cakes. "Then . . . maybe . . . perhaps . . . you should just go and hire yourself a professional and hear me out before you blow a gasket. Get yourself one of those escort services Lovell used when he was out cheating around on you and rediscovering his youth. You need to rediscover your femininity."

"A service? Have you been tipping the wine instead of putting it in your sauce? Besides, I shop, I pluck, I shave and dye, and I adore chocolate. I am feminine!"

"It's not as bad as it sounds as long as you choose carefully. I read all about it in *Cosmo*. 'Ten Steps to Finding the Perfect Gigolo.'"

"Holy mother."

"Lovell ruined you when he hooked up with the twenty-something tart in Atlanta. I should have cut his heart out with a spoon like I planned on doing."

Gloria held up her hands. "I survived the divorce . . . and my other little problem. I got custody of Dacey against Lovell and his highfalutin lawyers. You and I started Scrumptious and it's doing right well, except for the five pounds I've acquired by tasting everything. I won."

"You need to be thinking about fulfilling your wildest dreams." She reached into her apron pocket and pulled out a string of condoms. "Indulge yourself. Oh please, for me, for the whole blessed town?"

"For heaven's sake!" Gloria stuffed the packets in her purse to get them out of sight. She stood, hands to hips. "Of all the conversations we've had, this is the most outlandish. Even beats the one with us kidnapping George Clooney so we could have him all to ourselves."

"I haven't given up on the George idea."

"You're married, Sue Ellen. The Clooney ship has sailed."

Pouting, Sue Ellen slid a paper across the desk. "I can tell you're not listening to me one teeny bit, so you might as well take the meeting over at Magnolia House and land us that wedding catering job. I have these Savannah Dream Cakes to ice up for the high school bake sale tomorrow. Room 234. They're picking out accommodations and welcoming baskets for the bridal party and, for crying in a bucket, be nice. We can use the business."

Gloria batted her eyes. "Sugar just melts on my tongue."

"Too bad it's not some man melting in your arms," Sue Ellen muttered as Gloria slammed the door behind her. She stopped. Okay, that was a little over the top . . . the slam, not the man part. She *was* a little touchy these days. Maybe if she ate more chocolate that would take the edge off her over-active libido. Could she find that much chocolate in all of Savannah?

Crossing Abercorn to Broughton, April sun peekabooed through mossy oaks then settled on pink, purple, and white azaleas blossoming everywhere. Savannah does springtime, there was nothing better . . . except maybe a man in her life.

No men! Concentrate on Magnolia House with its scrolled ironwork and oodles of Southern charm. She couldn't concentrate, period! The elevator stopped on the second floor, the door to room 243 open across the hall, the maid inside. "I'm all done now," she said, breezing through the door as Gloria entered. "Just needed to drop off some goodies." She winked and closed the door.

Okay, this was better. Business, all business, except for the wink. Maybe the maid thought she was the bride? Gloria put her purse on the desk and her eyes focused on a bottle of champagne chilling in a silver bucket and a plate of choco-late-dipped strawberries. Nice welcoming package for the wedding guests . . . except for the note saying, *Take a ride on the wild side and enjoy yourself. Sis.*

Oh . . . dear . . . Lord! Gloria's knees buckled and she grabbed the edge of the desk for support. A hotel room? Champagne? Wild side and a wink? Sis!

The room did a quick spin, Gloria's vision blurred and she

stumbled out of her heels and staggered into the bathroom, closing the door. She ran cold water into the marble sink and splashed her face.

What was Sue Ellen thinking? If George Clooney walked through the door she'd pass out. Except it wouldn't be George but some male of a paid nature from Studs-R-Us. She needed to get out of here! She splashed more water, then yanked open the door to . . . to tall and delicious standing by the desk, reading the note. His head snapped up, blue eyes widening a fraction as his gaze met hers.

Now what? Flee? Fantasize? Faint dead away! Except . . . except he was really nice to look at. Not Clooney or Pitt handsome, but hunky all the same. About her age with blue eyes and a slow half smile that unexpectedly warmed her heart. Didn't look like a gigolo. Like she'd know!

"Uh, hi," he said and held out his hand. She took it, a reflex from meeting clients, except no client ever made her heart jump. "Well," he said, waving the note. "I've got to say you're not exactly what I expected." He smoothed back his short-cropped brown hair that didn't need smoothing. "I meant that in a good way. I think. I'm sort of new at this. Make that brand new. Good lord, what the hell am I doing here?"

"That's my line." She considered strangling Sue Ellen with her own apron. "Sisters have a way of butting in when they shouldn't. I'll just leave." She shoved her feet into her shoes but got the left shoe on the right foot, tangled her legs, and Blue Eyes held her arm to help her balance.

Time stopped, probably because she hadn't been *held* in a long time. His eyes darkened to cobalt and he wasn't breathing. Or maybe she wasn't the one breathing?

"Oh, what the hell." He sighed. "I'm here, you're here, and you're really pretty, no matter how corny that sounds." Then his lips took hers, his arms slid easily around her back, bringing her body tight to his, and corny was suddenly the best word in the English language. Her heart skipped around in her chest and the sensation of being kissed—and it was really a good kiss—drowned out any protest.

How the heck could this have happened? Because he was paid! Duh! But not enough, because this kiss was rapidly escalating to sensational. Always nice to get your money's worth, and then some.

She tripped on the half-on shoe and grabbed his firm shoulders, trying not to whine like some inexperienced teenager.

"You smell like vanilla and cinnamon."

"Savannah Dream Cake."

His eyes twinkled now, a great grin on his delicious mouth that she needed to taste again. "You are every man's dream and right now you're mine."

"Me?" She'd never been someone's dream girl before, and if she was ever going to break off clandestine affair 101, now was the time.

"Oh, yeah, you. Definitely you," he said in a throaty voice. "I can't believe I'm here and maybe I shouldn't be, but . . . but I don't want to leave . . . you." Then he let her go and flung off his shirt, revealing fine pecs and abs and . . . and now he was kicking off his shoes while undoing his belt.

Holy crap! Could she do this? His pants hit the floor leaving him in gray skivvies and nothing else. How could she *not* do this? Sue Ellen had paid good money. She owed it to her sister to see this through, and what there was to see was downright terrific, and the covered part looked wonderfully promising.

"My goodness." *Or badness.* What was a woman supposed to say to a near-naked man while looking him over like a Savannah pastry? He gave her a come-hither look, a devilish smile, and crooked his finger.

Yikes! It was now or never. Could she? Would she? Forget never! That put her in the meteor category and she so preferred the celestial body in front of her. *Do it! Just do it!* a naughty voice said inside her head. Where'd that come from? And did she care? Her body was okay . . . now . . . Not perfect, but better than she thought it would be. What the hell! She kicked off her one shoe and it landed in the champagne bucket.

"Oops," she giggled and blushed as he grinned, putting her at ease. She pulled off her suit jacket, then her blouse, sailing it over his head.

Blue Eyes's grin grew. "You are a tease."

"Nice undies." Nice package expanding underneath!

Her skirt pooled at her feet and he let out a whistle. "To borrow a line, nice undies."

"Bet you say that to all the girls." She added a little hip action and head tossing. Soccer mom does flirt.

"No other girls."

At least not for the moment, she thought as he snapped her into his arms, his breath hot on her lips, his skin warm and yummy and next to hers, the aroma of spice and spring and delish man invading her senses. He kissed her, adding some tongue. Lord have mercy, the man gave great tongue! Her insides burned clear up to her eyeballs. How long had it been since she'd been kissed like this? "You are too much for me," she panted.

His hips pressed to hers again, his erection hard and throbbing. She couldn't remember the last time something throbbed besides a headache. God bless rent-a-stud!

He shuffled her back till her thighs met the edge of the bed then toppled them onto the mattress. Both laughing, he broke the fall so as not to squash her. A gentleman and a stud. He smoothed her hair from her face. "You . . . are a complete surprise. Fun, exciting, not pretentious."

"Too chunky?"

"Too perfect."

"Far from perfect." He unsnapped her bra, nuzzled up the flimsy material, and she froze. Oh, God! What if he noticed, got turned off or . . . But he didn't say a word or even slow down with the nuzzling, and when he kissed the dip between her breasts all what-ifs vanished. "I'm falling apart here," she whimpered.

He levered himself up, his eyes blue and fathomless and genuine. "Me, too, sugar."

Her brain fogged and her sex drive roared. "Take me now?"

"I can do that." He looked around.

"Hey, I'm right here."

"Protection."

"My purse." She nodded at the desk. "There."

"Good girl. Lovely girl."

There was a time when she doubted she'd ever hear a man say that to her. He kissed her quick then rolled off, landing on the floor with a solid thud. This really must be his first time. A virgin gigolo, how sweet.

She peered over the edge of the bed. "Are you okay?"

He glanced at the bulge in his briefs. "Everything that's important still seems to be working." He winked, reddened, then scrambled to his feet, got her purse and unceremoniously tugged off his briefs. His technique really needed work. Then he turned back to her, ready for action, and the action part didn't need any work at all. *Blue Eyes was built for action.*

"I'm usually not this clumsy," he said, at least that's what she thought he said. "The problem is that you're beautiful and charming and I can't think straight."

"You're really beautiful yourself."

His eyes followed hers to his erection and this time he

turned crimson. She'd never felt more tender toward a man in her life. Her darling gigolo. She held out her arms, growled, and he dove on top of her, the bed creaking as they sank into the softness. She laughed and so did he, but as he slid into her in one long, hard thrust, the last thing on her mind was laughter.

"Oh God!" she gasped, arching her hips and taking him in, her legs tightening around his back. He thrust into her harder, filling her in places she'd never had filled before. Lovell had been . . . lacking! Of course, with him being her one and only, she hadn't realized that till now. But he had been lacking . . . a lot! Her body clenched. "Holy crap? Holy crap!"

"Is that a good crap?" He took her again, his voice strained.

"The best! Do it, do it now!" Then she climaxed in an explosion of pure, long-overdue euphoria of mind and body . . . especially the body, little pieces of Gloria shattering all over the room.

"Incredible," he finally whispered in short, hot breaths, his lips next to her ear, his torso mated to hers. "Best sex I've ever had. I mean that, I really do."

"Ditto. You are amazing."

He kissed her cheek and she stroked his damp hair. "I didn't think you'd be so . . . caring or so enthusiastic."

"I thought the same about you." He gave her a sweet smile, the kind that said it had been as enjoyable for him as for her, and that it wasn't just a job. Then again, maybe that's what she wanted to think.

He sat. "Let me clean up and we can enjoy the champagne." He paused, peered deep into her eyes while dragging his finger down her middle, stopping at the indent of her navel. He planted a soft kiss there. "You are something to celebrate, in and out of bed. How'd I get so damn lucky to wind up with you?"

She felt sexy and feminine and a little wicked and truly desired . . . at last! And it was great! He closed the bathroom door and she stretched out on the bed, heaving a big sigh except . . . except . . . Okay, now what? She quit stretching and bolted upright. Toast him for being a fabulous stud and she a needy woman?

Ouch! She needed to keep this fantasy perfect, just as it was right now—the red-hot mamma and the hunk—and not spoil it with forced conversation and strained moments and too many questions. Scrambling out of bed, she yanked on her bra, panties, blouse, and skirt, then grabbed her jacket, shoes, and purse, leaving all the money in her wallet for a tip. Then she slunk out of the door and into the elevator across the hall.

When the double doors closed she hit the stop button, dressed, tried to do something with her bird-nest of hair, then continued down to the first floor. *Don't run,* she ordered herself as the doors parted and she stared straight ahead. *Walk naturally.* But there was nothing natural about hooking up with a paid escort at Magnolia House.

She did the Southern amble out the front door, made her way to Abercorn and through the back door of Scrumptious. She collapsed into the chair she'd occupied an hour ago. Had it been just one short hour?

"Well, did you get it?" Sue Ellen asked, not looking up as she added pink rosebuds to the white-frosted Dream Cakes. "That was really fast."

"Get it? I suppose that's one answer. And it was too fast and what in holy blazes did you think you were doing, Sue Ellen?" Her voice approached a screech.

Sue Ellen glanced up. "Uh, getting us a catering job? Helping us pay bills." She did a double take. "And what in the world happened to you? You look like you were shot out of a cannon."

Gloria buried her head in her hands. "How could you do this?"

"Sugar, butter, vanilla, a little coloring. Voilà, you get icing and—"

"Don't play dumb with me." Gloria slapped her hands flat on the marble countertop. "The man, Sue Ellen, the man! The rent-a-stud! Champagne, strawberries, walk on the wild side? Sound familiar? It was all there just like you ordered up and I can't believe you did this to your very own sister."

Sue Ellen licked pink icing from her thumb. "What are you talking about?"

"The gigolo!"

Sue Ellen stopped, eyes huge, a dollop of pink on the tip of her tongue. She swallowed. "Huh?"

"The least you could do is look ashamed or squirm or . . . or something. The innocent routine isn't working."

Sue Ellen put down the icing cone. "Honey, what exactly happened over at that hotel?"

"I got my needs met just like you paid for!" Gloria banged her forehead on the counter. "I'm officially a Savannah slut. Bet tour buses start stopping outside and guides start pointing and saying, 'See, there. The local hussy!'"

Sue Ellen said in a too-quiet voice, "I swear on Grandma's bread pudding recipe, the one with the rum, I have no idea what you're talking about. And I think I'm really sorry about that."

Gloria snapped her head up, her eyes an inch from Sue Ellen's. "Oh . . . my . . . God!"

"Somehow I don't think it was a religious experience."

"If you didn't buy him, then . . . then who the heck was he?"

"Since your eyes are shining and you've got color in your

cheeks, I'd say he was really, really good. Gives a whole new meaning to room service. Who knew room 234 would see so much action?"

Gloria felt her heart stop dead in her chest. "234? Don't you mean 243?"

Sue Ellen sucked air between clenched teeth.

"Holy Moses, he must have thought I was what I thought he was! And sent there by a sister. Probably his." Gloria slapped her palm to her forehead. "See, this is why there can be no more men for me. They screw up my life. I just proved that beyond a shadow of a doubt. I'm going home now to a glass of something strong and I'm going to forget today ever happened."

But the next morning as she followed Dacey up the high school steps to drop off Dream Cakes for the bake sale, Gloria knew she hadn't forgotten squat. The events at Magnolia House were burned in her brain for all eternity.

"Are you okay?" Dacey asked. "You just walked into the trophy case and apologized to it. How many cups of coffee did you have this morning, Mom?"

"Not enough." They headed for the cafeteria. Should she go to Magnolia House, find Blue Eyes, and straighten out this whole mess? Give the experience some closure, put it behind her. Except . . . except Blue Eyes was standing right in front of her, just like he had been yesterday, but this time with clothes on. "You!"

His eyes bulged, his jaw dropped, the tray of cookies in his hands crashing to the floor, the clatter drawing the kids' attention. Oh, terrific, an audience!

Dacey looked from one to the other. "You two know each other?"

"Uh . . ." Gloria managed and Dacey continued, "Yesterday was Mr. Langley's first day as principal and he just moved here from Atlanta."

Gloria swallowed. "We met at Magnolia House. I was giving a quote for a catering job, got into the wrong room and we sort of collided over—"

"Over a birthday present from my sister," Rab rushed on, trying to keep his head from whirling right off his shoulders. "A bottle of champagne. What a . . . surprise." It took every ounce of self-control he possessed not to blush over what he had done with what he *thought* was his birthday present. "Seems we both have interfering sisters." Least that's the best explanation he could come up with.

He glanced at the crowd of kids staring at him and Dream Cake. He had to do something or this would get real embarrassing real fast. "So, would you have dinner with me tonight?"

"Excuse me?"

Rab grabbed her dish before it joined his on the floor. "Since we didn't have time to talk yesterday when we met."

"A . . . date?"

"As in going out together." He needed to do something respectable in front of all these kids since the meeting between him and Dream Cake was out in the open and there was obviously something going on between them that was a little out of the ordinary. "You can choose the restaurant. I'm new in town."

She took a step back, sliding on cookie shrapnel. "No." She shook her head and held up her hands. "I can't because . . ."

"If you say you have to wash your hair I'm going to look really pathetic here." He tried a smile and glanced at the kids, hoping she'd get the message as to why he was doing this here and now.

"I have to walk the dog."

"We don't have a dog," her daughter protested.

"We're getting one. I've got to go. Right now." Dream Cake hustled out of the cafeteria as if her hair were on fire.

"Well," one of the senior boys said as he put his hand on Rab's shoulder. "You have officially been shot down, Mr. Langley."

"Crashed and burned," added another boy with a look that suggested he knew all too well what it felt like, the other boys nodding in agreement. The bell for first period rang and the kids headed off, some patting him on the back, looks of sympathy in their eyes. At least he had made a connection with the kids, but now what? He tried to ask her out and it flopped. He could walk away now and everything would settle down and no one would think anything of them knowing each other now. He'd done the respectable bit, except . . . except he suddenly didn't want settled. He thought he did when he left Atlanta and his ex-fiancée, who ran off with the rich used-car salesman. But suddenly there was a note and a hotel room and one big misunderstanding and excitement and passion and a very pretty and electrifying woman.

Rab caught up with Dacey before she got into the hall. "Can I talk to you a minute?"

She stopped and they waited till the others left, the cafeteria door closing. "This is a little awkward, but are you okay with me asking your mother on a date? If not, just say the word and I'll back off. I don't want to be a problem."

Dacey gave a little shrug. "My mom dating the principal is not exactly my dream come true, that's for sure. If I could have my choice you'd own a big boat out on Thunderbolt or the Bebe store on Boughton."

His smile met hers. "Sorry, no boats or boutique."

"I can deal." She giggled. "You really seem to have shaken Mom up, and she needs that. She needs something besides work. And if she focuses on you for a while maybe I can get her to let me go on spring break to the Bahamas with my friends."

"So, I'm a decoy?"

"Sort of." Dacey wrinkled her nose. "She's a great mom. Be nice to her."

He watched Dacey leave and headed off to find a broom. He'd heard that Savannah was a hospitable old Southern town and now he believed it. He just had to figure out how to get one terrific Savannah Dream Cake to go out with him. The first step was to find out her name!

Thank God the day was over, Gloria thought as she collapsed onto the couch and plopped a plastic bag filled with ice on her forehead and took a bite of the MoonPie in her left hand. That the bag leaked and a trickle of cold water slid down her temple underscored just what kind of day it had been. What had Blue Eyes been thinking asking her out on a date in front of half the student body? Not that it mattered because she was never going near that high school, or him, again, no matter how good looking he was or how great a kisser or how fine in the sack. Why couldn't she stop thinking about this guy! She took another bite, marshmallow sticking to her upper lip, the music that invaded the house not helping her pain at all. She yelled upstairs to Dacey, "Turn your stereo down, honey, I can hear it all over the house, even outside."

Dacey yelled back. "Stereos don't exist anymore except in the Smithsonian. Music's coming from outside."

And it was getting louder . . . like a chorus of some sort and— The doorbell bonged. "Go away. Take your music with you."

It bonged again. Door-to-door CD salesperson?

"I'll get it," Dacey called as she trotted down the stairs and opened the door to louder music and . . . "Uh, Mom, the school show choir's standing in front of our house. I think they're here for you."

"I've been out of high school for twenty-five years."

"Mr. Langley's here with yellow roses and I'm willing to bet those aren't for me unless it's the newest way to deliver a detention slip."

Gloria bolted upright, ice sliding into her lap. Her gaze met Blue Eyes's as the singers started in on "I've Got a Crush on You" and Dacey gave her a get-your-fanny-over-here look.

"I know the Dream Cakes are good," she said when she stepped out onto the porch. "But this is a little over the top."

Blue Eyes grinned and handed her the flowers as the song morphed into "Pretty Woman." Yeah, that's what she was, all right . . . in her purple sweats and flattened hair, one side wet. She waved to the choir and they waved back.

"What do I do?" she asked Dacey.

"Smile."

She plastered one on her face as the choir started down the street singing "Don't Be Cruel," leaving her alone with Blue Eyes on the porch. And just where was Dacey now? Daughters were never around when you needed them. Bet if there was a plane reservation to the Bahamas she'd be there.

"What are you doing?"

"Courting you."

"Courting? I think that belongs in the Smithsonian with my stereo."

"I'm not sure what that means but I am sure I want to see you and I don't want to sneak around to do it. I have kids watching my every move, so I decided to use them and have a little fun."

"I think that makes me a school project."

"I want the boys to know how to ask a woman for a date, not give up when she turns you down, and to try again. And to be respectful and mannerly and show a woman that she matters and is important to him. So, do I pass?"

Did he have to be so charming and responsible and really care about the kids . . . and her? "Every woman should be so lucky, but—"

"Does there have to be a *but*? We got our priorities out of order . . . Magnolia House first, dating second . . . and now I want to catch up. We get along and have a real connection, and not just of a carnal nature. It's only dinner, Gloria," he said with a smile in his voice. "Got your name from school records."

"I . . . I went through a rotten divorce and it took me two years to pull myself together, start a business, and feel whole again after my lumpectomy."

His eyes widened a fraction and she rushed on because he needed to know. "I had breast cancer three years ago. Didn't you notice the scar?" She touched the side of her breast.

"I wasn't looking. I had other things on my mind, like you."

She took his warm, strong hand. He needed to understand. "It could come back."

"I could get run over by a bus." His forefinger slid under her chin and he tipped her head so her gaze met his and she wasn't just staring at his nose. "I had my life all planned out. Knew exactly where I'd be ten years from now. Married, two kids, a tan Volvo. Then I got left at the altar. Plans are good for about a week and after that it's all a crapshoot."

She put her face an inch from his. "Read my lips, can-cer. Not pretty."

"But you are. In fact, you're dynamite."

"I have a scar to prove it."

He pulled up his right pant leg. "Motorcycle accident five years ago."

"Oh, good grief. It's not the same."

"I know." He kissed her on the cheek, his lips lingering a breath longer than the kiss required, nearly sending her into a swoon right there on her own front porch. "I want to give us a chance and I'm not giving up because of what might be. I like you, and I think you like me. We're good together, and not just at Magnolia House. We have a connection. I can feel it and I know you do too or you wouldn't be so concerned over a simple dinner."

He strolled down the walk and pulled something from his pocket. Was that a harmonica? He winked back at her as "I'll Be Seeing You" filled the air. He was pretty good, had probably done his share of talent shows in schools.

"This is the most romantic thing I've ever seen," Dacey said beside her, her eyes dreamy. "I get a text message from Jake asking me to meet him for pizza and you get yellow roses and a moonlight serenade. I'm totally jealous."

Dacey gave Gloria's hand a quick squeeze. "Go for it, Mom. You deserve it and he might just be the one who deserves you." She headed for the stairs, the harmonica music fading.

Okay, Dacey was right, this was pretty romantic stuff. But just because some guy made her feel all warm and gushy inside didn't mean it would last. What if things fell apart and if the cancer came back and what if he freaked like Lovell had and left her?

Nope, she'd sworn to never get involved with a man again, and getting her heart broken for the second time was not worth with the risk.

"It *is* worth the risk," Sue Ellen declared as she served up a bowl of crab bisque and pecan chicken salad to a customer standing in front of the white counter at Scrumptious. Sue Ellen adjusted her yellow-and-blue-checked apron that matched the curtains and tablecloths covering the little bistro tables.

"That's because you're married and in love," Gloria said, packing up quiche, sweet potato soup, and praline cheesecake for Miss Jenkins's afternoon card party.

"You need to get yourself out there, girl, and . . ." Both stopped dead as a line of teens, each holding a flower, entered the shop. The line stretched out the door and a girl in front cleared her throat and said, "This is a special and personal delivery from Mr. Langley, hoping it will brighten your day."

She set a vase on the counter and put in a daisy, the boy behind her added a tulip, the next adding a daffodil, the next a sprig of peach blossoms. The kids streamed into the shop in single file, adding flowers and vases as needed until bouquets filled the counter and all the tables, the place looking more like a conservatory than a tearoom. Customers sat in wonder, others crowded in from outside, and at the end of the line was Rab Langley. "Pretty flowers for a pretty lady." He handed her another bunch of yellow roses.

Everyone applauded and the teens sang a quiet version of "Gentle On My Mind." Langley did a low bow. "Will you have dinner with me?"

"This is so romantic," a lady sitting at a table purred, clasping her hands to her breast and looking all moony-eyed. "The only thing my husband brings me is fish to fry up for him for dinner."

"My husband wouldn't know a rose from a rat," another groused. "I should bring him here for lessons."

Gloria smiled sweetly. "This is dirty pool, Mr. Langley. You're putting on the pressure."

"Because he really likes you," a lady in a pink sundress added. "If you don't do dinner with the man, I sure will."

Gloria resisted the urge to grind her teeth and Blue Eyes

continued, "This is my last offer. Take me now or lose me forever." He said it lightly but she knew he meant it.

Okay, this was good news, right? She'd tell him to hit the road and then get on with her life. Customers and students looked on. Waiting. Drat! She hated to turn Blue Eyes down in front of everyone. "I think you're a great guy—"

"Ah, there's another *but* coming, I can feel it."

"But I'm not up for dating or even dinner. I'm a single woman and I'm happy that way."

"And you're sure?" he said with a half smile.

"I am. And if I wasn't, you'd be the first guy I'd run after."

Customers shook their heads in disappointment and someone muttered *stupid, stupid woman.* Blue Eyes kissed the back of her hand then turned and left, the teens trailing behind.

"Have you lost your ever-loving mind," Sue Ellen wailed. "Women wait all their lives for someone like Sweet-stuff here to come along, and what do you go and do? Throw him back like some runt fish caught on your line. I'm here to tell you that man is no runt."

"I think that's my cue," said pink sundress. She headed for the door. "I'm coming, honey," she called down the street. "You wait up for me now, you hear." She ran out, skirt flapping, purse still on the table.

Gloria's stomach flipped and Sue Ellen took the purse for safe keeping. "You're not looking too good, Gloria. Could it be that even though you don't want Blue Eyes, you can't stand the thought of someone else having him? You can't have it both ways, you know."

"Well maybe I can." Gloria slid off her apron and cut through the back alley, finally spotting Blue Eyes making his way to the high school. The kids were out for the day but the principal's day was probably far from over. As he went by she snagged his jacket and yanked him into the alley behind a purple azalea big enough to conceal an army tank. She flattened him against the wall as his eyes rounded, a smile slowly forming on his great kissable lips, the heat from his body mixing with hers.

"Changed your mind, did you?" He kissed the tip of her nose. "Where do you want to have dinner?"

"Here. I mean I don't want dinner exactly, more like I want you . . . like this."

"Behind a bush?" He paused, his blue eyes dark now, and he shook his head slowly. "And I want a commitment . . . at least a one-date commitment that has the potential to develop into something more. I think it would, if you'd give it a chance."

"Since my divorce all I've done is take chances."

"Except you're not willing to take a chance on the one thing that matters most—your heart. Don't you want to share your life with someone who cares? You've got to take that leap of faith and believe in me, believe in us."

"I leaped once and *splat*. I can't go through that again."

"Then that's your decision and I'm sorry for both of us." He kissed her gently on the mouth then walked off.

"Wait."

He didn't even turn back. Blast the man! She ran after him. Taking his arm, she turned him around. "All right, all right. You win, I lose. I'll change, just like you want."

"This isn't about winning and losing."

"Then could we make it about sex? I think I definitely got the sex part down." She kissed him, throwing in some tongue of her own and groin-to-groin grinding that left nothing to the imagination.

He gently shoved her away. "That doesn't work for me."

"Worked pretty good last time and felt like it was doing fine this time, too." She grinned; he didn't.

"It's either the right way or no way. I'm the high school principal, and you're a mom and a respected woman in the community. We're both too old to be sneaking around and playing games."

"You're turning me down?"

"Flat as a pancake, sweetheart."

Her lips pursed. "Well, fine!"

"Actually, it's not, but there's nothing I can do about it. I'm not afraid of your cancer, Gloria."

"But I am!"

"I won't run if the going gets tough. I'd never do that to you." He rounded the corner and left her alone, all alone, standing on the sidewalk. *The rat!*

"Well, heck." She stomped her way back to the tearoom, the azaleas looking blah now, the sky more clouds than blue.

Sue Ellen arched an accusing brow as she entered and Gloria said, "Do not say a word. You got me into this, you know."

Sue Ellen gave her an evil look and Gloria recanted. "Okay, I got myself into this. Not that it matters. I mean, we . . . I have issues. Baggage problems. And I don't even know the man's name."

Everyone in the room shouted, "Rab!" and a man at the corner table added, "And we all have baggage, every one of us."

She held up her hands in surrender. "I get it." Or did she? Gloria peered at the older couple at the table by the window who'd been married so many years they looked alike. Always together, always sharing, and always there for each other. The young newly-married twosome in the corner with shiny rings and mesmerizing looks that rendered them the only people on earth. The mom, dad, and three kids having lunch, laughing and talking about the day.

She suddenly wanted that—or maybe it wasn't so sudden, but now she had the courage to admit it. Not that she couldn't exist just fine and dandy by herself as a single woman, but there was more in her life since she'd tripped out of her shoes at Magnolia House. There was Rab. He believed in her, helped her believe in herself again, and the most amazing thing of all . . . he believed in them together. How'd she get so lucky to find him? How'd she get so stupid not to run after him?

"I . . . I blew it, didn't I?"

"Gee, you think?" Sue Ellen smirked with perfect sibling sarcasm.

"Guess I could call him up and say something like, *Hey, Rab, how about a pizza?* That's a start, right?"

Everyone booed and Sue Ellen added, "That's a coward. You shot him down in public so you've got to make up the same way. It's only fitting." She swept her hands over the flowers. "The problem is, how in the world do you top all this?"

Rab sat back in his chair, reeling from his fifth mom conference this morning, along with his fifth invite for dinner, lunch, a beach picnic, midnight stroll, and two sleepovers. Some women didn't believe in beating around the bush when it came to what they wanted. Him! He stretched and stood as the most god-awful racket penetrated right through the walls of the school. A bagpipe with the flu? He did a quick trot down the empty hall and flung open the front doors to . . . Gloria? Gloria playing an accordion over a mic and singing the worst rendition ever of "I'm Sorry, So Sorry."

His ears hurt but his heart kicked into overdrive. Windows in the school flew open, kids and teachers leaning out. Some cheered, all clapped, and Gloria reddened but kept on playing. If he wanted the students to believe in romance and the power of love, here it was in their own front yard.

Gloria finished the song to more cheers. She untangled herself from the accordion straps and took the mic in her hand. "Mr. Langley," her voice boomed. "I've reconsidered your lovely invitation for dinner and would be honored to accompany you, except I think it should be for lunch."

"And," said Rab in his loudest principal voice. "Where would you like to have this lunch?"

"Right here is the perfect place."

A parade of people suddenly crossed the street carrying large pizzas, blankets, and cartons of soda. He recognized the people from the tearoom yesterday when he and the kids dropped off the flowers. A roar of approval ran through the school and students poured out the front door for an unscheduled picnic. Gloria shrugged, then picked up a basket and walked toward him, her yellow sundress fluttering in the breeze, her hair shining in the Savannah sun, her smile radiant. God, he could love her, and in time she'd realize she could love him, too.

"Lunch." She handed him the basket with an air of confidence he hadn't noticed before. "And me."

"A very lovely you. Are you going to teach me how to play the accordion?"

"Only if you teach me how to play the harmonica."

"A duet." He winked. "I like the sound of that." He took her hand. This was definitely the start of something big.

SALESMAN OF THE YEAR

KAREN KELLEY

·1·

JENNIFER GLANCED AT THE CLOCK ON THE DASH AS she pulled in the driveway, parking next to a black pickup. Probably the Realtor's. She was early. A sense of relief washed over her. Adam was easily irritated. Heaven forbid that she should annoy her fiancé more than once a day.

Now she was being bitchy and unfair. Adam had a lot on his mind with his clinic—*their* clinic—opening next month, and their wedding the following month. For him, everything had to be perfect.

She turned off the engine and got out of her car, looking up at the red brick house. Tall windows, massive entrance—ostentatious. Adam loved impressing people. She would've been just as happy in something smaller.

Her heels clicked on the sidewalk as she walked to the front door. Before she could ring the bell, the door opened—and she stepped back into the past.

Her heart fluttered inside her chest. Her skin went from hot to cold, and then back to hot.

"Hey, Jenny-girl, go to the prom with me." Devon ran a finger down the side of her cheek in a light caress.

She leaned toward him. He brushed his lips across hers. Heat flooded her body. She wanted to say yes, she did, she did . . .

And just like when she was a junior, and he a senior in high school, goose bumps popped up on her arms. She opened her mouth, but no words came out.

"Hi, Jenny." His words were spoken with a soft, southern drawl, jerking her back to the present.

He crossed his arms and leaned against the doorframe, a lazy smile lifting one side of his mouth. His dark hair was still a little too long, just like in high school. He hadn't cut it back then, either. He'd spent a lot of time in detention his senior year. The bad boy of Austin High. The rebel that had all the girls drooling, including her.

She cleared her throat, pulling herself back to the present. "Devon, what are you doing here?"

"I grew up and became a Realtor." His gaze lazily roamed over her again, bringing a flush to her cheeks. "And I see you grew up."

She might have drooled over him once, but she was engaged now, and his flirting wouldn't work. "Yes, I grew up and became a doctor."

She fingered the necklace beneath her sweater, then realized she was fidgeting, just like she had when Devon asked her to the prom. She'd really wanted to go with him, but her father had forbidden it. She'd always done what was expected of her.

"From animal doctor to people doctor," he said.

He remembered she'd wanted to be a vet? Her heart fluttered again. Not that it mattered, she quickly told herself. He'd wanted to get out of town and make a name for himself. Apparently, his plans had changed, too.

She shrugged. "Things change."

"Or people force them to change."

She cocked an eyebrow. "Are you implying something?"

He pushed away from the door. "What, that maybe your daddy convinced you being a physician was a much more noble profession? Of course not. I wouldn't dream of doing that."

"Sarcasm doesn't suit you." God, she sounded so prim and proper. "It's . . . It's good to see you again." And she really meant it. Maybe too much, though.

He moved so she could enter the house. She kept her back straight, eyes forward as she walked past him.

"You still smell nice." His voice was a whispered caress, skimming over her. "The same perfume. It drove me crazy all these years away from you. I couldn't figure out the scent."

"I doubt that. I'm sure you've had your share of women. You probably didn't think about me at all." She moved into the house, stopping in the first room she came to, which happened to be the formal living room. It was just as she'd expected—large, very overwhelming . . . and cold.

"You're wrong," he said.

She turned and looked at him, wondering if he'd read her mind about the house.

"I have thought about you," he continued. "I remember I asked you to the prom, and you wanted to go. But you said no."

She walked over to the fireplace, running her hand across the smooth surface. She'd been so young back then, and Devon was everything she wasn't supposed to yearn for. But she had.

"My father wouldn't let me."

"He didn't think I was good enough."

There was no anger in his words. He was just stating a fact. One they both knew.

"I wanted to go," she said before she could call back the words.

"I know. You never were the stuck-up kind. Only dutiful."

"I'm getting married—next month." Why had she just blurted that out? She sounded so defensive.

"Congratulations. Did your father pick him out?"

She was saved from answering when the front door opened, and Adam walked inside. She was relieved she didn't have to answer. If the truth be known, her father had introduced them. Maybe he'd steered her toward Adam, but she was the one who'd fallen in love with him.

Adam glanced toward Devon, then dismissed him. "Hello, darling."

She looked at the two men, noting the differences. Adam was just under six feet, blond hair and perfectly groomed. Adam would never be caught in a pair of jeans, unless they were a pair of designer jeans.

Adam's gaze moved to the ceiling as he inspected their potential home. She wished he would've kissed her cheek or at least draped his arm across her shoulder. But Adam didn't like public displays of affection. Too vulgar.

She looked at Devon. He raised an eyebrow. It would be just like him to push Adam's buttons. It wouldn't bother him a bit to take Adam down a peg or two, and Devon could do it.

She walked closer to Adam, smiling. "I was beginning to wonder what had happened to you."

Adam frowned. "I was going over plans with the interior decorator. Someone told her we wanted a pale yellow wall color. I wasted an hour with her. We'll go with a neutral color, beige, just like I'd planned. Yes, I'm late. I don't have all the time in the world—unlike you."

Heat rose up her face. "I'm . . . I'm sorry."

There was an uncomfortable silence.

"No, I'm the one who's sorry." Adam reached for her hand and squeezed it. "It's just been an incredibly long day."

"Of course."

His cell phone rang. "I need to take this." He strode to the other room, already talking on the phone.

"I think I would've preferred yellow," Devon said. "Beige is boring."

"That's what I thought, too." She fiddled with her necklace. "But Adam is much smarter in these things. He researches every detail."

"Did he research you before he asked you to marry him?"

Why was Devon doing this to her? She felt as though she were being pulled from different directions. Of course Adam hadn't researched her. But then, he'd already known her father was a well-respected doctor.

"Don't worry about it," he said. "Come on and I'll show you the rest of the castle."

She laughed. It bubbled out of her before she could catch it. She quickly looked toward the room Adam had stepped inside. His back was to her, and he still spoke on the phone. He hadn't heard her. Adam thought her laughter too loud, and he was right.

"I always loved when you laughed," Devon said. "I miss the spontaneity."

"Sometimes I'm too loud," she admitted.

"Why? Because a handful of jealous people tried to make you feel less of a person? Have you ever thought they might be the ones who are wrong?"

"We can continue now," Adam said as he stepped back into the room.

Saved from answering—again. Good. She wasn't sure how she would've responded. Adam was a good man, and a fantastic doctor. Her father approved of him one hundred percent.

Adam didn't mean to be critical, and he always apologized later, if not immediately.

Lately, she'd begun to wonder if getting married was a bad decision. Even before she'd seen Devon. She felt as though she were slowly sinking in the deep end of a very large pool.

They stepped into the kitchen. For the first time since entering the house, she liked what she saw. "Oh, it's beautiful," she breathed.

The kitchen was large, but it still felt cozy. The cabinets were a cream color, and it had all the modern appliances in a soft, off-white. A farmhouse sink with an antique, weathered-copper faucet rounded out the perfect picture of a family kitchen.

She looked at Adam, noted his frown, and her spirits dropped. "You don't like it?"

"You do?" He shook his head. "I thought you'd want something more modern. This just looks a little too . . . country, don't you think?"

"That's exactly what I like about it."

His sigh was long, deep, and unmistakable. "Of course, if you like it that much—"

"I do."

Devon chuckled, but quickly covered it with a cough. Adam turned his attention to Devon, his frown deepening.

"This is only the first house we've looked at," she quickly spoke up. "I'm sure we'll find one we absolutely love."

"You're right," Adam said.

When he smiled, she saw the Adam she'd first met. The one she'd fallen in love with. He looked boyishly handsome.

"Would you like to see the upstairs?" Devon asked.

"No, we wouldn't." He turned to Devon. "Do you have something you can show us with a more formal kitchen? We don't want to start off our marriage with a lot of remodeling."

And just as fast, Adam was back to the man she was starting to see more often.

·2·

DEVON PULLED IN THE DRIVEWAY OF THE SECOND
house that was on his list. Jenny parked beside him,
Adam directly behind her, but rather than getting out of his
car, Adam brought his cell phone to his ear. Jenny looked
anxiously behind her as she shut her car door.

Devon just shook his head.

He didn't like Adam. The guy was a jerk. Why couldn't
Jenny see that? He grimaced, already knowing the answer.
She'd been programmed to like him, to do exactly what was
expected of her.

If she followed through with the course she was on, he'd
be willing to bet that in ten years there'd be nothing left of
the Jenny he'd known in high school. Back then, he'd seen
some rebellion in her. Now, there was barely any left.

"I'm sure he'll be joining us soon. He's a cardiologist and
stays so busy." She fingered something beneath her sweater—a
necklace? Rosary? She'd need one if she married Adam.

"And what about you? Do you stay busy?"

She shrugged. "I'm a GP. Today's my day off."

"Let's go inside." He unlocked the front door, letting her
precede him. She not only smelled nice, she looked nice, too.

Except for the way she dressed and wore her hair now.
She'd pulled it up and twisted it into some kind of bun. He
supposed some would say it was a more sophisticated style.
He'd liked it better loose.

The dark blue skirt and white sweater she had on came
across as demure, just like he'd expect a doctor to dress. But

he remembered when she used to wear jeans and T-shirts. That was before her personality had been slowly sucked from her, and only a shell remained. Was his Jenny-girl lurking somewhere inside this woman?

"Tell me what you think," he said.

She glanced over her shoulder, her cheeks a rosy hue. It made him wonder what exactly she'd been thinking. About him, maybe? The passionate kisses they'd once shared? Or was that just wishful thinking on his part?

"About the house," he clarified. "If I know what you like or dislike then I can narrow the search."

She glanced toward the front door.

"Not what Adam thinks. What do you think?" He stepped closer, brushing some loose strands of her hair behind one ear. "I loved when you wore your hair down."

Her forehead puckered. "You left."

Lost in thought, it took a moment for her words to sink in. "You wouldn't have come with me."

She walked to the window. "You're probably right. Heaven forbid that I should upset my father," she spit out. "Sometimes I'd wish—"

"What?"

The door opened and Adam walked in.

"It's too late." She shook her head.

Adam glanced at his watch. "Of course it's not late. Sometimes you act as if you're an old woman, Jennifer." He glanced around the room. "It's small. Let's see the rest of the house." Adam marched past Devon and went toward the kitchen.

As Jenny walked by, he said, "It's never too late." She stumbled, caught herself, and kept walking.

"This kitchen is better," Adam said. "More to my liking."

"What do you think, Jenny?" Devon asked.

Adam raised an eyebrow. "Her name is Jennifer."

Devon leaned against the counter, "I guess she'll always be Jenny to me."

Adam looked from him to Jenny, then back to him. "What exactly does that mean?" His eyes narrowed.

"We knew each other in high school," she quickly interjected.

"High school?" Adam scrutinized Devon a little closer. "And then you became . . . what? A Realtor?" he smirked.

"Yeah, something like that."

"I think it must be a fabulous job." Jenny's words tumbled out. "You get to make dreams come true when people purchase their home."

Adam raised a sardonic eyebrow. "Of course, I can see the rewards one might have from being a . . . salesman. I certainly didn't mean to imply that it couldn't possibly compare to, say, a cardiologist."

Devon's smile widened. He knew Adam's game. Trouble was, he could play games, too. Except he never played by the rules. "No offense taken."

"What college did you attend?" Adam asked, looking as though he were really interested. Devon knew better.

"I didn't go to college," Devon replied. "I dropped out of high school my senior year." He nodded toward a set of French doors. "Would you like to see the pool?"

"If you're looking for some extra money, we need someone who can clean up around the clinic. It would be only temporary until we can hire someone full-time."

Adam's expression was easy to read. He thought he'd already won.

"I'd love to have a pool," Jenny said, casting a look of apology in Devon's direction, then regretted her intervention when Adam frowned.

"It would help you keep the weight off, too," he said. He

looked at Devon again. "Jennifer's weight has a tendency to fluctuate. She has to constantly watch what she eats. Exercise would do her good." He stepped out on the patio, and glanced around.

"I've never had a problem with my weight!"

"But wouldn't you love to have a pool, darling? I want to keep my wife happy." He smiled at Jenny.

"I think her weight looks pretty darn good." Devon let his gaze wander over her. "In fact, I would imagine you'd have to be careful someone didn't steal her away from you."

Adam bristled. "And what about your wife?"

"Me? Not married. I was in love once, but I let her slip away."

"This house won't do at all." Adam put his arm around Jenny's shoulders and pulled her close. "We're looking for something high-end. Do you handle the more expensive properties or will we need to see someone in your company who might have a greater degree of knowledge?"

Jennifer wanted to die. Adam was being so rude, but his words didn't seem to bother Devon. They just rolled off him. She wanted to tell him one's job didn't matter as long as he loved what he was doing.

"I'm sure Devon is top in his field. Not everyone wants to be a cardiologist—or a physician, for that matter."

"This isn't like you, Jennifer." Adam moved away from her and marched toward the front door. "Your hormones must be acting up."

She opened her mouth, but his cell phone began to ring. She just stood there fuming and wanting to inflict bodily harm.

"Here." Devon handed her a ceramic dish that was out for display. "Throw that at him."

She laughed, some of her tension draining. "I'm not sure it would help."

"Why are you with him?" he asked as they walked toward the front of the house.

"He's not always like this."

"You mean he's not constantly putting you down?"

"He doesn't mean to. Adam has a lot on his mind. We're opening a clinic, and then there's the wedding the following month and . . ." She frowned, her shoulders slumping. "He wasn't this bad in the beginning."

"If he's different now, then why are you still planning on marrying him?"

Adam snapped his cell closed. "Could we please leave for the next house? It's not like I have all the time in the world."

He went to his car, not waiting for them. Adam apparently assumed they'd follow suit. And they did. But as Jenny went to her vehicle, she pulled the clip from her hair and shook it out. Much, much better. She ran her hands through her hair.

Wearing her hair up was a pain in the butt. It was thick and heavy. Usually by afternoon, she'd have a headache. When had she started wearing it up? Had it been her father or Adam who'd suggested the style? She couldn't remember, but a cold shiver ran up and down her spine when she thought about how similar the two men were.

Just before she got in her car, she glanced at Devon. He grinned and winked. She knew he referred to her small act of rebellion. And it *was* small, but, darn it, she felt a lot better for it.

As she followed Devon to the next property, she began to wonder when she'd given up all her dreams. She *had* wanted to be a veterinarian rather than a physician. She loved animals.

And she'd wanted to go to the prom with Devon. Her father had forbidden it, so she'd chosen to stay at home. Her defiance had infuriated him.

That night, she'd vowed she would be her own person. She'd wanted to tell Devon she was sorry, but he'd left school. No one knew where he'd gone. She went as far as to go over to his parents' house. They were both drinking, said he'd left, and they didn't know where he'd gone. They didn't seem to care, either. So much time had passed, but it seemed like only yesterday.

Devon pulled into another driveway. Her mouth dropped open. He couldn't be serious. It looked more like an office building than a home. It was all sharp angles and flat surfaces.

"This is more like it," Adam said as he got out of his car.

Devon didn't look in her direction. A good thing, too. The look she would've given him might have been strong enough to cause physical harm. This monstrosity was not a home. It wasn't even close.

They went inside, and it was even worse. Would anyone be able to make it feel warm? It wasn't a task she'd want.

"We could put a couple of white sofas opposite each other in this room. And a glass coffee table between them."

She shook her head. "I don't like it. Doesn't it feel cold to you?"

Adam clamped his lips together. "I'm trying my best to juggle everything that has to be done before the wedding, Jennifer. Would you rather we spent our honeymoon in your father's home?"

Her father's home? "I thought we were going on a cruise?"

He refused to meet her gaze. "I had to cancel that. I don't have time to take off." He walked to the far side of the room.

"And when exactly were you going to tell me that we aren't going on a honeymoon?"

He faced her. "Don't be so childish, Jennifer." He frowned. "You've lost the clip from your hair."

"No, I haven't. I wanted to let my hair down. It was giving me a headache."

Adam's frown only deepened.

"Would you like to see the rest of the house?" Devon asked.

"Yes, of course," Adam said.

He would do anything to drop the subject, and she knew it. But it wasn't the end of their discussion. Not by a long shot.

The kitchen was worse than the front room. It looked like something right out of a futuristic movie. With all the polished chrome, who needed a mirror? And she'd be willing to bet she'd be the one doing the polishing, too. Adam had already said he didn't want to hire a maid because she would go through his things.

"This house is perfect," Adam said again as he walked into the kitchen.

She might as well not even have an opinion. "I said I don't like it," Jennifer told him again, talking a little slower so he might understand exactly what she was telling him.

"You're upset about the honeymoon, aren't you? Your father was afraid you might rebel."

"My father knows we aren't going on a honeymoon? You talked to him before you did me?"

Adam stood taller. "I respect your father's opinion."

"I do have another house that might work," Devon interrupted.

There was so much more that she wanted to tell Adam, but there was something about the way Devon looked at her. It made her hesitate. She couldn't quite put her finger on it though. He was plotting something.

"We'll look at it but I'm sure this is the house we'll choose," Adam said.

I think not, Jennifer thought to herself, returning her attention to Adam. Why *had* she agreed to marry him? He could be a real ass sometimes.

A flutter of excitement swept through her. It was almost as though the old Jenny were emerging, breaking through the shell that had encapsulated her.

·3·

DEVON WAS TAKING A CHANCE AND HE KNEW IT. HE glanced in his rearview mirror and wondered what Jenny was thinking. Yeah, he'd known she'd hate that contemporary monstrosity. It was everything she disliked. He had a feeling he knew her better than she knew herself.

And he was cheating, pushing all the right buttons, fighting dirty. He grinned.

He pulled in front of the house that he wanted them to see. It wasn't as large as the other homes, but it sat high on a hill and a person could almost see forever. Large plate-glass windows framed a view that looked down on the tops of trees, and made one feel as though they were in a tree house.

He got out of his pickup, shutting his door. When he looked at Jenny, he knew from her expression it was exactly what she was looking for in a home.

If things didn't go just right, he might be in trouble for showing this place. Sometimes life was all about taking chances, chasing your dreams.

"It's beautiful," she said as she came to stand beside him.

"And it's in the middle of nowhere," Adam complained as he joined them. "I don't want to live in the country." He wrinkled his nose in distaste.

"Let's at least look at it. We're already here." Jenny didn't wait to see if he followed, but walked toward the front door.

Devon produced a key, and quickly unlocked it.

She stepped inside. "Oh, someone is living here."

"It's not vacant."

Adam pushed past Devon. "I told your company that we needed to start moving in as soon as possible."

But Devon wasn't worried about what Adam wanted as he watched the expression on Jenny's face. It was pure joy, as though she knew she'd come home.

"I love it. It's open and airy." She walked closer to the windows. "A tree house." She laughed.

"No," Adam said with a shake of his head. "This won't do at all. I refuse to live here. This house is too small, and not nearly as dramatic as we want. A home should make a statement."

Jenny faced Adam. "That's exactly what's wrong with you. A home shouldn't make a statement. Unless it's a statement attesting to the love inside."

Adam's lips thinned. "You don't know what you're talking about, darling. I'm sure when you think about it, you'll realize I'm right."

"No, I won't."

"I refuse to live here," Adam said.

Devon noticed that Adam's face had begun to turn red. He wondered if he knew that getting this pissed off could cause a coronary. Probably, since he was a cardiologist.

Devon looked at Jenny and grinned. He could see from the expression of defiance on her face that the old Jenny had pushed her way past all the barriers and restrictions that had been thrown up in front of her.

"Then don't live here," she said, crossing her arms in front of her.

Adam relaxed. "Good, I'm glad you see it my way. We would never be happy here."

Jenny tugged off her engagement ring and handed it to Adam. Dumbfounded, he took it.

"What's this for?"

"You're right, Adam, we would never be happy together."

"That's not what I meant, and you know it."

"When I first met you things were different between us. I thought you loved me, but you don't. You loved what I could bring to the marriage. But you know what? You're a first-class jerk." She poked her finger at his chest. "You love dominating people and that isn't what love is all about."

"I'm going to call your father!"

She laughed. "Yes, call my father. You're two of a kind. I'm sure you can carry on quite a conversation about how I've gone off the deep end."

"It's his fault!" Adam pointed toward Devon. "I'll have your job for this! Who's your supervisor?"

Devon reached into his back pocket and pulled out a business card, handing it to him. "That would be me."

Adam looked at the card, then at Devon. "You're the owner of Two Hearts Property Management," he mumbled, staring at the card.

"Two Hearts?" Jenny's gaze swung to Devon.

"You're worth millions." Adam was still staring at the card.

Jenny looked around. "This is your house, isn't it?"

"Remember the day we talked about what kind of house we wanted to live in someday?" Devon asked. "You laughed and said you wanted to live in a tree house."

She reached inside her sweater and pulled out her necklace. Two hearts entwined. He'd given it to her for her birthday.

"Isn't this cozy," Adam snarled. "Lovers reunited and all that crap. You can have her." He looked at Jenny with contempt. "You would have never made a decent wife for me. I need someone who will complement me. I doubted you were good enough from the start. Not at all like your father." He nodded toward Devon. "And he'll see that, too, eventually."

Devon had had just about enough of this guy. "Get out of my house."

"Gladly!" Adam turned on his heel, slamming the door as he left.

"I didn't think he'd ever leave," Devon said.

"You planned this whole thing," she said.

"Guilty."

"You don't look guilty."

"I don't feel guilty, either." He stepped closer, taking her in his arms and lowering his mouth. Her lips were warm against his. She tasted sweet, just like he remembered. When he ended the kiss, he continued to hold her close. "I never stopped loving you."

"Me, too." She drew in a deep breath. "I wish you hadn't left."

"I needed to. I couldn't ask you to go with me when I didn't even know where my next meal was coming from."

"Do you really own your own company?"

"Yeah, I did well in real estate. I had a great mentor. I bought a small company, and it sort of grew from there. I can take care of you now."

"We'll take care of each other."

He smiled, hugged her tighter. "I'm ready to take life a little slower now. Want to get married?"

She pulled back just a bit and stared up at him. "That's taking life slow?"

"Well, yeah, we'll wait at least nine months before we start having children. You do still want children, don't you?"

"At least a half dozen." She laughed. "You always made me feel good about myself."

He turned serious. "Don't ever let anyone tell you that you're not good enough to do or be whatever you want. No one has that right. You are a wonderful person, Jenny-girl."

She smiled, resting her head against his chest. "Yes, I am."

DANCE
THE FANDANGO

ROSEMARY LAUREY

"MOM, YOU REALLY MUST MAKE SOME DECISIONS."
Magda Stephenson smiled at her daughter, Barbara. "Yes, dear. I know."

"It's been a year since Daddy died," Josie, two years and three months Barbara's senior, added, just to get her two cents in, Magda suspected.

It had been one year and nine days since Sam died and one year and five days since his cremation. But pointing that out was picky and would put their backs up. They were good girls, all of them. She smiled at Annie and Theresa, who were leaving the others to launch the subject. Magda almost chuckled at Theresa's encouraging smile. *Bear up, Mom,* it seemed to say, *be brave. We, your supportive daughters, are here for you.*

And, truth to tell, they were. But Magda wasn't ready for the sort of support they were about to offer.

There had been gentle hints, subtle comments over the phone, and now this confrontation around the dining room table.

The respective spouses had all disappeared, with the amassed grandchildren, to feed the ducks in the park, leaving the women to do the dirty work. Oh! Yes, this was a planned performance, but Magda had her own plans. "Tell you what, dears, if we're having a little chat, I'll get myself another cup of coffee. Anyone else want one?"

"Mom, coffee isn't good for you. Think of your heart," Josie said.

"You're right, Josie. I'll get something else." Magda stood and made for the kitchen. "Anyone else want a gin?" she called over her shoulder.

Surprisingly, Josie and Theresa did. Nikki asked for a glass of white wine. Barbara echoed her, and Annie, always different, wanted a soda. With half an ear cocked to catch the whispering from the dining room, Magda loaded a tray. "Here we are." She handed the drinks around, daring Josie to make a comment. All she said was a clipped, "Thank you, Mom," no doubt convinced if she commented on a G and T that her mother would hit the neat gin.

"Now, my dears," Magda said after taking a sip and savoring the sweet perfume smell. "You wanted to talk about the future." Might as well take the initiative. She might not keep it, but she'd at least start off where she wanted. "Josie's right. I do need to make some decisions and I've been doing some thinking." At least they didn't gape in shock at their ancient parent actually thinking.

"You've got to look toward the future, Mom," Annie said.

Did they really think she was looking to the past and the three heart-rending years when Sam sickened and faded in front of her eyes?

"At least you've taken our advice about going about more," Theresa said. "It's done you good to get out of the house. You used to spend all your time here."

Apart from the outings to the doctor and the hospital, but why dwell on that? "Yes, I have enjoyed getting out."

"I think your trip to the beach did you a world of good," Nikki said. "You came back so relaxed."

"I was, dear, utterly. I needed it." Better not mention it wasn't Garden City she went to. Time enough, later, to mention Juan's house on the north coast of Spain.

"Have you thought any more about selling the house and looking for sheltered housing?" Barbara asked. "There's a really nice place near us in Cambridge. John and I could put your name down."

Did Barbara really think she was that old and feeble?

"Now's a good time to put it on the market, you know. Wait much longer and you'll be into fall and the market tanks once school reopens." So spoke Annie, the veteran of two house purchases.

Time to drop Magda's first surprise. "That's all taken care of, girls. No need to worry."

"You've listed it!" Surprise always raised Josie's voice a tad. "We agreed you'd use Alan's cousin."

They might have agreed, Magda hadn't. But best not stir up too much at one time. "I would have, dear, if I'd had to list it. But as it happens, I was lucky enough to sell it privately and save myself a bundle in agent's commission." By the look on her face you'd think Josie had personally been deprived of a share in said commission. Maybe she had. No, that was an unworthy thought.

"It's sold?" Nikki, Simon's wife, asked.

"Yes. We exchanged contracts last week and they get possession the middle of September. Gives me time to settle somewhere else." More specific plans she'd share when this dust storm settled.

"A little hasty weren't you, Mom?" Annie asked.

"They made a good offer and it seemed plain foolish to refuse."

"No doubt they wanted to rush you and take advantage of a widow." Barbara never gave up.

"Did you get a good price?" Josie asked. "Alan told you what to ask. Did they try to knock you down?" She sounded almost hopeful. She'd always been good at "I told you so," even as a little girl.

"We had two, independent valuations, and since they came in just five thousand apart, we agreed to meet in the middle." As Josie opened her mouth to speak, Magda went on, "Alan's cousin was a bit off the mark. He must have been going by Connecticut prices and this is Ohio. I got nearly a hundred thousand more than he estimated." She'd mention later that price included some of the furniture and the boat Magda knew she'd never use again.

"Who are these people?" Josie all but demanded.

"A nice family in the neighborhood. They have a house up on Elm. They have four children and the wife's expecting another just before Christmas."

"And I suppose they just knocked on the door and made an offer," Barbara said.

Oh dear, she was sounding snippy. "No, they telephoned first. They looked over the house and I looked over them. We called in agents to value the place and worked things out between us." Every single one of them, Nikki included, was stunned into silence at the thought of their ancient and decrepit parent being capable of navigating a house conveyance. Magda smiled. They were good girls really, but . . . "This house is meant for a big, loud family with lots of children running through the rooms, falling down the stairs, and poking the handles of tennis raquets through the hall window." The last she said with a little grin Annie's way. "It's far too big for one lone woman." Concession to Josie and her Alan here. "Once I pay off the last loans we took out to get you lot through grad school," she nodded in Annie and Theresa's direction, and gave an invisible nod to Simon in the park with the offspring, "I'll have a nice little nest egg. I should manage nicely."

She'd stunned the lot of them into silence. For a full five seconds.

"Where will you be going?" asked Nikki, a worried crease between her brows.

Now was not the time to drop *that* little thunderbolt. "I have until mid-September."

"You might have consulted us. We are your family, after all." Barbara sniveled. It was truly the only word for it. "And it sounds shifty to me, buying a house but not moving in for three months! Are you sure they're not swindling you?"

"Absolutely not!" Magda forgave herself the note of tartness. "Saul Laurence handled it for me and he commented on what reasonable buyers they were. Wished they'd been around when he was trying to sell his house."

That hushed Barbara for a minute or two. Long enough for Annie to get in, "Is there anything we can do to help, Mom?"

Magda smiled at her eldest daughter. "Right this minute, no. I'll have to have a big tidy out. I'm selling some of the furniture. You all took your pick after Sam died, but if there's anything you or the children would like, we can talk about it later on."

Barbara was about to say something when the front door opened. Four boys and two girls burst in, followed by their respective male parents, bringing with them the warmth of the summer night and several jars of lightning bugs. Josie's Alan brought up the rear with little Twig (what a name!) in the baby carrier on his back.

Quite a clan.

Brought back memories of her lot clutching jars full of little flashing yellow lights. "Brilliant, my loves!" Magda said, reaching out and hugging children and arms and jars. "Aren't they beautiful, but we must let them go before you get in bed." She well remembered the tears of shock and horror when her children awoke to find little corpses instead of flickering lights.

"Do I have to, Grandma?" young Peter, Annie's eldest, asked. With a bit of a whine, Magda couldn't help noticing.

She preempted any discussion or negotiations here. "Yes, you have to."

"You also have to get to bed," the elder Peter announced, the male voice cutting off any more argument.

"Is it really bedtime?" Paula, Simon's one and only, asked, with a definite wheedle in her voice.

"Yes." Simon sounded ready for bed, even if his seven-year-old wasn't.

"If it's dark enough for lightning bugs, it's almost bedtime," Nikki said, backing up Simon. Those two did very well together.

"It's my bedtime," Magda said, "and I'm getting into the shower before you lot take all the hot water." A virtual impossibility, given the size of the water heater, but the idea put little grins on dirty faces. Magda turned to her daughters and Nikki. "I really am tired, and tomorrow is going to be busy, so I'm off to get my beauty sleep."

A dedicated, noble, self-sacrificing grandmother would no doubt stay to help wash behind ears and supervise teeth cleaning. But she'd done plenty of that over the years. Time for the next generation to wield the washcloths.

"You okay, Mom?" Simon asked with an anxious, questioning glance toward Nikki.

"Fine but tired. I'll see you all in the morning. You know where to find towels. If there's anything else you need, go forage."

Leaving behind the echoes of scampering feet on the stairs, Magda crossed the hallway to the downstairs bedroom Sam and she had moved into when he fell ill. As the last pair of feet sped upstairs, the silence fell around her, Magda let out the sigh—several of them, in fact—that she'd pent up all day. They were children to be proud of, and despite the nagging and fussing, were genuinely worried about her. But really. Sheltered accommodation! She had far better plans for the years she had left.

Magda reached for her cell phone—one never could be

sure if a little hand wouldn't start playing with the land line—and pressed speed dial.

"*Amante*, is all well?"

The warm, deep tones of Juan's voice seeped into her soul. Was all well? She couldn't lie to him. "Apart from me going to bed early since I'm worn out and a trifle irritated at my concerned and loving daughters, yes, all's well."

He caught her sarcasm. "They're unhappy with you?"

That was going it a bit strong. "I wouldn't go that far. Barbara seems to think I'm ancient and decrepit and need sheltered housing. Josie is astounded and a trifle put out that I can arrange and negotiate a house sale without her telling me what to do. Nikki is clearly worried about me. And Theresa is worn out herself, being seven months gone. Still, they have accepted I've sold the house."

"But our plans, they're okay with us?"

How many times had they gone around on this one? "They will be." She'd dunk all their heads in the pond in the park if they weren't. "I'm telling them after they meet you on Sunday."

"Of course. They know you've invited us?"

"Not yet. I'll announce that tomorrow at breakfast. I'm fixing pancakes. Even Barbara wouldn't dare gripe after pancakes."

His laugh wrapped around her soul. How she loved him.

"*Querida*, I miss you. Two days is a long time."

"You're right there! I'm tempted to leave my bedroom window open but I don't want to see my daughters dropping dead from shock if they decide to bring me a cup of early morning coffee."

"True. No point in scandalizing the young. They shock so easily."

"You can say that again."

"I would rather say, 'I love you.'"

"I love you, too, Juan." Wondrous really, after losing Sam she'd been empty, hollow. Juan had changed all that.

"Tell me, my love, would Sunday be the time for me to ask their permission to marry you?"

"You don't need to ask anyone but me, and I've already said yes."

"It might help."

He was right. Much as the thought rankled. "Ask Simon. The sons-in-law can go sing and the girls will probably want to debate it and take a vote."

She loved his laugh, full of life and energy. She shut her eyes a second, letting his love and merriment wash over her. Darn! She wanted him. Sixty-five—minus two days—was not too old to feel burning lust. If her worried daughters had any idea . . .

"You're sure this is the right way?"

"Can you think of a better? They'll meet Iñes and Rob and their family, and what's more natural than they bring Iñes's father who is visiting?" she paused. "I could always introduce you as my Spanish lover. The man who made love to me in the pine woods."

That chuckle was downright lascivious. "You could."

"Better not. I think Annie has high blood pressure. Wouldn't want to send it soaring." Although if they really thought all she and Juan did was hold hands . . .

But since they didn't even know Juan existed . . . "One step at a time with my lot, Juan."

"Understandable. Iñes doesn't know the extent of our feelings, although she has dropped the most enticing hints that you are a really nice woman and I should invite you out to dinner again."

"Why don't you?"

"Would you accept?"

"I'd have to think about it."

"Think hard, *amante*."

"Hard's good!" She let her snicker last until she ran out of breath. "Think about me."

"Every waking minute, Magda. Every second. *Buenas noches*."

"*Buenas noches*. Goodnight, my love. Sleep tight."

She'd only just pressed the Off button when the door opened.

She should have guessed.

Barbara bearing a mug.

"Were you talking to someone, Mom."

"Yes, dear. On the phone."

"I didn't hear it ring." She sounded downright put out at the omission.

"It didn't. I called someone to chat." And share a little naughty talk.

"Oh!"

Bless the girl, or rather woman, she stood in the doorway, nonplussed. Magda could satisfy her curiosity but was just too darn tired to face the possible furor. Besides, she had her plan and was sticking to it. "Is that a drink you've brought me?" Comments like that no doubt reinforced her failing faculties in her daughter's mind.

"Yes, Mom, we thought you'd like a cup of mint tea. It'll help you relax."

She didn't need relaxing. Not after the generous gin she'd poured herself. "Thank you, dear. Just put it here and I'll sip on it later. I want to go over my plans for the party before I go to sleep."

Barbara came over, but after setting the mug on the night stand, she plonked herself on the side of the bed. "Are you sure this isn't too much for you, Mom? We could all take you out to dinner instead."

"Why not do that on Monday? It'll be that or leftovers."

Not the reply she'd hoped for. "I just think it's a lot of work and fuss."

"You're so right, dear, but surely you haven't forgotten how much I enjoy all that work and fuss? I loved putting on parties with your father, and now I'm doing this one for my-self . . . and all of you," she added hastily. "It's not every day a woman gets to be sixty-five."

"My point exactly, Mom. You're not getting any younger."

"None of us are, dear. You won't see thirty-seven again, will you?"

A wee bit nasty, but justified. Magda reached over and took a sip of the tea for form's sake. Too darn sweet though. She set the mug back down. "Now, dear, I have a suggestion for you and your sisters and Simon. Get those children into bed as soon as you can and follow them there. I'm going to work you all hard tomorrow." She kissed her on the cheek. "Goodnight, dear."

At least she took the dismissal in good part, but it didn't take much to imagine the talk in the kitchen.

She's hell bent on the idea. I suggested we take her out but she's so stubborn.

Yes, but Magda wasn't the only stubborn one in the family. And no doubt one day Barbara would frustrate and irritate little Jane in her turn.

Funny how it all worked out.

She woke early—a habit she'd acquired nursing Sam through his illness—and drawing back the curtains, stretched and treated herself to twenty minutes of yoga in front of the open window. Later it would be hot, but now the morning coolness wafted in and she was tempted to throw off her nightshirt and indulge in glorious nudity. But who knew when a little person in footed pajamas might burst through the door?

With that thought in mind, Magda locked the bathroom door when she showered, and so almost missed Juan's call. Dripping wet and half-wrapped in a towel, she grabbed her cell phone.

"*Buenas dias, mi amante!*"

"*Buenas dias*, my sexy lover!" A quick glance over the shoulder reassured her the door was still shut tight. "I dreamt about you last night."

"I thought about you all night long. I want you in my bed."

"When?"

"Now?"

"Sorry, love, I've got to fix pancakes for sixteen."

"You're cooking now?"

"Not yet. I just got out of the shower."

"Ah!" How could one syllable hold such a wealth of meaning? "You are naked, Magda?"

He wished. So did she, come to that. "Except for a sagging towel, yes."

"If only I were there, to take care of the sagging towel."

"How would you tighten it around me?"

"I wouldn't tighten it." Dear heaven, he had a lovely, dirty, sexy chuckle. "I'd toss it out the window, and carry you in my arms to the bed."

"Sounds good but, darling, I have lots of hungry mouths to feed." Didn't stop her longing for his hungry mouth, though. "Tomorrow."

"Ah yes, *mañana*. Will they be truly upset, do you think?"

"You know, Juan, if they are, they can go suck eggs! I've done my bit for them all these years. They have good lives, happy marriages, beautiful children, and successful careers. I did my bit for Sam because I loved him, but now it's time for Magda to get my attention, and, love, I'm ready."

"Give me the word and I'll stand beside you."

"I know."

"Or lie beside you."

And with that thought echoing in her mind, Magda pulled on her "If you follow the rules, you miss all the fun" T-shirt and a pair of walking shorts—she'd had her legs waxed two days ago; might as well show them off—slipped her feet into comfy sandals, and crossed the hallway into the kitchen.

She had the flour sifted and was reaching for the eggs when the first pair of little feet appeared. It was Paula, Simon and Nikki's one and only, her beautiful dark curls still tousled from sleep and the imprint of her clutched blanket still red on her left cheek.

"Good morning, my sweet." Magda shoved the eggs aside and swept her granddaughter up in both arms and kissed her. "Did you sleep well?"

"Until I woke up and Mommy and Daddy said to go in and see Tom and Pete, but I'd rather see you."

"What a wise and sensible girl you are. This way you get to learn the secret of perfect pancakes."

Paula set to stirring batter with gusto, giving Magda time to put on the kettle and get a pot of coffee going. By the time the first batch (which of course Paula agreed was hers by right) was ready, the others arrived in ones and twos and Magda was well into her second mug of coffee.

Pancakes disappeared as fast as she flipped them out of the pan.

"Real maple syrup," John said as he reached for the pitcher. "What a treat. You should get it, Barb. Forget that flavored colored stuff."

Not a tactful comment. Some men never learned. Although how he could ignore the furrow in Barbara's brow, heaven alone knew.

"Should you be drinking all that coffee, Mom? You know caffeine is bad for you."

She should have expected that, drinking from a bright red mug with "Give me caffeine, caffeine, and more caffeine" on the side. Maybe she should admit to drinking decaf for the past seven or eight years, ever since those heart palpitations gave her a scare.

"Oh, leave Mom alone, Barbie." Simon never missed a chance to disagree with the bossiest of his sisters or to use the nickname she hated. "I guess she needs the jolt to see her through cooking for all of us."

"Speaking of cooking . . . I have a bunch of last-minute jobs lined up for everyone," Magda announced, producing her stack of lists and papers. "If everyone pitches in, we should be done by early afternoon, and then we can all collapse and put up our feet until tomorrow."

She went through the list. "Annie and Barbara, if you'd get all the plates and glasses up from the basement and wash them. Alan and Peter, you take the boys—might as well put swimsuits on them first—and get out the tables and chairs from the garage and hose them down. They're probably covered with cobwebs and worse. Simon, if you and John would put up the little awning in the corner by the lilacs, I want to set the bar up over there, and I'd like to have it up before they deliver the big awning I rented for the tables. That's coming at ten. Paula and Jane can help Josie polish sliver. And Theresa and Nikki, I'll need your assistance with the food. Most is done or at least prepared, but we'll need a marathon session to get it all ready."

"Mom, you should have called in caterers."

Barbara never gave up. "Bear with me, Barbara, I like doing this." It made her feel like a general commanding her army. Wasn't often these days she got to tell her crew what to do.

"Right, Mom." Simon stood and the sons-in-law rose with him.

"Swimsuits, boys," Peter told his pair. David obviously included himself and the three scampered upstairs, pulling Andrew after them.

"Seventeen chairs then, Magda?" Peter said. "Plus the high chair for Twig."

"No, make it thirty." Might as well drop the first surprise when they were sated with pancakes and syrup. "I think there's three dozen, so pick the best, and I must warn you, the tables are a bit wonky. You may need to use duct tape on a few of them, make sure they don't fold on us."

"Thirty, Mom?" Annie was almost as predictable as Barbara. "Not counting Twig, we're seventeen including you."

"I can add up you know, dear. I'm inviting the Wallaces, who are buying the house, so you can meet them, that's six more. Seven, since I've invited Iñes's father, who's visiting. And a couple of other friends: the Downes and the Pattersons and Saul and Henny Laurence."

Everyone dispersed, no doubt to hold anxious conversations in the garage and the basement, but no one had outright protested or complained.

They were too darn busy.

Nothing like a few chores to keep them quiet.

Everyone set to, and things went well, apart from a bit of excitement when David, waving the hose with sheer boyish enthusiasm, half-doused one of the delivery men (who took it in good part) and a minor panic when Twig (why on earth had they given the child such an outlandish name) slammed her hand in the pantry door. But that was nothing a bag of ice and a couple of cookies couldn't fix, and by late afternoon, all was ready. Food was on dishes or in the fridge ready to be served; every piece of silver, china, and glass was spotless and gleaming; and the tables were set end to end under the long awning. Nikki, bless the woman, had ironed the tablecloths and every single napkin and they waited, neatly folded.

Alan decided they needed more coolers and had nipped out and bought six extra, and he and Simon were to buy the ice first thing after breakfast tomorrow.

It was as ready as it could be, and the lot of them—apart from those with ages in single digits—looked as tired as Magda felt.

She retired to shower, leaving them arguing over what pizzas to order for dinner.

Pizza was quite the success and yanking out the old home movies Sam had transferred to video was sheer inspiration. Magda half-suspected the parents enjoyed them even more than the grandbabies, but it was hard to decide amid the laughter and the giggles.

In fact they were so engrossed, she nipped out under the pretext of dumping the old pizza boxes and called Juan.

"*Amante*."

"My darling."

"Are you well? You sound tired."

"Juan, I'm ready to drop. I'm half-inclined to think Barbara and Theresa were right and I should have had this whole bash catered, but all's set. The only things lacking are a nice day tomorrow and a garden full of guests."

"It cannot rain. I will not allow it."

"Fixed the weather, did you?"

"Of course. For you I would do anything."

Men were full of it. "Just turn up tomorrow and keep the skies blue and I'll marry you."

"I'll hold you to that, *amante*." His voice changed. She knew the tone and a sweet shiver of anticipation snaked down her spine. "What are you wearing?"

She hated to spoil the moment, but why lie? "Shorts and a ratty crumpled T-shirt."

"Easy to imagine taking them off. Once your family leaves, I'll be tapping on the door, carrying roses and a bottle of massage oil, and I will oil every inch of your body, stroke, and caress you and not stop until I have you begging for me to be inside you."

"Can't wait." But she was going to have to. "Juan, I want you so much it hurts."

"Good. I'm hard just thinking about you, Magda. I want you naked, under me. Crying for more. Shouting with a climax."

If he went on much longer it might just happen over the phone. "Until tomorrow."

"No, call me tonight, when you're in bed. And be naked."

"All right. If you insist."

"I do, my love, I do."

And after that she had to go back and empty the dishwasher. Yes, one of the children would have done it willingly, but it beat rejoining the noisy crowd in the sitting room when she wanted to be alone with her thoughts.

Was she handling this the right way? Should she perhaps have had a small, family dinner and introduced Juan to them that way? No. Wouldn't have worked. They'd never have come home from all directions across the country just for a dinner. It had to be a once-in-a-lifetime event, hence her big birthday bash.

Magda woke early; it was her birthday, after all. The sun was already bright and the dew fast drying off the grass, just as if Juan had laid on the weather for her delectation.

Maybe he had. He seemed the sort of man who could do anything.

Grinning like a silly girl—okay, a silly old girl—Magda nipped into her bathroom, opted for the indulgence of a nice soak in lavender bath oil, and emerged, not exactly relaxed, but with a building excitement about the day ahead.

And the horrid worry that her plans would all backfire. That her family would dislike Juan on sight, would kick up a frightful stink and . . . Hell! In that case, they'd elope and really give them all something to tut over!

The unmistakable aroma of frying bacon brought her back to the here and now. No point in borrowing trouble when breakfast awaited.

Not just breakfast. The whole gang of them waited, in various stages of dress and undress. Theresa was turning bacon and sausages in the pan, and what looked very much like mushrooms in another. Barbara was pulling a tray of biscuits out of the oven. Across the kitchen, a heap of gifts covered Magda's chair and her place at the table.

But it was all blurred by a resounding chorus of "Happy Birthday" and her grandchildren clutching her by the waist or knees, depending on their reach.

"We have breakfast for you!" Paula said.

"And lots of gifts. Hundreds of gifts," little Pete said.

"It's a surprise, were you surprised?" David asked.

"I am beautifully and wondrously surprised," Magda replied, smiling down at them and across to her children and in-laws, "Ecstatically surprised, thank you."

"Have a seat, Mom," Annie said.

Simon moved aside her own chair, now heaped with packages, and produced another with a flourish. Barbara brought her a cup of coffee, and even grinned as she set the mug down.

"Drink up, Mom, you'll need it today."

"Open the gifts, please," Paula pleaded. "I want you to see what I gave you."

"Oh . . ." Magda feigned hesitation. "Perhaps we should wait until after breakfast, maybe until after all the guests go home."

That suggestion went down pretty much as she'd expected. Everyone protested and gathered around as Magda started pulling off bows and snapping ribbons.

"Do you like your birthday surprises?" Andrew asked after all were opened.

"I love every single one." From the basket painstakingly constructed out of Popsicle sticks by Paula, to a sinfully extravagant cashmere blanket from Barbara and John, a bookstore gift certificate in an astonishingly generous amount from Simon and Nikki, and a plethora of luxuries in between.

She had wonderful children. Surely they could understand what Juan meant to her?

"You look sad, Grandma," young Peter said. "What's the matter?"

"Nothing, darling. I'm just thinking how much I love you all and what wonderful children and grandchildren I have."

"And the same wonderful grandchildren need to get washed and dressed as soon as we have breakfast," said Josie as she put a platter of bacon and sausages on the table.

"So, get in your seats and let's tuck in." Annie set a basket piled high with biscuits on the table and hustled her lot into their seats.

Simon refilled her coffee when Barbara was busy decanting scrambled eggs into a serving dish.

Yes. It was going to be the perfect birthday.

Fingers crossed under the table.

At everyone's insistence, Magda took her coffee into the garden while children were washed and dressed and breakfast cleared.

She did not sit down and put her feet up as urged, and resisted the temptation to call Juan. He was no doubt coping with his own loving family. Magda strolled around, double-checking everything, before popping into the now-empty kitchen for tablecloths and cutlery. Might as well get something done. In a couple of hours everyone would be arriving.

Simon and Tom departed to pick up ice. Children started appearing washed, brushed, and dressed, and settled to watching videos; a desperate maternal attempt to keep them spit-polished. Magda recognized the tactic and wished them better success than she'd ever had. She retreated to her bathroom and got dressed. Luckily no one offered to assist their aging parent with the zips and buttons. Magda wasn't quite sure what they'd make of red silk underwear adorned with heavy black lace.

The fabric felt like a second skin. All right, a much younger skin, but one was never too old to dream, and Juan didn't have any problems with a few wrinkles and stretch marks. Come to that, neither did she. It was the man beyond the wrinkles she loved. The man for whom she was now snapping on a red lace bra, even if the chances he'd actually get to see it were pretty much close to zero. Too many loving and caring children hovering, unless they skived off and abandoned her own party. Something she wouldn't do to her children, even for Juan.

Children who seemed quite impressed with her appearance.

"Wow!"

"Mom, you look fantastic!"

"Grandma, you're so pretty."

"Purple, Mom?" Dear Barbara was so predictable.

"Yes, love, it sets off my grandmother's pearls." She obviously hadn't read a certain inspirational poem. Maybe if Magda had indulged in a red hat to match . . . "Now, girls, help me put out the hors d'oeuvres. Simon, please check the champagne is cool enough, and . . ." Heck, if it wasn't done by now, it wouldn't get done and no one would miss it.

The Downes were the first to arrive—Arthur had been one of Sam's fraternity brothers—the Laurences and Pattersons came shortly after. And then, not ten minutes later, Iñes Wallace walked through the gate with her sons and daughter, and behind her came her husband . . . and Juan.

One look at his dark eyes and the sexy smile that set a dimple low in his left cheek and Magda wished the lot of them, minus Juan of course, on the opposite side of the moon, or at least in Michigan.

And one glance into the depths of his dark eyes and she knew he felt the same.

Why, oh why, had she ever thought this was a good idea?

"Magda, may you have a wonderful birthday." His hands enclosed hers, but she wanted them other places, she wanted his arms around her, holding her tight against him so she felt the pressure of his erection against her belly and the strength of his male body against hers. She wanted their clothes to evaporate and to lie naked with him on the grass.

What she wanted and what was going to happen were very different.

"Thank you for coming, Juan. Lovely to see you. Now let me introduce my children."

That took a good ten minutes and helped her heart rate to settle a bit. Except for when she glanced back in Juan's direction. Good thing everyone was too caught up in the introductions and passing out drinks and trays of nibbles to notice that two members of the assembled company were panting for each other.

Everyone was getting along nicely: Theresa and Nikki were swapping obstetric stories with Iñes; the children seemed happy to share the swings and climbing frame; the males of all ages were clustered by the drinks table, no doubt talking football.

It was going to be a lovely party.

"Mom, think we should get the salads out?"

Annie was right. "Why not, dear." Magda looked around for Simon; he seemed to be in deep conversation with Juan.

"Give it another ten minutes dear. Why not round up the children to wash their hands? Then they can help bring out the salads."

"Look, forgive my bluntness, but what is it between you and my mother?" Simon knew that to be utterly tactless and totally uncalled for. The man was a guest, for heaven's sake. And yes, he was Spanish, but that hardly gave him license to ogle Mom.

"Your mother, Magda," Juan Hernandez smiled, "is a beautiful woman."

Yes, Simon supposed she was, and she did look rather splendid in that swirly purple thing, but . . . "Okay, but . . ." How the hell did you tell a man old enough to be your father to keep his beady eyes off your mother? "Have you known my mother long? You've met her before, right?" Christ, this was not easy.

Juan Hernandez smiled. "To answer your question, Simon, I've known her three months. As for what she is to me, I had hoped to initiate this conversation, but since you brought the matter up, she is the woman I plan to marry. You have no objection?"

Damn lucky he wasn't drinking or he'd have snorted champagne.

"You want to marry her? After three months?" Damn! The man had just said so, hadn't he?

"I've known her three months, but I wanted to marry her the moment I met her."

"A bit sudden, don't you think?"

"No." The man had a permanent smile. "How long was it after meeting your wife—Nikki, isn't it—did you know she was the one for you?"

That was different. Or was it? Simon had to smile back. "Thirty seconds, I think. Maybe twenty-five." The man had made his point. "Look here, fair enough, but you know about Dad, I mean, and . . ."

"I know your father died after a long and harrowing illness that wore your mother out. She loved him and mourned him. I find myself flattered and honored that she's willing to take her chances with me. I lost a spouse, too. Maria died many years ago. I've met a lot of women since then, many beautiful, many charming, but Magda is the first one to catch my soul and heart. I want to marry her.

"When I asked Maria's father for her hand, I enumerated my career prospects and my ambitions and my ability to provide for a wife and family. Now . . ." He gave a little shrug. "I have a pension, savings, and a house. Do you have any objections?"

The man was a comedian. Simon chuckled and shook his head. "As if my objections, if I had any, would carry any weight with my mother. I don't think anyone has ever been able to tell Mother what to do. If I had the temerity to object, she'd no doubt whisk you off to Reno."

Judging by the grin, the man obviously knew Mom well. "I believe she did mention that alternative. I'd prefer a wedding, here. So all our respective offspring can attend."

"Any idea when?"

"Before the end of the summer. It's soon, I know, but at our age it really doesn't pay to dally."

Definitely a comedian. Simon held out his hand. "Welcome to this insane family. Just make Mother happy, although I think you've done that already. Treat her wrong and I'll cut your balls off."

Juan grasped his offered hand. "I think Magda would beat you to it."

Simon turned as Annie called his name. She was getting all het up about something. So, it seemed, was Barbara. "Better see what they want. Sisters can drive you round the twist."

"I know. I have three."

Simon grinned. Nice at last to have a family member who understood the sister situation.

Magda surveyed her guests. It was a wonderful party. And if she was enjoying herself, everyone else had to be, right? One look down the long table convinced Magda. One look down the long table and she met Juan's eyes, as she had at least five hundred and seventy-two times during the meal. The girls were splendid, bringing out dishes and press-ganging the children into helping clear plates. All Magda had to do was eat, chat with anyone within talking distance, and think of Juan. So close, and yet several feet away.

Between the salad and the peach soup, Juan stood and proposed a toast to her birthday, and her incredible cooking, and wished her a long and happy life. She was tempted to propose a toast to his incredible lips, but instead replied how thrilled she was to have everyone there and how happy she was to hand over her house to Iñes and Rob.

The sun was shining, she had the people she loved most around her, and the man she adored smiling in her direction, lust blazing in his eyes. What woman could ask for more?

After the salmon, Simon proposed a toast welcoming Iñes and her family, and wishing them as happy a life in the house as he and his sisters had grown up in. Nicely done.

As they cleared the plates, Annie whispered anxiously that they needed her help with the desserts. Arranging raspberries around crème brûlées hardly needed her supervision, but the agitation in her daughter's eyes convinced Magda something had gone wrong. She'd noticed all the children had been sent back to their seats. Oh, dear, had to be a big mess. There was always the emergency stash of ice-cream but . . .

She dropped her napkin on her chair and followed her eldest daughter into the kitchen.

Where the lot of them all but pounced on her.

"Mom, what is going on between you and Mr. Hernandez?"

Easier to handle than thirty smashed desserts. Or was it? Barbara spoke the question repeated in three other pairs of eyes.

"Something is going on, isn't it?" Annie sounded just like the schoolteacher she was.

This was not exactly how she'd planned on breaking the news, but maybe . . . "What makes you ask?"

"Give over, Mother!" Theresa shook her head and seemed almost ready to shake her finger. "You and he are practically ogling each other."

Had they really been so obvious? She smiled. What the heck? "I think you've guessed my dears. I'm in love and I'm going to marry him."

Just as well the crème brûlées were safe on the counter. The empty tray Barbara held hit the floor with a resounding crash.

"When?" Nikki asked, while the others tried hard not to hyperventilate.

"Soon, before school starts. We haven't booked anything and it won't be a big event. Just you and Juan's family."

"Christ almighty!" Barbara seldom swore. She was upset.

"You're dead serious, aren't you, Mom?" Annie asked.

Magda nodded. "I am, my dears. After your father died, I

felt no one could replace him. Juan doesn't. He's very different from Sam, but I love him, too. He's a widower. Both our families are grown and we love each other." She picked up the tray still sitting on the floor. "I think we'd better get the food out there, or people will think there really is a crisis in here."

"How can you be so calm about it?" Theresa asked.

"I'm not calm, darling. I'm bubbling, burning, and bouncing inside. I'm also gloriously happy to have you all here together. Wish me joy." The last was a plaintive entreaty. They had to accept Juan. They had to.

"He's not the least like Dad," Annie said.

"No," Magda conceded, "but we love each other."

Barbara broke the deadlock, hugging Magda tight. "He'd better treat you right or I'm going after him with a frying pan."

They ended up in big, five-way hug, and Magda had to stop to blot a few tears as the girls tossed raspberries onto the desserts and carried them out.

Simon interrupted the dessert for another toast. "I've some news Juan and I want to share, with Mom's permission," he added, with a sly smile.

"We know what it is!" Annie and Barbara chorused.

"Yes, we do," Theresa said.

Josie added, "You're late, bro."

Nikki chuckled. Simon's face was a picture.

"Sheesh! Beaten to the post by my sisters again."

"Then let me announce it," Juan said.

This was not what she'd planned, but what the heck? Juan smiled at her and she stood, nodded, and smiled back.

"My family, Magda's family, her old friends, I am a truly fortunate and blessed man. Your lovely hostess has agreed to be my wife, so we will invite you all back to sing and dance at our wedding."

Tim Downes almost choked on his crème brûlée. Good thing it was soft and went down easily so he recovered fast. Everyone stood and wished them well and Magda just knew she was grinning like a fool in love. Which was, after all, an altogether nice thing on your sixty-fifth birthday.

"Are you really getting married, Grandma?" Paula asked as they all sat down and tucked into the last of their desserts.

"Yes, dear, I am."

"Can I be bridesmaid?"

"Of course, you, Twig, Jane, and Iñes's Alys. All our grandchildren will be bridesmaids.

"I won't!" Little Peter said.

"Of course not," Jane told him. "You're not pretty enough."

A quick glare from Annie stifled that little spat before it took off.

Magda looked down the table at Juan, her lover, her man. What more could any woman of any age ask for? A wonderful family, loyal friends, and a future with the man of her dreams. She raised her glass to Juan, and wondered how soon everyone was leaving.

THE GIRL
NEXT DOOR

JANICE MAYNARD

JASON RATCLIFF STOOD ON TOP OF A HIGH, GRASSY hillside and looked out over his rural southwestern Virginia home. In the early summer sunshine it was peaceful and serene. The farmhouse in the distance might have been part of a Rockwell painting. But in truth it had seen its share of heartache.

For Jason, the memories were bittersweet. Especially now that he was leaving. He'd sold the property, all fifty-two acres of it, and finally his dreams were about to become a reality. The dreams he'd put on hold the day his parents died in a car crash six years ago.

For a nineteen-year-old young man, it had seemed like the end of the world. In the midst of his grief, leaving the university to come home and care for his two younger sisters was merely a blip on the radar. It was only later that he realized how much he had given up.

But Rita and Pam, both still in high school, had needed him. And he had needed them. The three siblings were a team.

Jason had managed to bring in his dad's crop of feed corn that first year, and there was plenty of fresh produce to help with the grocery bill, but he wasn't the farmer his dad was, nor did he want to be. Instead, he'd found work wherever he could. He'd rented out part of their land for grazing. He'd hired on at other, bigger farms as a laborer. And he had managed somehow to keep the wolf from the door.

But his two beautiful, funny, smart sisters were on their own now. Both of them were doing well at college, and though they'd gotten a late start because of financial woes, both were now about to graduate. Despite his initial protests, the girls had been the ones to insist he sell the farm and go back to the University of Virginia to finish his degree.

He was going to be an architect. He'd said it a million times in his head, but it still seemed unreal. In two years he could have a job and the career he'd dreamed of. It was nothing short of a miracle.

But as neatly as everything appeared to be falling into place, there was still one big, unanswered question. What in the heck was he going to do about Felicity?

Felicity Jones was running out of time. Not for Mrs. Pirkle's color. That still had another nine minutes to go. Felicity double-checked her watch just to make sure. The elderly woman loved changing her "look" even at her advanced age, and today she had opted for Tahitian Sunset. The red color might shock some, but Edith Pirkle had the personality to pull it off.

Felicity sighed and glanced out the window. It was a sad day when an eighty-one-year-old woman had more spunk than her sixty-years-younger hairdresser. But that was going to change.

Her heart beat faster as she thought about what she had to do. The man she loved was ready to disappear from her life, and if she didn't act fast, she would lose him for good.

Not that he was really hers to lose, but a girl could dream. She'd been in love with him since she was fifteen, about the time he had come back home to look after Rita and Pam. Felicity and Pam were best friends, and watching Jason's gentle strength, his loving care of his two lost and hurting sisters, had won Felicity's heart.

Those feelings had grown and matured in the years since, but, sadly, Jason looked at her and apparently saw the little kid she used to be and not the full-grown woman who wanted to jump his bones.

She rinsed Mrs. Pirkle's hair and rolled it on brush rollers, all the while keeping up with the lively conversation even though her stomach was tense with anxiety. What was she going to do? Jason was leaving. Permanently. He'd sold the farm. He was moving.

No matter how many times she told herself, it didn't sink in. The Ratcliffs and the Joneses had lived side by side for years. They were the best kind of over-the-fence neighbors, and as hard as it had been for Felicity to say good-bye to Pam and Rita, her two dearest friends, it would be infinitely worse when Jason walked out of her life.

She was in love with him. The real thing. Bells and whistles. Until death do them part. But she had been such a coward up until now, she'd preferred to remain in limbo rather than express herself.

They flirted, under the pretext of friendship. She was pretty sure that Jason felt something for her as well. But it was scary to imagine being the one to lay her heart on the line. And what if Jason saw her declaration as simply another responsibility to tie him down? She wouldn't wish that on anyone, certainly not the man she loved.

He'd borne the weight of the world on his shoulders, and god knew he deserved some time for himself.

But the thought of him heading off to Charlottesville and finding another woman to hook up with just about shredded her heart.

So she had to quit being a coward. What was the worst

that could happen? He might politely let her down. Tell her he didn't reciprocate. It would be embarrassing and painful, but he would leave after that. She wouldn't have to see him day after day.

And wasn't *knowing* better than not knowing?

She tucked Mrs. Pirkle under the dryer and grabbed a broom to sweep up the remnants of an earlier haircut. Her dithering had to come to an end. A strong woman couldn't wait for life to *happen* to her. She had to seize it by the horns and wrestle it into submission.

Ha. With that improbable image in her head, she refilled a shampoo bottle and tried to push Jason Ratcliff out of her mind.

Jason looked in the mirror over the sink and grimaced. He was about three weeks overdue for a haircut, and he couldn't put it off any longer. But that wasn't as simple as it sounded. Felicity had been cutting his hair for the last six months, ever since her mom and dad had moved to Florida for Mr. Jones's asthma. Felicity's dad had built the beauty shop on the back of their house, and Felicity, who had learned all the tricks of the trade from her mom, now kept up with a steady business on her own.

At first, it had been fun having pretty, dark-haired Felicity cut his hair. They joked and laughed and teased with the familiarity of longtime friends. But somewhere along the way, that teasing had taken on a sexual undertone. He noticed things about her that he'd never paid attention to before. Her soft, rounded breasts brushing his arm. Her long-lashed green eyes. The way her curvy ass filled out a pair of jeans.

Yeah. He noticed. And in the beginning, it had embarrassed him. Hell, this was Pam's best friend. But Felicity had grown up and then some. Leaving him with a very awkward attraction that was sometimes hard to hide. Hard being the operative word.

He glanced at his watch and turned to jog down the stairs. His appointment was at three and he wasn't rude enough to make her wait. She had a business to run and clients to keep happy. He vaulted the fence and crossed the expanse of yard that separated the two houses.

Her face lit up when she saw him come through the door, and something in his chest unfurled in a warm jolt of recognition. She quickly toned down her smile, but that first second or two her eyes had been full of a woman's awareness, her expression open and vulnerable.

He had to wait for five minutes or so. Felicity was cutting a kid's hair, the mom looking on with worried pride. Felicity was good with children. She entertained the little boy with silly stories, and yet managed to trim his unruly locks without missing a beat.

When it was Jason's turn, he kissed her cheek casually and sat down in the chair. She fluffed a cape over him and snapped it behind his neck. Even the brush of her fingers on his nape made his whole body stiffen with tension. When she lowered the chair and tipped him back to put his head in the sink, he got a whiff of her perfume. He closed his eyes and prayed he wouldn't make a fool of himself. He steadied his breathing and tried his best to make his mind go blank.

That lasted until Felicity squirted shampoo on his head and started massaging his scalp with her long, talented fingers.

Sweet Jesus. Now he had the beginnings of a boner. She rubbed firmly, pausing now and again to brush suds from his ears. He nearly groaned out loud when she began rinsing and stroking through the wet strands to remove all the soap. By the time she finally sat him up and towel-dried his hair, he was a mess, his hands shaking and his chest heaving.

He wanted to kiss her. Badly.

She picked up a pair of scissors and met his gaze in her mirror, her face cheerful and happy. "How much?"

He gaped at her. Then the question registered. "Short," he muttered. "I don't know when I'll have a chance to get it cut again."

Her smile dimmed. "How soon are you leaving?"

He shrugged, prompting a scold from her. Then he sat up, straight and still. Those shears were sharp. "I have to be out in six days."

She wasn't looking at him in the mirror now. She was concentrating on the back of his head, quickly snipping and nipping until most of his hair drifted onto the cape and then to the floor. She picked up the electric clippers to do his neckline. "You need any help packing?"

Her voice was casual, her face devoid of any expression. His heart thudded in his chest. He had to clear his throat before he could speak. "Sure. I hate to sound sexist, but women seem to have a knack for this moving stuff. I'd probably end up with boxes full of broken glass if I do it all myself."

She picked up a shaving brush and wielded it firmly across his neckline, removing the bits and pieces of hair that clung stubbornly. Her grin was wry. "Don't oversell it, Jason. I've already agreed to help."

After she removed the cape, he stood up and handed her a folded bill. "Come over this evening around five, if you can. I'll cook some steaks on the grill and we can work afterward. How does that sound?"

They faced each other in the silent shop. Through the large window he could see Felicity's next appointment coming up the walk.

Felicity brushed his cheek with gentle fingers, ostensibly to remove one last errant piece of hair. "I can do that."

He acted on instinct, catching her hand against his cheek and holding it there. "I'm glad," he muttered. And then he kissed her.

Felicity managed not to butcher her last few customers, but it was a close call. How could a woman be expected to concentrate on work when a man had just knocked her legs out from under her? Wow. She had imagined Jason's kisses over the years, fantasized about the taste of his lips. But nothing had prepared her for the reality, the quick shock of electricity.

If only Mrs. Paretsky hadn't opened the door right about then, that lovely kiss might have gone on and on.

Two hours later, Felicity locked up the shop, turned out all the lights and walked through the house to her bedroom. It was still a shock to find her parents absent. But the medical diagnoses, from a trio of doctors, had been unequivocal. Her father couldn't survive another allergy-ridden spring or cold, damp winter.

Her parents had been gone since right after Christmas, and only Jason's presence next door had enabled Felicity to say good-bye to them with equanimity. Now he was leaving her, too, and she wasn't ready for that to be the last word.

She showered and changed quickly. It was hot and humid outside, so she put on a light cotton sundress striped in aqua and green. The halter neck left her shoulders and upper back bare. No bra, of course, and her clean undies were teal with tiny pink hearts. She looked wistfully at the new silver and bronze sandals she had bought last week at the mall in Bristol, but they weren't made for walking in the grass. With a sigh of resignation, she slipped her feet into plain white flip-flops.

After all, the dress might be a tad over the top. Perhaps a

bit too much for a casual next-door cookout. But she wore jeans or khakis for work every day, and she wanted Jason to see her in something else tonight.

She wanted Jason to see the woman. Not the friend or the hairdresser. She wanted Jason to see possibilities.

He was as good as his word. When she rounded the corner of the house and started across the side yard, the wonderful aroma of cooking meat assailed her nostrils. Her stomach clenched in hunger. As she came in sight of him, she donned her usual breezy smile. "Smells wonderful." But food was really the last thing on her mind. Jason's broad shoulders stretched the seams of his blue cotton Henley, and his fair, wavy hair was mussed from the breeze. From past experience, she knew his eyes would reflect the color of his shirt.

He looked up, spatula in hand. "Hey there, gorgeous. Do you mind checking on the baked potatoes? They should be about done."

She grinned and nodded, escaping inside on rubbery legs. That kiss stood between them like a big pink neon elephant.

Jason's kitchen was as familiar to her as her own. At that round oak table he had tutored Pam and Felicity, both in geometry and second-year algebra. The fact that Felicity had barely squeaked by was not Jason's fault. She had struggled with a learning disability all through school, and the night of her high school graduation was one of great relief.

She was smart and she had good business sense, but she was done with traditional schooling. Inheriting her mom's business by default had been a win-win situation. She knew she could make a go of it. But with Jason leaving, did she even want to? What else might there be in her future if she had the guts to pursue it?

Jason interrupted her musings, holding open the screen door with an elbow and triumphantly bearing a plate laden with two steaming steaks. They worked together in companionable silence, setting the table, serving the salad, and at last cutting into the perfectly cooked beef.

They chatted lazily over the meal. Jason's eyes had widened appreciatively when he saw her dress, but he didn't comment. Now he watched her with a small smile on his face. "How are your parents?"

She wiped her mouth on a napkin and laid it aside. "They're good. Up until now, they've been living in an apartment, but they've found a really lovely retirement community. Expensive, but lovely. They'll have to sell the house to be able to afford it."

He frowned. "What will you do?"

She shrugged. She'd been born when her parents were in their midforties and they had given up on having a baby, so they were much older than Jason's parents had been. "I'm a grown woman. And my profession is portable. I've already told them to do it. They'll fuss a bit and worry about me, but I can convince them. They've worked hard all their lives. They deserve a chance to enjoy their golden years."

He still looked troubled. "But how will you relocate?"

His sincere concern warmed her through and through. "They own a lot of land, Jason. Some of it near the interstate. It's been in the family since my great-granddaddy bought it in the early nineteen hundreds. But the time has come to sell, at least according to my dad. There will be enough money for them to get settled permanently, and a bit for me to set up a shop wherever I like."

"Where will you go?"

She bit her lip, wondering what to say. "They want me to move to Florida."

·2·

JASON'S STOMACH CLENCHED. FLORIDA? THAT WAS damned far away. When he imagined himself in Charlottesville, he'd had this hazy picture of visiting Felicity on the weekends. But how could he do that if she was all the freaking way in Florida? He swallowed hard. "I see."

She had a funny look on her face, but he was too frazzled to try and decipher it. He scowled at his plate. "Let's dump all this in the dishwasher and get started on the packing."

She followed him into the living room. He'd already cleared out the bureaus and closets upstairs. Pam and Rita had moved most of their stuff. Only a few stray boxes of "girly" things remained. Some of the furniture would go into storage until Jason finished school. His sisters had already taken the pieces they wanted. All in all, the house was pretty empty even now.

It made him a bit sad, especially when he thought back to the many years he'd spent growing up here. But without their parents, he and his sisters were simply marking time until they could move on with their lives.

Felicity had already assessed the situation and made a plan. She headed for a corner cabinet filled with his mother's antique teapots. "Shall I start with these?" She looked at him over her shoulder, and he felt his pulse jump. The smooth skin of her back made him want to run his hands over it and see if it was as soft as it looked.

He shoved his hands in his pockets. "Sure."

He paused to watch her bend over and take something from the bottom shelf. Her skirt rode up just enough in back for him to see her long, slender legs from ankle to almost ass-high. Then she straightened and the moment was gone. He sighed and started removing paperbacks from the bookshelf. Time to get busy.

In an hour and a half they made incredible progress. Felicity filled two boxes to his one, but he was responsible for taping them shut and stacking them, so they worked out a steady rhythm.

When she passed by him to get another empty box from the hall, he grabbed her wrist. "Let's take a break. You want a beer?"

She frowned, but she didn't pull away. "We've barely gotten started."

He rubbed his thumb over the pulse in her wrist. "I had ulterior motives for accepting your offer to help."

"Oh?" Her eyelids lowered and he couldn't read her expression.

He tugged her closer. "Yeah."

Their lips met as easily as if they had been doing so for weeks, months, years. He traced the seam of her mouth with his tongue. He was so very conscious that she was practically nude beneath her dress, and he wasn't sure he could keep this light and fun.

He felt her sigh as he gathered her more tightly into his embrace. She was a tall woman, and their heights matched perfectly. He ran his hands over her back. "You're beautiful, Felicity." He moved his mouth over hers, keeping the kiss languid, unhurried.

Her arms came up around his neck. The expression in her eyes was unguarded. "I wasn't sure you noticed. Sometimes you look at me as if I'm still fifteen."

He abandoned her lips and concentrated on the soft curve

of her neck. She was so damned smooth . . . everywhere he touched. "I noticed." He groaned, cupping her butt and drawing her into the cradle of his thighs. There was no way she could miss his erection. And her tiny, almost inaudible gasp told him he was right.

She turned her head. Her lips grazed his ear. His whole body shook. She was pressed up against him like warm, sensuous temptation. Their bodies were sweaty, their breathing labored.

He wanted her beneath him, flat on her back. Now. But this was crazy. He couldn't make himself take things to the next step. Not when the consequences were so dangerously volatile.

His hands were kneading her ass, playing with the line of her panties through the thin fabric of her skirt. She didn't protest. Not even when he eased her back enough to tease a nipple and then pinch it firmly.

The sound she made sent him from erect to steel-hard in half a breath. "God, Felicity." He groaned her name, literally paralyzed with indecision. The man in him knew exactly what to do. But the friend, the neighbor . . . that guy wanted to know what the hell he thought he was trying to pull.

His heart slammed in his chest. He either had to cool things down really fast, or they were going to do something they both might regret.

Felicity bit his bottom lip . . . lightly . . . and then soothed it with her tongue. Her pretty grass-green eyes were hazy with arousal, and a tiny smile on her lush red lips taunted him. "Jason?" Her voice was husky . . . strained.

"Yeah?"

"What would you think about me coming to live in Charlottesville?"

His minute hesitation cost him dearly. As did the unmistakable way he tensed up. Shit.

She went from cuddly to caustic in a split second. She jerked out of his embrace so suddenly she almost fell over a nearby pile of boxes. Her eyes were bright. With tears? The possibility wounded him. She backed away, heading for the door. "Oh, shoot," she said, her voice wobbly. "That was just the hormones talking. Forget I said anything. I'll see you later." And then she fled.

Felicity ran from his house to hers as though pursued by a pack of ravening wolves. Sadly, it was wasted effort. Jason didn't bother to follow. Inside her quiet, lonely room, she stripped off her dress and tumbled into bed, sobbing into her pillow and calling herself every name she could think of. It was hours before she fell asleep.

The next morning was Sunday. She made herself crawl out from under the covers and then confronted her image in the mirror. Her eyelids were swollen and her hair was a rat's nest. It was an appalling reflection.

She cleaned up, dressed, and ate a banana and yogurt, even though she didn't want to. As her mother had drilled into her head, breakfast was the most important meal of the day, and she needed her wits about her.

She smeared sunscreen over every inch of skin bared by her navy tank top and khaki shorts and then grabbed a water bottle from the fridge. It was time for Felicity Jones to do some serious thinking. And she knew exactly the place to do it.

This part of the state was famous for its picturesque rolling hills, and the high knob behind Jason's house was a familiar destination. From there you could see for miles on a clear day, range after range of sun-dappled peaks in the distance. As kids, all four of them had loved playing king of the mountain. She huffed and puffed her way to the top, flopping down on her butt at the summit to catch her breath.

A lone oak dominated the crest, providing pleasant shade. She shielded her eyes with her hand and looked down on her childhood. Part of her wanted to cling to the place, to the memories. But another, more grown-up voice in her head said it was time to let go. To quit hanging on to the past. Time to see what the future had to offer.

It was daunting and scary and exciting and exhilarating.

She chided herself inwardly for her cut-and-run act the night before. She hadn't even given the man a chance to answer her. Perhaps his statue imitation had been surprise and not horrified shock.

She lay back in the grass and closed her eyes. God, it had felt wonderful to be in his arms. To feel the strength of his embrace. His hard chest. His gentle, and at times forceful, kiss.

What would have happened if she had stayed? Would he have made love to her?

She was still a virgin. Not going away to college had limited her opportunities for sexual experimentation. She'd heard stories from Pam and even Rita about the guys they had dated, the good and the bad. And surprisingly, she hadn't been jealous in the least. Not with the guy she wanted right next door. But it was going to be a tough pill to swallow if he didn't want her back.

And that word "wanting" was ambiguous. It was clear even to a twenty-one-year-old virgin that Jason had been aroused last night. But whether he was prepared to act on it was another thing entirely. And even if he had made love to her, that was worlds away from what she wanted in the end.

She wanted him to be hers and her to be his. It was that simple. And that complicated.

When she sat up, the breeze played with her ponytail and tossed runaway strands in her face. It was much too hot to leave her hair down. Even in the shade, the air was thick with humidity. She leaned back on her hands and closed her eyes, listening to the faint sounds of bees and cows and lawn mowers.

When two warm hands closed over her face and cradled her head, she squeaked in surprise. She might have been scared but for the fact that she recognized Jason's aftershave instantly. It was a common brand, not expensive. But on him it might as well have been a rare aphrodisiac.

She wiggled in his embrace and turned to face him. "I can't believe I didn't hear you." She should have been embarrassed after the way they parted the night before, but her foremost emotion was wistful happiness. Each moment they spent together was precious and fleeting. He looked relaxed and casual in a plain white T-shirt and faded jeans.

He came down beside her, leaning his back against the tree trunk. "You were lost to the world. Problems, Fliss?"

Hearing the old nickname on his lips squeezed her heart. He hadn't called her that in years.

She nodded slowly. "Lots to think about."

He put his hand on her knee. "Am I one of those problems?"

Her skin burned where he touched. And her stomach did a free fall. She wasn't going to get any better opening than this. It was now or never. She sucked in a quick breath. "Yes," she said bluntly. "As a matter of fact, you are."

His gaze was wary, his eyes narrowed. "How so?"

She sank her teeth into her lower lip to keep it from trembling. "Because I'm in love with you."

His face went blank with shock, and she wanted to smack him. Were men really that dense?

He blinked twice, and now a pleased expression replaced the look of disbelief. "Since when?"

He smiled at her. The knot in her stomach eased a bit.

She shrugged. "Hard to say. It started out as a crush and somewhere along the way turned into the real thing." She paused, painfully aware that she had bared her soul, and other than a smug, male grin, he had yet to say a word about his own feelings.

Suddenly pissed, she jumped to her feet. "Never mind. This is pointless. You're leaving."

She didn't make it two steps before he grabbed her arm and tumbled her into his lap with a firm jerk. "Slow down, Fliss. Give me a chance here."

She opened her mouth to protest, and he claimed it urgently, moving his lips over hers with drugging hunger. Thrusting his tongue between her lips into the warm recesses within. One of her hands lodged against his collarbone. The other slid around his neck and hung on for dear life.

He groaned deep in his chest and settled her cross-legged in his lap. That maneuver aligned their bodies in interesting and dangerous ways. She moved instinctively and felt him hard and warm against the part of her that ached so fiercely.

His hands were under her tank top now, stroking, cupping, caressing. She was in way over her head, and still he was mute on the one important issue. With her final puny ounce of willpower, she reluctantly broke the kiss, scrambled to her feet, and propped her hands on her hips. She glared at him. "What in the heck are we doing? I didn't tell you that as some sort of good-bye package deal. I want the truth, Jason. Am I nothing more to you than Pam's little friend?"

He looked up at her, all five feet ten inches of her, with a wry gaze. "Little? I don't think so."

She kicked his leg halfheartedly. "I'm a vulnerable woman. I have delicate feelings. Be nice."

He snorted and rose to his feet. "You're one of the strongest women I know." He topped her by a good four inches.

The look on his face was all dark, predatory male, and it sent a shiver of arousal down her spine. She'd given him way too much ammunition

She tapped her foot. Or she would have if she hadn't kicked off her sneakers earlier. Now her toes curled in the grass. "I'm waiting for a response, Mr. Ratcliff. Maybe *get lost. I like you. You're embarrassing me*. Take your pick."

He moved closer. She backed away. He took her shoulders in his hands. "What if none of those is appropriate?"

She licked her lips. "You could improvise." She whispered the words, her heart in her throat.

He lifted his hand and brushed his thumb over her lower lip. His eyes were bluer than the summer sky. "You make me ache," he said huskily. "You make me believe in home and happiness and new beginnings. You make me smile when I wake up knowing I'm going to see you every day. You make me groan and shake and want you when I lie in bed at night. I love you, Felicity. So much it hurts."

Her chest tightened, even as her legs trembled. "You don't have to say that." Her voice was unsteady. She wanted so badly to believe.

His lips twisted in a wry half-smile. "I sure as hell do. I've been racking my brain over how I was going to concentrate on finishing up at school when my heart was back here with you."

A single tear escaped even though she blinked rapidly to keep it from falling. "I won't be your burden or your responsibility, Jason. I want you to have freedom to hang out with the guys. To study. To play. All those things you missed out on."

He tucked her face against his chest, and she could feel his heart beating beneath her cheek. He sighed. "College is supposed to be a time for growing up, Fliss. But I did my growing up here. With the girls . . . With you. And as hard as it was, I wouldn't change a thing, unless of course if I could bring Mom and Dad back. I learned the difficult lessons that books and frat parties and finals can't ever teach. And it gave me you."

She buried her nose in the soft fabric of his shirt. "I'm not as smart as you are."

He jerked and held her at arm's length, his expression stern. "Never let me hear you say that. Don't be such a goose. You're amazing, and you'll make a success of whatever you do in life."

She sniffed. "How do you know?"

He kissed her softly. "You just did a hell of a job with your first marriage proposal."

"Marriage?" she squawked, her jaw dropping.

He assumed a look of innocence. "Surely you didn't say *I love you* just to get me into bed. I'm shocked."

She winced. "About that bed thing." He was nibbling her neck now, so it was awfully hard to concentrate.

"I'm listening, sweetheart." His words were muffled, making his sincerity suspect.

She arched her neck and shuddered when he hit a sensitive spot. "Jason. I need to tell you something."

Now he cupped one breast in his hand and ran his thumb over the nipple. Fire shot from her breast to her womb, and she moved restlessly. He dropped to his knees and tongued her navel just above the low-slung waist band of her shorts. Her knees lost their starch. Gooseflesh broke out all over her skin, and she sure as heck wasn't cold.

Her hands clenched in his hair. It was soft and thick. She played with it absently, while she tried to regain control of the situation.

He unfastened the single button at the top of her zipper. "Felicity." He said her name on a low breath of sound that made the hairs on her arms stand up.

Somehow they were both on the grass, his broad shoulders looming over her, his thigh heavy and warm against her hip. He was hard and ready, and her need made her dizzy.

He licked her nipple through her shirt, wetting the fabric. "Talk to me, sweetheart. What were you going to say?"

Her whole body was a puddle of liquid, aching want. How was she supposed to think straight? His hand toyed with her zipper again, and she sucked in a breath. "I'm a virgin, Jason. I hope that doesn't complicate things."

He went so still that she couldn't even hear him breathing. And her eyes were squeezed shut, so she couldn't see his face.

He flopped to his back beside her and started laughing. But when she opened her eyes, the look on his face was more pain than humor. She sat up and poked him, disgruntled and frustrated. In more ways than one.

"It's not a laughing matter."

He grinned up at her and brought her hand to his lips. When he sucked one of her fingers into his mouth, she wondered if she had the courage to attack *his* zipper.

He must have read her face, because his smile went from naughty to tender in a heartbeat. "It's no laughing matter at all," he said quietly. "But it's amazing and humbling and I sure as hell don't want to mess this up. I can wait."

She pouted dramatically. "What does a girl have to do to lose her virginity these days?" She rubbed him daringly, and his eyes rolled back in his head.

He clenched her wrist in a bruising grip. "I can't face your mom and dad if I seduce their baby girl without a ring on her finger."

She bent over him and kissed him . . . with a fair amount of determination. "They're busy getting settled in Florida. You're moving in six days. Seems to me a quick trip to the courthouse would solve all our problems."

He sat up and cupped her face. "What about the bridal magazines, the giggling wedding showers, the fancy dress and cake?"

She studied his face, his dear, wonderful, handsome face. She thought about waiting, and in a split second she decided that six years was long enough. She sighed softly and kissed him. "All I want this summer is you, Jason. That's all I've ever wanted."

He returned the kiss lazily. "And how about a ring?" he teased.

She lifted an eyebrow. "That goes without saying, Mr. Ratcliff. The bigger and gaudier, the better."

He chuckled and hugged her tightly.

Suddenly an unpleasant thought dented her mood of euphoria. "So what would have happened if I hadn't chased you down and professed my eternal and undying love?"

He tugged her ponytail with one hand and caressed her butt with the other. "Why do you think I climbed this hill, Fliss? That kiss yesterday was a giant wake-up call. I was ready to leave my house . . . this place. But I couldn't imagine leaving you."

She got all teary again, but he managed to distract her rather nicely with a hot, spine-melting kiss. She nuzzled closer into his embrace, imagining a world of possibilities. "It's hard to believe this hilltop won't ever be home again after we leave."

He shook his head, dragging her to her feet before they both succumbed to temptation. His smile was whimsical and full of anticipation. "You're all the home I'll ever want or need, Felicity. Home, sweet home."

CHICKEN SOUP
FOR ANNIE

LuAnn McLane

"HELLO . . . ?" ANNIE CALLED OUT IN THE COZY thrift shop half hoping that no one would answer so that she could turn on her heel and head right back out the door. Glancing around she noted that the shelves were crammed full of everything under the sun from clothing to furniture to canned goods. Boxes overflowing with miscellaneous items were stacked in the corner, making it obvious that the shop was a work in progress and certainly could use some helping hands. Releasing a sad little sigh, Annie remembered that not very long ago she would have jumped at the chance to volunteer for such a worthy project.

"Hello there?" she ventured again and looked down at the name written on her note from Mrs. Greene, her warmhearted but meddlesome employer. "Mr. Wainscot? Are you here?"

"Mrs. Hathaway? Oh, so you're feeling better? Excellent." The reply was muffled but masculine and came from somewhere near the rear of the store. Annie spotted a dark head poking above some shelving, but before she could correct him he said, "Come on back. I'm in the toy . . . *whoa!*" A thud followed by a crash, a moan, and several more ouches and crashes had Annie running to the back of the room.

"Mr. Wainscot?" she asked breathlessly while searching for the source of the commotion. At first all she saw was a huge pile of scattered toys but then she spotted a blue Nike running shoe and a jean-clad calf poking out from beneath a big red teddy bear. One hand slowly emerged while clutching a Mr. Potato Head but the rest of the body was buried beneath board games and Barbie dolls.

"Mr. Wainscot?" Annie knelt down beside the groaning pile and started pushing the toys aside. "Oh my gosh, are you okay?"

"I'm . . . fine . . . um, I think." The reply came from under a Monopoly game, a chess set, and a toy keyboard that was playing a tinny version of "Old MacDonald Had a Farm." "I just hope nothing's broken."

"Oh no! You think you might have some broken bones? What hurts? Your arm? Your leg?" Annie frantically slid the keyboard aside to reveal a plain white T-shirt hiked up a few inches, exposing some surprisingly nice abs.

"No, I mean I hope the toys aren't broken."

Shaking her head, Annie pushed away chess pieces and Monopoly money to reveal dark wavy hair, light blue eyes, and a full mouth that did funny things to her stomach. A little shocked, Annie ignored the unwanted attraction and frowned down at him. "How in the world did you manage to get yourself buried beneath all of these toys?"

With a grimace, he pushed up to a sitting position. "It's all Mr. Potato Head's fault. I was checking the box to see if all the pieces were there, because if you don't have the mustache and glasses, what's the point, right?"

Annie nodded at his pointless question but smiled. "Right."

"I was attaching his nose when I heard you call out. I sort of twisted on the ladder to see the front door and lost my footing, something I'm prone to doing. I grabbed the shelving and caused the toys to fall like an avalanche on top of me. I was lucky that the shelves tipped back to the wall and didn't fall on me as well. That would have really caused some bodily harm." He flexed his wrist with a wince.

"So . . . you were playing with toys while standing on a ladder?"

"Guilty," he admitted with a smile that made his mouth even more attractive. "Did I mention that I'm accident-prone?"

"Yes, which is why you should refrain from playing with toys while perched on a ladder."

"I'll make a mental note of it." His grin deepened, making a dimple visible in his left cheek. "So I'm guessing you're filling in for Mrs. Hathaway?"

Feeling heat creep into her cheeks, Annie hesitated. "Um . . . I . . ." she began, trying hard to swallow her pride, but it stuck in her throat. "Uh . . . *yes.*" She waved her hand over the toys. "And it looks as if I have my work cut out for me."

"Sorry about the mess."

"We'll have it cleaned up in no time." Thankfully it was her day off from her job at the bookstore. "But, Mr. Wainscot, I have to pick up my daughter from school by three o'clock. And by the way, my name is Annie Alexander."

"Oh, please call me Josh." After pushing up to his feet, he offered his hand. "Mr. Wainscot makes me feel old."

"Which is what I was expecting the pastor of First Christian Church to be," Annie admitted and then felt the heat of another blush.

"Well, that makes us even, because Mrs. Hathaway is seventy-eight," Josh said while engulfing her hand in his large, firm grasp, making Annie feel feminine in comparison. When his fingers slid from hers the rough calluses on his fingers made her realize that he might be a man of the cloth but he was no stranger to physical work.

Another unexpected little zing of attraction tingled in her fingers, making her take a step back while rubbing her hand against her jeans. "We had better get to work," Annie said briskly and began sorting through the stack of toys.

"Right," Josh nodded but he couldn't help but smile at his cute little volunteer. The sudden rosy color in her cheeks had him hoping that the attraction that he was feeling was mutual. Although she had mentioned a daughter, her ring finger was bare, so he assumed that she was a single mom and he intended to find out before her shift was over. He decided not to come on too strong since she seemed rather skittish . . . not that he was a smooth operator. No, quite the opposite. When it came to women, Josh tended to get tongue-tied. "So are you a friend of Mrs. Hathaway?"

"Um, no," she answered without looking up from the Old Maid cards that she was stacking together. "Why do you ask?"

"I didn't remember your name from the volunteer sheet so I guessed that you were filling in for her as a favor."

After a slight hesitation Annie said, "Actually, I was sent here by Betty Greene. I work at her bookstore and live in the apartment over the shop. I've only been in town for a couple of months."

"Oh, that explains it. Betty is a kindhearted soul. She holds back all of the Spider-Man comic books for me."

"You read comic books?"

"Since I was a kid," Josh admitted while sliding board games back on the shelf. "Of course if you ask my mom she'll say that it's because I never grew up." Josh plunked a felt pirate hat on his head and swished a plastic sword through the air. "Arrrrgh, don't know why she thinks that." He was rewarded with a giggle from Annie.

"No, I can't imagine."

"Yes, everyone thinks I started this thrift shop as charity work but it's really an excuse to play with toys," Josh joked with a smile, but to his surprise Annie didn't smile back. "Hey," he said quietly. "I didn't mean to sound flippant. This store began as a Christmas project last year but I decided that we needed to help the less fortunate all year round," he explained with a more serious note in his voice. "We hand out vouchers to those in need so that they can have the pleasure of shopping for what they really like and want instead of having a basket dropped off on their doorstep with food they don't enjoy or clothes that don't fit."

"It's a worthy cause," Annie answered with a solemn nod.

Josh tried to coax a smile back to her pretty face but she remained rather quiet and he wished he could take back his flippant comment. His attempts at casual conversation, with questions like where she was originally from and her reason for settling in Prescott, Ohio, seemed to make her uncomfortable to the point where Josh gave up. "Um, I'll be in the back working on some broken toys," he announced after a long stretch of silence.

"Oh, okay. When I finish here I'll dive into those boxes over there," she said, pointing at the mess in the far corner of the store. After glancing at her watch she said, "I've got another hour or so before I have to pick up Cassidy. It's her last day of school before summer break. She'll have a lot of stuff to carry home so I don't want to be late."

Josh nodded. "Sure, I understand. By the way, we have a fun summer Bible school program if you're interested. There are sign-up sheets on the counter over there."

"Okay, thanks," she replied, but to his surprise didn't seem all that interested. For someone willing to volunteer at a church-related project, this didn't quite add up. "And I'd love to see you at Sunday services. I promise that my sermons aren't that long," he added with a grin.

"Thank you for the invitation," she replied with what Josh thought was a rather sad smile. He got the impression that she wouldn't be there but didn't pry.

"Well, I'll be in the repair room if you need me," Josh said while backing away.

"Oh, watch out!" Annie's warning was too late and Josh bumped into the shelves, dislodging several toys.

"Ouch!" A Magic 8 Ball bonked him on the head and landed with a soft thud on the carpet. "Tell me I didn't just do that," Josh said while rubbing his head.

"You didn't just do that," Annie said and had to giggle. "Go!" She shooed him with her hands. "I'll take care if it." Annie watched the gangly but cute preacher leave the room but then mentally shook herself when she realized that she was admiring him way too much. Oh, how she wished that her circumstances were different and that she really was there just to help out.

For the next hour Annie worked on organizing the shelves, grinning when she heard an occasional crash, thump, or a muffled *ouch* from the back room. She imagined that Josh's sermons would be energetic and inspiring but she hadn't been inside of a church since the funeral for her husband. It wasn't just Matt's death but the circumstances leading up to his fatal car crash that had left Annie's life shattered and her faith shaken to the core.

Annie glanced over at the stack of Bible school sign-up sheets and felt a stab of guilt thinking that, if nothing else, she could at least enroll Cassidy in the summer program. Pushing to her feet, Annie brushed off her jeans while feeling the familiar surge of depression weighing her down. After a long sigh she was about to tell Josh that she was leaving when she spotted the Magic 8 Ball where it had rolled to the corner of the room. Not wanting Josh to trip on it, she walked over and picked it up. "Will my luck *ever* change?" Annie asked darkly. She turned the ball over and watched the little white triangle tilt and bob in the liquid.

Without a doubt it read and Annie chuckled without mirth. "Yeah, right." After placing the ball on the shelf she went to say good-bye to Josh.

He was so intent on his task of fixing a battered bike that seriously looked to Annie as if it should be trashed that he didn't hear her enter the cluttered room. His dark head remained bent over the chain, and for someone who had trouble putting one foot in front of the other, his long fingers deftly looped the links back in place.

"Um, I'll be going, now."

"Oh!" Startled from his concentration, Josh looked up. His wavy hair was tousled as if he had been running his fingers through it, and a black smudge of grease sliced across the bridge of his nose. "Will I see you again?"

"I . . . um . . ."

"I mean, you know, to volunteer," he explained with a shy but warm smile that thawed a frozen section of Annie's heart.

Annie nibbled on her bottom lip. "Right. Well, now that Cassidy is on summer break I'm not sure that I can swing it."

"You're welcome to bring her," Josh offered.

"I'll keep that in mind but her birthday is next week so I'll be pretty busy . . . you know with plans and everything."

"Sure, I understand."

When his smile faltered a bit, Annie once again wished that her circumstances were different. He was such a nice guy, not to mention attractive, but Annie didn't know if she could risk opening her heart up to love or trust ever again.

"How did it go?" Mrs. Greene asked Annie as soon as she entered the bookstore.

"Fine," Annie said as she sat Cassidy's overstuffed backpack down on a table but avoided looking directly at her employer.

"Thool'th out for the thummer," Cassidy excitedly lisped through her missing front teeth. "Now we get to play and thwim all day!" She twirled in a happy circle and gave Mrs. Greene a toothless grin.

Annie smiled but didn't know how to tell Cassidy that there would be very little swimming since they were no longer able to afford a swim club membership. So much had changed since last summer when she and Cassidy had packed up a picnic lunch and gone swimming almost every day. At least since Matt had been an absentee father for the better part of two years, Cassidy didn't feel the pain of missing him as much as she might have. Of course, little did Annie know that his so-called business trips had actually been visits to the casino boats where he had gambled away their savings.

"There're chocolate chip cookies and a glass of milk waiting for you on the kitchen table if it's okay with your mommy," Mrs. Greene said to Cassidy.

"Sure, but only two, and drink all of the milk. And don't just dip the cookies in it."

Cassidy held up two chubby fingers. "I *promith*! Yummy! Chocolate chip ith my favorite!" she shouted and scampered off to Mrs. Greene's apartment at the rear of the store.

With her fists on her ample hips, Mrs. Greene said, "Well, Annie Alexander, I see you're empty-handed. Didn't you use the vouchers?"

Annie felt heat creep into her cheeks and it had nothing to do with the warm summer day. "Um, there was a bit of a misunderstanding."

"Go on."

"Josh . . . well, thought I was a volunteer."

"Oh, Annie, and you didn't set him straight?" Mrs. Greene asked gently.

"Well, I *was* going to tell him after I dug him out from beneath the pile of toys but he thought I was there to help."

"Dug him out from a pile of toys?"

Annie managed a chuckle. "Don't ask. But Mrs. Greene, he needed help so badly that I thought I would tell him the real reason for my visit afterward . . ." Annie hung her head and continued in a whisper, "But I was ashamed."

Mrs. Greene walked over and rested her hands on Annie's shoulders. "You are in this situation through no fault of your own, child. There is no shame in asking for help."

"I know. I'll tell him tomorrow morning before the bookstore opens. I've decided to help him out when I'm not working here and then at least I'll feel as if I'm earning my way instead of taking a handout."

Mrs. Greene nodded her head so hard that her gray bun bobbed and slid to the side where it normally rested by the end of the day. "You're a good girl, Annie Alexander. Mark my words, your string of bad luck is going to change."

"So I've been told," Annie commented dryly.

"Well, I'd better get busy. I've got a stack of comic books to sort through," Mrs. Greene said and reached for a big box. She zipped it open with a razorblade.

"Any Spider-Man in there?"

"Ah, so you like him do you?"

"Spider-Man? Who doesn't like Spidey?"

"Oh, don't give me that." Mrs. Greene waved her hand at Annie. "I meant *Josh*. He's quite the . . . *hottie*. Why do you think I never miss Sunday services?"

"Hottie?" Annie repeated shaking her head. The slang that came out of Betty Greene's mouth never ceased to amuse Annie, especially since the elderly woman bore a striking resemblance to Aunt Bea from *The Andy Griffith Show*. She bakes chocolate chip cookies that melt in your mouth, can quote passages from the Bible . . . and can sing along with the Black Eyed Peas.

"Hey, I might be old, but after I got my cataracts removed

I was like *wow* that dude is smokin' hot. Why, just last week that preacher-boy was mowing the lawn in one of those muscle shirts . . . Wowee. I about swallowed my false teeth."

"Mrs. Greene!" Annie squeaked.

"What?" Mrs. Greene asked while batting her eyelashes.

Annie laughed, instantly lightening her mood. Although the past year had been horrific, she had to admit that running out of both gas and money in front of Betty's New and Used Books had been a stroke of luck. While Mrs. Greene couldn't afford to pay Annie more than minimum wage, the small but cozy apartment came with the job, enabling Annie to put a roof over her head and food on the table.

"But, Annie," Mrs. Greene began in a more serious tone of voice, "remember that everyone falls on hard times. There's no shame in that."

Annie nodded. "In theory, I know this . . . but it's hard, you know?"

"Sweetie, I know."

"I'll tell Josh, though. I promise."

The next morning Annie walked over to the thrift shop while rehearsing her Josh-I-need-to-explain-something speech in her head. The summer sun felt warm on her face and friendly waves from towns folk reminded Annie that she couldn't have found a nicer place to raise her daughter. She was already thinking of Prescott, Ohio, as home.

Mrs. Greene had offered to watch Cassidy and had encouraged Annie not to return to the bookstore until noon. But when Annie entered the shop Josh was nowhere to be found. She was afraid to call out and cause another mishap, so instead she headed for the workroom. She found him attaching the back fender to a bicycle. "Wow, is that the same bike that you were working on yesterday?" Annie exclaimed.

Josh's head shot up. "Annie! What a nice surprise. Yes, doesn't the bike look great? I spray-painted it last night. It's almost ready to go."

Last night? Annie looked a little closer at him and noticed dark circles beneath his eyes. "What time last night?"

"I'm not sure." Josh shrugged. "Sometimes I lose track of time when I get busy on something. Because it's summertime I don't get as many volunteers, what with the kids out of school and people taking vacations. I'm glad that you were able to come back to help. I can use it."

"You need to get more rest," Annie scolded. "You'll end up making yourself sick."

"Yes ma'am," he said with a salute.

Annie giggled. "Sorry. It's the mom coming out in me. You did have breakfast, right?"

"Two bowls of Peanut Butter Cap'n Crunch."

Annie rolled her eyes.

"I warned you that I was just a big kid," he said with a grin.

With his plain white T-shirt stretched across his broad shoulders and tucked into worn, low-slung Levi's, he certainly didn't resemble a kid to Annie. He looked deliciously rugged and all male. Mentally shaking that thought out of her head, she said, "I can help out for a couple of hours but then I have to work at the bookstore."

"I appreciate it, Annie."

"My pleasure," Annie answered, and to her embarrassment her voice had a husky edge to it that made her innocent response sound . . . suggestive.

Josh's blue eyes widened a fraction and his mouth moved but no words came out.

"I . . . I mean . . . *you know*, I'm happy to do it . . . *volunteer*, that is."

Josh swallowed, making his Adam's apple bob in his throat.

Annie put her palms to her cheeks. "I'm so sorry. I didn't mean to sound like I was flirting with you."

"Well, darn."

Annie blinked at him in surprise. "Excuse me?"

"You had me hoping. Women tend to keep their distance from me like I'm off-limits or something."

"I guess it comes with the territory," Annie said with a small smile.

"Yeah, I guess it does," he agreed in a rather tired voice. "But in reality I'm just a guy. Flirting with me is perfectly okay. Encouraged, even." With a half-smile he met her eyes briefly and then bent his head to work on the bicycle.

"I'll get to work now," Annie said softly and headed out to the shop. She had to wonder though if Josh was lonely. She supposed that people tended to walk on eggshells around him when it sounded like he just wanted to be treated like a normal guy.

Annie was surprised at how fast the morning went, and with a glance at her watch realized that it was time to go. Looking around, she was pleased with her progress. But after calling out a quick good-bye to Josh she had to hurry to the bookstore. She told herself that her quick departure was her reason for not using her vouchers and made a mental promise to tell Josh the truth tomorrow.

"Mommy, Mommy!" Cassidy shouted as soon as Annie entered the bookstore.

"Hey, babycakes," Annie said while kneeling down to brace herself for the impact of her daughter running to her at full speed. Cassidy wrapped her small arms around Annie's neck and gave her mother a fierce squeeze. Her baby-soft hair brushed against Annie's cheek and she smelled like crayons and grape Kool-Aid.

"Mommy, I made my birfday lith," Cassidy announced and ran back over to the table to get it. "Mith Greene helped me thpell the hard words," she announced with a smile.

"She knew most of them," Mrs. Greene said and Annie felt a surge of pride.

"Wanna hear, Mommy?"

"Sure," Annie answered, hoping that they were gifts that she could afford.

" 'Kay," Cassidy said as she frowned in concentration at her list. "I want a thoccer ball."

"Good choice."

"Thummer clothes cuz my shorts are too tight. A new bathin' thuit."

"Good idea," Annie agreed with a nod and breathed a sigh of relief. *And not too expensive.*

"Oh, and a two-wheeler bike. Either blue or pink or maybe red."

Annie's heart started to thud when she realized that a bike was out of her price range. But then a picture of Josh working on the red bicycle popped into her head. "Um, Mrs. Greene, would you mind if I ran an errand? I won't be long."

"Sure, Annie."

"Can I go with you, Mommy?"

"No, baby, but I won't be long."

"Okay . . ." she said a bit glumly.

Annie took off down Main Street and ran the three blocks to the thrift shop. *Please don't let the bike be gone.* Panting, she came to an abrupt halt when a young couple came walking out of the store with the shiny red bike. A lump formed in Annie's throat and she wanted to slither to the concrete sidewalk in a heap of tears.

She had weathered losing her beautiful home and all of her savings to her husband's gambling addiction. When Matt had perished in the car crash she had somehow remained strong. After learning that Matt had cashed in his life-insurance policy just days before his death she bucked up and vowed to start over, for Cassidy's sake.

But suddenly she started to crumble. Her knees felt as if they were made of water and she had to put her hand out to the brick wall for support. This was stupid, she told herself. It was only a bike.

A bike!

Annie put her other palm on the rough, sun-warmed brick, trying to absorb the heat into her suddenly cold hands. She took a deep breath and willed her heart to stop pounding so hard.

"Annie? Hey, are you okay?"

Josh's deep, soothing voice washed over her like gentle summer rain. After another cleansing breath she looked at him through the shimmer of unshed tears. "Um . . . yeah. I'm," she gulped and then said, "fine."

Josh wasn't buying it. "You don't look so fine," he said gently.

Her mouth trembled for a second but then her chin came up. "I'm . . . fine. *Fine!*" she insisted but then swallowed hard.

"Okay," Josh replied barely resisting the strong urge to gather her into his arms. "Would you like to come inside for some iced tea? It's hot out here and I just made a fresh pitcher."

"Um . . . no," she said while taking a step backward. "I have to go. But . . . thanks."

Still concerned, Josh frowned. "But why did you come back? Did you forget something?"

She shook her head but didn't answer. "I really have to go."

"Annie—" Josh began but she turned on her heel and hurried away. Threading his fingers through his hair, he watched, confused, and wondered if he shouldn't go after her and get some answers. With a sigh, he turned to go back inside but paused when he noticed a couple of familiar yellow vouchers that his secretary handed out to needy families scattered on the sidewalk.

"Aw . . . *no*." Josh groaned as he bent over and picked the vouchers up. "How could I have been so blind?" It hit him like a sucker punch to the gut that Annie had come to him for help and he had put her to work. It worried him that he still didn't know the cause of her distress so he hurried inside and looked up Betty Greene's phone number, hoping to get some answers.

"Hello?" Betty said in her singsong voice that never ceased to make Josh smile.

"Mrs. Greene, this is Josh Wainscot. I need to ask you some questions about Annie Alexander."

"Wait a minute, Josh. She just walked back into the store. I'll have to take this call in my office."

"Sure." Josh heard Mrs. Greene tell Annie that she was going to take her lunch break.

A moment later Mrs. Greene said in a hushed tone, "Okay young man, tell me what's up."

"Well, I'm afraid I made a stupid mistake. I thought that Annie was a volunteer when in fact she was coming to the thrift shop for assistance."

"So she finally came clean, did she?"

"Um, not exactly. She dropped some vouchers on the ground."

"Oh . . ."

"Do you know what she was coming here for?"

"It might have been a bike for her daughter. Do you have one?"

"Oh . . . no."

"Let me guess. You *did*."

Josh sighed. "I had been restoring a cute little two-wheeler all week. Why didn't she say something?"

"Because Cassidy just now gave Annie her birthday list and a bike was on it. And in case you haven't noticed, Annie has her pride."

"So she won't use the vouchers?"

"Well, I think she might, but only in exchange for working."

"Mrs. Greene, you're brilliant."

"Why, thank you. Oh . . . and Josh, maybe take her out to lunch sometime? Poor thing brings a thermos of chicken noodle soup to work just about every day."

Josh grinned. "Not a problem."

"Ah, so you're into her, are you?"

"*Into* her?" Josh chuckled. "Yes, I guess you could say that."

"Good, because I do believe that she's into you, too."

Josh smiled as he hung up the phone. Now if only he would get a nice used bike in. . . .

As luck would have it, the very next day Josh got not one but two bicycles, along with a whole truckload of items left over from a yard sale. He was sorting through the huge pile when Annie walked in.

"Hi," she said a bit shyly. "Looks like you got quite a windfall there." Her eyes lit up when she spotted a worn but fixable pink bike.

"Yes, hope you're ready to work."

"I'm only here during my lunch break . . . But about that. I have a confession to make."

"Before you do, may I ask you a favor?"

"Okay."

Putting down the Rubik's Cube that he had been twisting, he said, "I need regular part-time help. I can't afford a salary but I could pay in these vouchers that we give out. You could use them in the store like real money."

"Really?" Annie asked innocently.

"If you're interested."

Annie glanced over at the bike. "Yes, I think I could manage to work part-time, if it's okay to bring Cassidy sometimes."

"Sure." Josh grinned. "I'll put her to work as well and she can earn some vouchers, too."

"Cassidy would like that." Annie smiled. She knew that she had dropped her vouchers so she was on to Josh's little game. It warmed her heart that he was trying to save her pride. "That would work out well . . . when she isn't in your summer Bible camp, that is."

"You signed her up?" His eyes lit up.

Annie reached in her purse and handed Josh the forms. "Yes. It's time that we regained our faith."

Josh gave her one of his big smiles that made the dimple pop out in his cheek and her stomach filled with butterflies.

"Now about my confession . . ." She took a step closer to him.

"Oh, Annie, you don't have to—"

"No, you need to know." She nibbled on her bottom lip, suddenly losing her nerve.

"Really, Annie, you—"

"Shh!" Annie arched up on tiptoe and gave Josh a soft but lingering kiss on the lips.

"Th-that was your confession?" he asked with a husky note in his voice that made a hot shiver slide down Annie's spine.

"Yes. I've wanted to do that ever since I dug you out from beneath the pile of toys."

"You did?"

Annie nodded. "You're quite the hottie, preacher-boy."

"What?" His dark eyebrows shot up.

"I'm quoting Mrs. Greene."

Josh chuckled as he wrapped his arms around her. When

he dipped his head to capture her lips, Annie threaded her fingers through his hair. She melted into the kiss and felt the hope of a new beginning sing through her veins.

When Josh finally pulled back, his arms remained around her waist. "I'd love to take you to lunch today, Annie."

"I brought chicken noodle soup." She pointed to a green thermos and brown paper sack.

"Maybe you'd like a change of pace . . . A burger or club sandwich in town?"

Annie smiled up at him. "I'd love to eat lunch with you but I'll stick with the soup."

Josh angled his head and asked, "But why?"

"You're going to think I'm silly." Annie took a step back and put her hands to her cheeks.

"No, I won't."

"Promise not to laugh?"

"I promise." He gently pulled her hands away from her face and threaded his fingers through hers.

"Whenever I got sick my mom would always make chicken soup for me. I know it was all in my head but it never failed to make me feel better. To this day just the smell lifts my spirits. It makes me feel . . ." Annie shrugged and said softly, "*Loved*." With a soft chuckle she shook her head and said, "I've gone through gallons this past year. See, isn't that silly?"

"Not at all."

Annie smiled. "I brought enough to share. Oh, and tons of crackers."

"You gotta have crackers."

"And I have homemade chocolate chip cookies, courtesy of Mrs. Greene."

"Now we're talkin'."

Annie gave him a slow smile. "So, does chicken soup sound good?"

"Yes, it does, but in return I want to take you to dinner."

"I promised Cassidy pizza. It's kids-eat-free night. Makes taking her out affordable."

Josh grinned. "Can I tag along? After all, I'm just a big kid. Maybe I can eat free, too?"

"Hey, it's worth a try. Wear the pirate hat, okay?" Annie said with a grin as she unscrewed the thermos. Closing her eyes, she inhaled deeply. "Never fails." When she opened her eyes she spotted the Magic 8 Ball and grinned.

"What?" Josh asked and turned to follow her gaze.

"You know the other day when the Magic 8 Ball bonked you on the head?"

"Yes, it left a lump," he said reaching up to rub the spot.

"Well, it rolled to the corner and I picked it up so you wouldn't trip over it."

"Smart thinking," Josh said while nodding slowly. "Oh, so you asked it a question?"

"I sort of growled a question," Annie admitted. "You want to know what I asked it?"

"Of course."

"I asked it if my luck was ever going to change."

"What did it say?" he asked while crumbling crackers into his soup.

"Without a doubt."

"And you believe in the Magic 8 Ball?"

Annie grinned. "I do now."

Josh leaned across the table and kissed her. "Hey, you know what?"

"What?"

"I do think that being a Magic 8 Ball believer entitles you to free pizza, too."

"Really? Think I qualify?" Annie asked innocently and then slurped a noodle through puckered lips. "Imagine that."

"Ah, a woman after my own heart." Josh laughed and then clinked his mug to hers.

Of course Annie knew that Josh was merely teasing. But in that moment when his eyes met hers something warm and wonderful passed between them, renewing her hope and re-kindling her spirit.

NO ANGEL

Lucy Monroe

A LOUD BUMP SOUNDED AGAINST THE WALL BEHIND Cheryl Gentry's desk, startling her. Then several thumps and a string of curses sounded from her boss's office.

She leapt to her feet and rushed into the adjoining room. Amusement warred with concern at the sight that greeted her. Zack Alexander, the CEO of Citywide Construction, was on the floor.

His office chair was not behind his desk where it was supposed to be, but tipped over, resting drunkenly beside him. One of its casters had come off and rolled to a stop a few inches from where Cheryl now stood. The glass from two shattered light bulbs decorated the man as well as the expensive designer carpet around him.

"I told you to wait for maintenance to change that."

He glared at her with narrowed dark brown eyes, the tanned skin of his angular face going dusky. "I'm six-foot-six. I can change my own damn light bulb."

"And the ceilings on this floor are ten feet high. You told me you ordered them that way so you wouldn't feel claustrophobic."

Running his fingers through his black hair to dislodge bits of the super-thin glass, Zack rose to his impressive height. His Italian suit did nothing to disguise the bulge of muscles caused by the movement, and Cheryl forced herself to once again suppress her reaction to the sight.

He might dress like the high-powered businessman that he was, but he looked like he could be one of the many construction workers employed by the company he ran. In fact, he was bigger than most of them.

And cranky. Man, Zack knew how to frown. "I would have been fine if the stupid chair hadn't gone out from beneath me."

"Perhaps you should have chosen a perch that was not on wheels." She didn't even crack a smile when she said it. Go her.

He didn't deign to answer her impudent remark, but went to dust the glass shards off his suit.

"Stop!"

If anything, his frown intensified. "What?" he asked in a dangerously low voice that seemed to intimidate most everyone else.

It had no effect on her. She knew the sound of a man about to do you harm—either physically or emotionally—and Zack was so not there. "You're going to cut yourself. Just hold on a second and I'll get the whisk broom."

"I don't need a broom."

"You didn't think you needed maintenance, or at the very least a stepladder, either. However, I was aware of the necessity of one and would have suggested the other if I'd known you were going to be so impatient about getting the bulb replaced."

"Rub it in, why don't you?" Even angry, his gorgeous Texas drawl made things inside her quiver she'd rather not acknowledge.

"That's my job."

"I thought your job was to assist me."

"I am assisting you," she said before walking out to her desk.

She pulled open the bottom drawer and grabbed the small broom and dustpan she kept stored there. She returned to the scene, glad to see that despite his arguments, her boss had listened and hadn't tried to dust off the glass with his bare hands.

She walked over to him and started whisking with the broom. "Now, hold still."

"I'm not going anywhere." He sounded like a petulant little boy, and why that should be endearing rather than annoying, she had no idea.

Being this close to him wasn't doing good things for her equilibrium either.

"What in the world?" The shocked voice sounded from the doorway.

Zack turned to face his former fiancée and Cheryl adjusted her own stance so she could both see the other woman and continue her task.

"Hello, Leslie. What are you doing here?"

"Daddy wanted me to invite you to dinner tonight. The mayor's coming and he hopes to discuss that upcoming expansion at city hall."

"I'll check my schedule and get back to you."

Leslie turned her attention to Cheryl. "What about it? Is Zack free tonight?"

It was just another example of the hundred ways that the owner of Citywide Construction's daughter manipulated people. She wanted a positive response and assumed if she asked Cheryl in front of Zack, she'd get what she wanted.

"I'll have to look at the calendar," Cheryl replied in a firm voice.

The petite woman's mouth twisted in a moue of frustration. "Please . . . you remember everything."

Cheryl simply ignored the other woman and finished her dusting. If Zack wanted her to answer, he'd say something. He didn't and she stepped back after examining him for any missed bits. "I'll call someone to come up with a vacuum."

Zack nodded. "Do that. Ask for another desk chair while you're at it."

The man had insisted on trying to change his own light bulb despite a ten-foot ceiling, but wouldn't attempt to put a caster back on his chair so he'd have something to sit on while he worked. *Men.*

She stifled the urge to shake her head and simply said, "Will do."

"If I hear one more word about Leslie, the angel, I'm going to blow something up." Cheryl leaned back against the huge oak tree in the downtown park where she and her best friend often shared lunch.

She took a bite of her apple. Today's lunch. Was an extra eight pounds really worth starving herself over?

"Maybe you should have taken classes in explosives instead of office management," her friend Esperanza teased as she sat on one of the benches under the tree's leafy branches.

"I'm serious. It's bad enough that he was engaged to her at all, but the way everyone talks like it's such a tragedy they aren't engaged anymore just annoys the pee out of me. The people I work with are so clueless. Zack and Leslie are totally unsuited."

"You're just cranky because you're dieting again. When are you going to listen to Paulo? Huh? A man likes a body he can cuddle, not sharp edges that will poke him just when things start to get interesting."

"I'll listen to Paulo when he divorces you and starts dating me."

Esperanza's eyes flashed. "It will never happen."

"I know." Cheryl was thrilled her friend had found a good man to share her life with and Esperanza knew it.

"*Escucheme* . . . listen to me, *amiga*. It is time you started dating again."

If anyone else had said those words, Cheryl would have

been furious, but she and Esperanza shared more than a friendship. They shared a similar history.

They'd met in a support group for victims of domestic violence. As different as they appeared on the surface, their lives had been eerily similar.

Cheryl had grown up in Beverly Hills and attended private schools all the way through university where she'd gotten a supremely useless degree in ancient French literature. She'd married a man already on the fast track to political power the summer after she graduated.

Esperanza had been raised in one of the *barrios* of LA, got married her final year of high school, and never went to college. She'd had two children by the age of twenty-one and the same number of broken bones.

Cheryl's husband hadn't started out physical in his abuse, like Esperanza's had, but he'd gotten there in the end. And it was at this point that their stories merged.

Her family had been furious when she'd had the audacity to leave her husband. Even more so that she had derailed his political career by pressing charges against him after he'd put her in the hospital. He'd been one of her father's protégés.

No one had understood her belief that political ambition did not excuse domestic annihilation. Her mother had tolerated Cheryl's father's emotional abuse for decades. She and both sets of grandparents had been scandalized by Cheryl's unwillingness to be her own husband's "stress relief."

Esperanza's entire family had disowned her when she had filed for divorce from her first husband. Both her mother and grandmother had been married to men who used their fists to get their points across. They thought Esperanza was weak for refusing to stay in a similar situation.

Despite their different economic and educational backgrounds, Cheryl and Esperanza had become friends the first night they met in group session.

Four years later, they were as close as sisters. Which was why when Esperanza had moved to Dallas with her children and her new husband, Cheryl had followed. Her blood family treated her like a pariah and she had no reason to stay in California.

The Hispanic woman was convinced Cheryl needed a new environment to start life over. And that was exactly what she'd done, taking classes to augment her impractical degree before landing a job as Zack Alexander's personal assistant.

Cheryl had been Esperanza's only attendant when the other woman had started her own new life and married her Paulo. He was a truly decent man who would no more hit his wife or stepdaughters than he would jump in a vat of boiling oil. In fact, he'd probably jump in the oil first.

He was gentle and patient . . . everything Esperanza needed in a man, but not what Cheryl wanted. Cheryl was drawn to strong, powerful men . . . men like her ex-husband. For obvious reasons, that made her less than enthusiastic about dating.

She finished chewing another bite of her apple before speaking. "There's only one man who interests me and even if he shared my interest, the relationship would be impossible."

"Not to mention scary, no?"

"Yes."

"But this man, this hottie boss of yours, he is nothing like your ex."

"I didn't say it was my boss."

"Please." Esperanza rolled her eyes. "Give me some credit . . . I am your closest friend. I know these things."

"The angel is petite, probably a size zero, soft-spoken—"

"And as manipulative as she is lovely."

"But he asked her to marry him . . . She's the type of woman he wants."

"Like your ex is the type of man you want?"

Cheryl grimaced. "It's not the same."

"You do not think so, *amiga*?"

"Zack Alexander would never be interested in me." At five-nine, she was taller than average. "I had bigger thighs in middle school than she has now. She's a blonde; I've got red hair and it curls like crazy. I've even got freckles now that I'm not using that facial cream my mother always insisted on buying for me." Cheryl was also outspoken, a brown belt in Tae Kwon Do, *and* his personal assistant. "Besides, he doesn't date employees."

"Has he said so?" Esperanza asked.

"Well, no . . . but he doesn't have to."

"So, you are reading his mind?"

"Why not? I do it in the office all the time."

"You are good at what you do."

"I had six years of training for it. The perfect political wife is often little more than a glorified personal assistant."

"But not such good training for taking a risk."

Cheryl was considering Esperanza's words later that afternoon as she sat at her desk answering e-mail for her boss. No, marrying Darren had definitely not been good training for taking a risk.

But if she accepted that, then she ceded him the power to control her future and she had spent enough time being controlled by him in the years they were together.

Darn, maybe it *was* time to start dating, if only to prove that she could.

The next morning, Cheryl had little time to ponder her decision to start dating again because Zack was in a foul mood. His normally exacting standards were in overdrive and that meant he kept her hopping.

Finally, after he'd bitched about the way she answered an e-mail he never would have bothered to even acknowledge, she demanded, "What is the matter with you?"

He gave her a chilly stare that sent others running. "Nothing is the matter with me. This is about the way that you do your job."

"I'm great at my job."

A bark of laughter escaped him before he was scowling again. "You have no shortage of confidence, do you?"

If he only knew what a hard-fought battle that had been. "Not in this area, I don't."

He said nothing.

She crossed her arms and met him glare for glare. "You're in a rotten mood and you seem intent on taking it out on me. You want to tell me why?"

"No."

"Do it anyway."

He ran his hand over his face. "Fine. I spent an uncomfortable evening with Leslie and her parents because you couldn't be bothered to make something up for my schedule last night."

"You expected me to lie to her to get you out of the dinner invite?" Cheryl asked in shock.

"I thought it was obvious. You read my mind about practically everything else, why not that?"

Okay, so maybe she'd sensed a little reluctance on his part. "I refused to confirm you had nothing on your schedule."

"Not good enough."

"I don't lie. Not for you. Not for anyone."

"You could have hedged around the truth."

"If you didn't want to go, why didn't you simply say so?" she asked with exasperation.

"I couldn't."

And obviously he hadn't been real hot at making up his own lie either. "Let me get this straight. You wanted me to make up excuses so you didn't have to face telling a little slip of a woman you didn't want to have dinner with her?"

"It was with her family, not just her," he clarified, sounding even more put out. "I didn't want to hurt Leslie's feelings. It's important to her that we remain friends."

"Even though she broke off your engagement."

"Yes."

"And because you don't want to bruise her delicate sensibilities, you wanted *me* to *lie* for you?"

"Yes," he ground out.

She opened her mouth to blast him when a discreet throat clearing sounded behind her. She turned and there stood the marketing director. He was also one of Zack's friends.

"Hey, guy, why don't we get some lunch?"

"It's only eleven o'clock," Zack said impatiently.

The other man shrugged. "I'm hungry."

Cheryl wasn't buying it for a minute. She'd seen this happen before. The marketing director ran interference for Zack with Leslie and other people as well. Frankly, Cheryl didn't understand why. Okay, so Zack had a temper, but he controlled it. Always.

And it wasn't even a struggle for him. She could tell; she'd had six years experience watching a man submit to his temper rather than making it submit to him.

Zack wasn't that weak.

Her frown matched her boss's as she looked at the other man. "Stay out of this. I'm no angel. I don't need you or anyone else, for that matter, to protect me from Mr. Alexander's temper tantrums."

"Temper tantrum?" Zack demanded.

She turned her less than happy look on him. "What is the point of this little tirade?"

"Little tirade? Point?"

"Yes. Point. You say I can read your mind. I say that you have to know me well enough to know I'm not going to jump into a situation you should be grown-up enough to handle on your own with a convenient story to cover your cowardly behind."

"Cowardly behind?" This time it was David, the marketing director, repeating her, and he sounded like he was choking back laughter.

She gave a short nod to let both men know she wasn't taking it back.

"If you recall, you were the one who wanted to know why I was in such a bad mood," Zack said.

"So, now I know . . . I'm still looking for the point in your complaints. Is all of this going to end with the dramatic announcement that I'm out of a job?"

"You think I'm going to fire you?" Disbelief laced his tone.

Good. She didn't for one minute think that, but somehow both he and David needed to realize that she wasn't worried. That Zack's mild bad temper didn't intimidate her. "Are you?"

He cursed. "No."

"Glad to hear it." She stood and grabbed her purse from the top drawer of the filing cabinet.

Zack moved in front of her before she made it out the door. "Where are you going?"

"David had a good idea. I'm going to lunch. Then, I'm taking the rest of the afternoon off. It's been a trying day."

"It's only eleven a.m.," Zack said repeating himself from earlier.

She simply gave him a look that told him he knew who to blame for her current mood. She was nobody's doormat, and he knew her well enough to be aware of that truth, too.

Without another word, she sailed past him and out the door. Stopping just in the hall, she looked back over her shoulder at David. "Have a good weekend."

"We'll be seeing you on Monday, then?"

"Of course. It's not a holiday that I know of."

"Uh, I think you have one pissed-off personal assistant there, Zack-buddy."

Zack shook his head, trying to clear it, but it didn't work. He wanted to charge after Cheryl and demand she come back to the office. She belonged here, with him. He didn't do it only because he had no desire to mess up more than he already had.

"It might have been unreasonable to expect her to get me out of dinner with Leslie's family," he admitted.

David chuckled. "Only a little. Truth is, since you hired Cheryl, you've gotten used to her making your life easier. But this time your expectations were a tad on the irrational side."

"She spoils me."

"You can say that again. I wish my PA was half as efficient and able to anticipate my needs as Cheryl is for you. Hey, maybe she'll be looking to move on after your *little tirade*."

Zack's mood went south again. "Don't even think about it."

David put his hands up in a placating gesture. "I was just kidding, bro. You *are* in a bad mood, aren't you? What's the matter? Are Leslie's parents still hoping you'll get back together?"

"I don't think so, but it's uncomfortable just the same. They all treat me like some poor unfortunate soul. Even Leslie. The looks of pity get really old after the first half-hour."

"I can imagine . . . especially when you consider that *you* think you had a lucky escape."

"I can't exactly tell them that, can I?"

"Nope. Not unless you want Leslie crying all over you and her daddy."

"I can't believe I let myself get involved with someone from work."

"Leslie doesn't work here."

"That's what I told myself when we started dating, but it's just as awkward."

"Does this mean you're trying to talk yourself out of pursuing the stick of dynamite that just flounced out of here?"

"I might be annoyed . . . embarrassed even . . . by how things turned out with Leslie, but I'm not stupid."

The blond man smiled. "Then you'd better call the florist."

"What for?"

"A dozen roses make a nice apology."

Zack nodded. Easier than actually saying he was sorry, that was for sure.

Zack came into his office on Monday morning, and, as usual, Cheryl was already there.

He stopped in front of her desk. "Have a good weekend?"

She looked up from her computer, a small smile of welcome on her lips. Just like most every other morning. "Yes. How about you?"

It had been frustrating as hell. He'd expected her to call about the flowers, but she never had and he'd spent two and a half days wondering why. He'd been engaged to Leslie and never given her that much thought.

He couldn't stop himself from asking, "Did you get my flowers?"

"Yes." She went back to her computer.

He didn't leave, though he'd clearly been dismissed. "Is that all you have to say?"

"What do you want me to say?"

"Did you like them?"

"They were lovely."

"Did they last?" Okay, so it was a dumb question, but semi-legitimate. Sometimes the most beautiful buds did not bloom, but simply wilted on the stem.

"It became a moot point."

"What? Why?"

"I fed them to the garbage disposal stem by stem."

"You what?" He wasn't angry, but rather startled by her audacity.

She contemplated her nicely manicured nails. "I thought about tossing them. The image wasn't quite as satisfying."

"Do you make it a habit of sending someone's apology down the garbage disposal?" he asked dryly.

"Is that what it was?" Her brow lifted. "An apology?"

"Yes. Damn it. What else would it have been?"

"I don't know. Maybe it's just me being paranoid, but I guessed that David talked you into sending them."

He winced at the accuracy of her guess.

She looked smug. "Or perhaps I didn't see the sincerity in your apology since you had the card signed 'Regards, Zack.' No mention of the word *sorry* at all. Yes, that could definitely have been it."

"Well they were an apology," he huffed.

"Say it."

"You want me to say that I'm sorry?"

"Yes."

"Isn't that a little juvenile? I've already told you the flowers were meant to convey that."

"So, say the words."

"Fine. I'm sorry for the way I treated you Friday morning and for expecting you to lie to get me out of a tight spot."

"That wasn't so hard, was it?"

He grimaced. "Hard enough."

She laughed. "You are forgiven."

And why those particular words should make his dick go hard as granite, he had no clue, but he wasn't knocking it.

He wanted the feisty redhead and he was set on having her.

Cheryl was feeling hunted.

Zack kept giving her these looks. Ones that made her insides melt in a way her ex-husband never had. Her boss also began invading her personal space at the slightest opportunity. And he made comments . . . innuendo that left her almost sure he wanted something more from her than mere workplace efficiency.

He was gone on-site and she'd been enjoying the respite from all the emotions he awoke in her. The sound of movement in her doorway caused her to look up, certain her break was over. But it wasn't Zack. It was Leslie.

"Is he in?" the other woman asked.

"No. He's on-site."

Leslie's mouth turned down. "I'm sure he doesn't need to check up on the progress personally. After all, there's a foreman on every site, but Zack has a controlling personality."

Yeah, right. Cheryl knew controlling behavior and Zack was not guilty of it. He had an opinion that he voiced, but he listened to what others had to say. "From what I've heard, his hands-on management style has saved your father a lot of money and downtime over the years."

The petite woman just shrugged. "You've got to watch out with Zack or he'll steamroll right over you."

"I haven't had that problem yet."

"It's why I broke off our engagement," Leslie went on as if

Cheryl hadn't spoken. "There had been signs before, only I ignored them. But our honeymoon was the last straw."

"Your honeymoon?" They hadn't even gotten married.

"Yes. I wanted to go to Hawaii and I made sure he knew it. Lots of subtle and not-so-subtle hints."

"I see." But she didn't. Zack was a wealthy man. He could have taken his so-called angel anywhere. Why would she choose Hawaii for this once-in-a-lifetime trip?

"He made the plans, but wouldn't tell me where we were going. I got nervous."

"He probably thought surprising you would be more romantic."

Leslie looked at Cheryl pityingly. "That's what he said, but I didn't buy it. It was all about his need for control."

Cheryl didn't think it sounded like Zack was the one with the control issues.

"What happened?" she heard herself asking.

"I had to resort to trickery to find out where my honeymoon was going to be. I called the travel agency pretending to be his secretary and got the details."

She'd lied to get the details. Some angel.

"You'll never believe what I found out."

"What?" She was breathless with anticipation. Not.

"He had booked a week on the French Riviera. Can you imagine? I took Spanish in high school, not French. If he was going to take us someplace foreign the least he could have done was choose Spain. Not that I remember much Spanish, but still. Not only is he very controlling, but he's not the least bit considerate. Why, he never once sent me flowers."

Cheryl thought guiltily of the roses she'd fed to her garbage disposal. She also saw them in a different light. Even if David had suggested Zack send them, the fact that he wasn't in the habit of doing so made them special.

"So you broke off your engagement?" In Cheryl's opinion, the *angel* was cracked mentally if she preferred Hawaii to a villa on the French Riviera.

"Yes. You can understand, of course. I realized that this was just the beginning. Our marriage would be full of times when he would make a decision, ignoring my input, and I couldn't deal with it." She let a tear slide down her cheek before artistically wiping it away. "He's a control freak, a throwback to a time when men made all the choices and women meekly obeyed."

"Funny, I've never seen that side of him and I've worked here almost a year."

Leslie opened her mouth to answer but was forestalled by a deep masculine voice. "Hello, Leslie. Have you been regaling my personal assistant with tales of an engagement gone wrong?"

The petite woman had the grace to blush. "Why, of course not. I simply stopped by to see if you needed help planning the dinner for the group from Houston."

Only good manners and iron-clad self-control kept Cheryl from calling the other woman on her lie. However, she did say, "The arrangements have all been made."

"Perhaps I should check them over."

"That won't be necessary." This from Zack. "Cheryl is very good at her job."

"Well, if you're sure," Leslie said, sounding doubtful.

"Never more so."

"I'll pop in and tell Daddy it's all under control then."

Zack leaned against Cheryl's desk, his sexy backside temptingly close. "Already done."

"I see." Oh, the angel sounded pissed.

Cheryl had to stifle a smile.

The other woman left with a barely civil good-bye.

"Did you ever get the feeling that you weren't the one with the control issues?" Cheryl asked.

Zack smiled. "A bit late, but yeah."

"I can't believe you loved her." She couldn't believe she'd said that. "I mean . . ."

"I know what you mean. What can I say? I was taken in by her soft-spoken manner."

Cheryl understood being deceived by appearances. Hadn't Darren seemed like the perfect man . . . right up until the day after they were married? "At least you figured it out eventually." And didn't it make her feel better to know that? "The two of you are completely ill suited."

"According to her, I'm ill suited to anyone."

"Well, that's understandable."

His eyes flashed dangerously. "Why? Because you agree?"

"Don't be silly. It's understandable because she wouldn't want to accept blame for the breakup. It doesn't go with the perfect angel image."

"No, it doesn't."

They were both silent for several seconds. She didn't know about him, but Cheryl spent the time growing increasingly light-headed from the need to cover the distance across the desk between her hand and his thigh.

"So, you don't think I'm responsible for the breakup?" he finally asked. "You don't think my plans for the honeymoon were indicative of a control freak nature?"

"Actually, I found your plans very romantic, but that's just more proof of how unsuited you two were. She really wanted to go to Hawaii. It's safe. They speak English."

"I don't intimidate you, do I?"

"Nope."

"You don't find me controlling?" he pressed. Man, the angel had done a number on him.

"I was married to a psychotically controlling man for six years. Trust me, I know the difference between having an opinion and needing to dictate every detail of another person's life."

"Did he hurt you?"

She couldn't believe they were having this conversation here in the office, but she found herself answering anyway. "Yes, but I healed."

"You're a strong woman."

"I'm glad you think so."

"Will you come into my office with me?"

Her answer was to stand up. She followed him into his inner sanctum. He shut the door . . . and locked it.

He turned to face her, his hand touching her cheek lightly before dropping back to his side. Somehow, they both moved and ended up a short breath apart.

"This has nothing to do with your job."

"I understand that."

"If you turn around and walk out of here, it won't impact our working relationship."

She believed him totally, which said more about how much she instinctively trusted him than even her admission a moment ago about her ex-husband.

He looked like he was going to say something else, but then he groaned and pulled her body flush with his.

The kiss he laid on her lips rocked her world and shattered her concept of intimacy and sensuality. Never had she been so impacted by something so small. Though calling his kiss small was like saying Mount Rushmore was a tchotchke.

His hands were everywhere, caressing her body as if he couldn't get enough of touching her. Darren had never been this intense. And that was the last piece of real estate her ex was getting in her thoughts for the duration of this interlude.

She let her own hands roam over Zack's thick muscles, getting drunk on the freedom he gave her with his body. His erection was big and warm and really, really, really hard. Yum.

They were half naked and writhing together on the floor when a tiny thread of sanity decided to rear its ugly head.

She broke her swollen lips from his. "What exactly are we doing here?"

"We're making love." He kissed along her jaw and down to her breasts. "You are so beautiful. I want you. You can feel how much."

"Making love as in making a commitment or making love as in a euphemism for sex?" she asked, wishing it didn't matter. Wishing she could be more casual about this, but knowing it wasn't possible for her.

"Don't play word games with me, Cheryl. Not now. I want you too much. We're both adults and we know the score. Making love doesn't always mean a lifetime commitment. Let's take this one step at a time."

Her heart squeezed. "The first step being sex and the next being . . .?"

"Whatever we want it to be."

She pulled away, rolling to a sitting position and searching for her top. "I have a feeling we won't want the same things."

"I want you and I know you want me. How much simpler can it get?"

"You said we both know the score. Unfortunately, I don't think we're keeping it for the same game."

"What the hell are you talking about?" He grabbed her shirt. "Stop getting dressed. We're going to work this out."

"We are?" she challenged.

"Yes. For some reason, your mind-reading capabilities where I'm concerned are obviously on the fritz, or we wouldn't be having this conversation. I guess that means we'll just have to talk it out." His tone was long-suffering, but he smiled.

She found herself smiling back even as she gave up her grip on the shirt. "So, talk."

"You're perfect for me."

"I'm far from perfect."

"Maybe that's what makes us such a good team. We complement each other and you aren't going to expect me to never make a mistake."

"If you do, you can send me some very expensive, very lovely long-stemmed red roses to feed to my garbage disposal."

He pulled her back into his arms. "We're going to have to do something about your fetish for feeding perfectly good flowers to the garbage disposal."

"I suppose if you sent them as something other than an apology, I might."

He grinned. "Consider it done."

"I was going to leave." She might have been more convincing if she wasn't busy divesting him of the rest of his clothes.

"I have a better idea . . ."

Three months later Esperanza stood beside Cheryl as she spoke her vows of love and commitment to her former boss. They were partners now, in every sense of the word, having started a small construction business that specialized in projects too small for the big guys.

Cheryl had moved to Dallas to start a new life and she'd found a new love, a real and lasting one.

ANGEL IN THE ALLEY

PATRICIA SARGEANT

To my dream team:

- My sister, Bernadette, for giving me the dream
- My husband, Michael, for supporting the dream
- My brother Richard, for believing in the dream
- My brother Gideon, for encouraging the dream
- My friend and critique partner, Marcia James, for sharing the dream

And to Mom and Dad always, with love.

My very sincere gratitude to Lori Foster and Dianne Castell for offering me this opportunity. You ladies are the best!

HAT IS THAT?

Sara Barber shifted her grip on the long, rectangular box of newly printed menus and shut the door of her used Jeep Wrangler with a bump of her right hip.

She crossed the parking lot to take a closer look at the monstrosity in the alley behind Baked Fresh, her soon-to-be coffee shop. The pile of boxes—cut open, flattened and taped together—looked like . . . shelter.

Oh, no way. This hadn't been here when she'd left yesterday. How could someone have constructed a home between nine o'clock Friday night and six o'clock Saturday morning? This couldn't be happening. Baked Fresh was opening in three days. She couldn't have a shantytown popping—

"May I help you?"

The deep, lyrical voice came from everywhere and nowhere. Sara nearly jumped out of her skin. She steadied the three-pound box, which was growing heavier by the minute, and spun toward the speaker.

How could such a large man sneak up on anyone? Sara took a careful step back, the box held in front of her. The stranger was six-plus-feet tall. At least eight inches taller than her five feet five inches.

His skin glowed the color of burnt sienna. His eyes were coal black and piercing. Thin, brown braids hung past his shoulders and were restrained at the nape of his neck. A neatly trimmed mustache traced a well-shaped upper lip, and a tidy goatee cupped a strong chin.

He seemed slim, perhaps half-again her weight. It was hard to judge his size beneath the worn cream overcoat.

Why was he wearing a coat in June? Granted, this was Columbus, Ohio, but it got hot in the summer here, too. She was warm in her red capris and copper top, a color a few shades darker than her skin. But he wasn't even sweating.

Sara nodded toward the cardboard structure behind her. "Do you . . . live . . . here?"

"Yes." His tone was matter-of-fact.

Sara struggled to keep her stress from transitioning to panic. "But you can't."

He remained unruffled. "Why not?"

She adjusted the box of menus again and nodded across the alley toward Baked Fresh. "My coffee shop opens Monday. People won't come if—if there's a makeshift community next door."

Her voice dwindled with the little courage she had. How would he react to her words? Sara's gaze shifted left and right, assuring herself of unobstructed escape routes.

The man looked over his broad shoulder toward Baked Fresh, then his gaze slowly circled the alley. Sara knew what he saw—the asphalt driveway that widened into a rear parking lot, commercial-grade Dumpsters, and the brick walls of neighboring buildings. But what was he thinking?

His surveillance complete, the homeless man returned his attention to Sara. "I have nowhere else to go."

He spoke without inflection, but a chill swept through her. How many times over the years had she thought those same words? *I have nowhere else to go.* So she'd gone nowhere.

"Can you go to a shelter?"

He shook his head. "There is no room."

There hadn't been any room for her, either. No one to turn to. Nowhere to go. And now this man found himself in the same situation. A neighbor in need of help. A kindred spirit in search of a fresh start.

He seemed harmless. He was courteous and clean. Her gaze dropped to the clear plastic bag in his hand. It carried a small bar of soap, a toothbrush, and a small tube of toothpaste. All used.

She studied his face. "What's your name?"

"Raphael."

She waited, but he offered nothing more. "Raphael what? What's your last name?"

"Just Raphael."

From whom was he running? The mob? The police? Or someone else?

·2·

SARA'S GRIP TIGHTENED ON THE BOX AS SHE REALIZED what else they had in common. They were both alone, and they were both runners.

Slow down. You don't know him. Raphael may look harmless, but looks could be deceiving. On the other hand, her ex-husband had told her he'd loved her. It had taken her heart years to accept what her mind and body had realized long before: Her ex-husband was a liar.

With Raphael, her mind and heart were in agreement. He needed help. Perhaps if there had been someone to help her, she wouldn't have ended up in emergency care three times.

She relaxed her grip on the menu box. "My shop opens in three days, and there's a lot left to do. I could use some help."

Raphael's thick, black brows knitted. "Are you offering me a job?"

"With pay. And you can sleep in the back room until you can afford a place of your own. Are you interested?"

He smiled and took the box from her. "Lead the way."

"Lunch time." Sara carried a tray with two bowls of soup, two glasses of iced tea, and a sandwich to a booth beside the window. "You've been working nonstop for hours. You need nourishment."

Raphael set aside the cloth and recapped the cleanser. "I will wash my hands."

Sara watched him walk past her to the men's restroom. His speech pattern interested her. He didn't use contractions. English must not be his first language.

And what was it about that coat? He still hadn't taken it off. Perhaps his clothes embarrassed him.

He returned to the dining area and sat across from Sara. "May I say grace?"

Sara bowed her head and waited for Raphael to say the blessing over their food. His simple, heartfelt words touched her. They were beautiful in comparison to the clumsy, desperate prayers that had kept her going the past five years. But God kept answering her.

"Amen." She lifted her head. "Thank you."

Raphael nodded. He spooned up some soup as he looked around. "I like the atmosphere. It is very cheerful."

Sara smiled her pleasure. "That's what I was trying for."

She enjoyed the spring green and sunrise orange walls, and the knickknacks she'd hung around the room and tucked into corners. Frills and bright colors. That's what she loved.

She was tired of restraining that part of herself so she

could be accepted in a monochromatic world. Her ex-husband's world. It was time to share her true colors—the complete rainbow of them.

Raphael picked up his sandwich. "What would you like me to do next?"

Sara sipped her iced tea. "I need to pick up a few more supplies today. I'd appreciate your help with that."

"Whatever you need. I am here to help."

Sara tilted her head. It wasn't what he'd said that seemed strange so much as how he'd said it.

Raphael swallowed a bite of his sandwich. "The greeting card on your counter matches the colors of your shop. Did you get it from a friend?"

Sara's lips curved in a small smile. She didn't have friends anymore. "It's from the bookstore manager." She gestured toward The BookEscape next door. "I haven't been able to thank him in person yet. I'll try again before we get the supplies."

Raphael was right. It was uncanny the way the green and orange colors of the card almost matched the decor of her shop. The card was blank inside, except for the hand-written note: *Welcome to the neighborhood. G, The BookEscape manager.*

The envelope's return address had read "Archer," with The BookEscape's information. The manager wasn't anxious to be recognized. Nor was he an easy man to meet. Each time she'd gone to thank him, he'd been either out or in meetings.

After lunch, Raphael helped Sara clean up. Then they locked the store as they left for their errand.

Sara glanced at her watch. "I'm going to see if Mr. Archer is in."

"I'll wait for you in the parking lot."

Sara entered The BookEscape and immediately felt the lure of the rows of dark hardwood bookcases. She resisted the pull, turning instead toward the customer service desk. Her sneakered feet tread silently across the black tiles.

She stopped in front of the cashier. "Is Mr. Archer in?"

A young African American woman with a wealth of glossy curls smiled at her. "Mr. Archer isn't in right now. Is there something I can help you with?"

"No, thank you." Sara was tempted to question whether G. Archer existed. But this same young woman had previously assured her Mr. G. Archer was real, and he was the store manager. "Do you know when he'll be back?"

The clerk gave her a regretful smile. "I'm sorry, I don't."

Sara thanked her and left. Perhaps she'd try again tomorrow. Sooner or later, G. Archer would have to make an appearance.

Half an hour later, Sara pulled her silver Jeep into the industrial supply store parking lot. As she and Raphael walked toward the store entrance, she tossed a smile toward a woman seated behind a display requesting donations for a homeless shelter. She made a mental note to drop some change into the collection pail on her way out.

Sara pulled out her shopping list. "This shouldn't take too long." Her jaw dropped in surprised dismay when she saw the swarm of people in the store. It was Saturday afternoon. She should have known the store would be crowded.

Raphael placed a bracing hand on her arm. "Should I get the shopping cart?"

Almost two hours later, Sara stood watching the register, hoping the bill wouldn't be too far from what she'd anticipated. Raphael waited patiently beside her.

Sara stilled when the cashier announced her total. It was much more than she'd expected.

She looked at the packed bags. "I think I may have been double-charged for some items."

The middle-aged woman cracked her chewing gum, giving Sara a condescending stare. "You weren't."

Sara tensed at the woman's belligerence. "I kept track of my purchases, and that total is quite a bit higher."

The clerk's voice was flat. "You added wrong."

Sara started to tell the woman she'd used a calculator. That's when she became aware of long sighs and shuffling feet. The patrons behind her were getting restless, and she was making a scene.

Blushing, Sara pulled out her credit card and waited for the cashier to process the charges.

Raphael steered the cart out of the store as Sara fumbled to put the receipt, her card, and her wallet into her purse. Her hands were shaking.

As she walked past the shelter's display, she gave the volunteer an embarrassed smile. She couldn't afford to make a donation today. Still, the woman smiled back as though greeting an old friend.

"Did you look at the receipt?" Raphael's calm voice soothed her frayed nerves.

"No, I—"

He stopped in the middle of the parking lot. "Look at it now."

Pausing beside him, Sara pulled the receipt from her wallet. "She double-charged me for four items." She was angrier with herself than with the clerk. No, not angry. Disappointed. Why hadn't she insisted the other woman double-check the bill?

Sara wiped her brow. The summer sun seemed even hotter above the asphalt lot. Raphael still hadn't broken a sweat.

He swung the cart around and pushed it back toward the store.

"Wait." Sara hurried after him. She felt a spurt of panic. "What are you doing?"

Raphael stopped. "She has to correct your bill."

Another confrontation. Sara shriveled inside. "I don't want to make a big deal out of this. Let's just forget it." She tugged on Raphael's upper arm. His muscles remained taut beneath her fingers.

"Sara, you cannot afford to forget this." The understanding in his voice cancelled any blame.

"I'm just not comfortable with confrontations." She resisted the urge to wring her hands. Barely.

Raphael looked toward the store, then returned his coal black gaze to her. "You are not comfortable standing up for yourself, but could you do it for the shelter? Could you face your fears to help someone else?"

Sara stilled. If it were just her, she'd take the coward's way out and walk away. But Raphael's question forced her to see the greater consequences of her actions—or inactions.

If she returned to the store to correct the billing error, she'd get some money back. She would donate that money to the shelter, which would use her donation to help others in need. People like Raphael, whom she'd found the courage to help that morning.

Sara straightened her spine, squared her shoulders, and led the way back to the store. Raphael followed.

She returned to the clerk and showed her the receipt. "You charged me twice for these four items." Her voice was polite but firm.

The clerk looked at the receipt, looked at the cart, then looked at Sara. "Oh, honey, I'm sorry. Let me get my manager to credit your bill."

Minutes later, Sara strolled out of the store and donated a fistful of money to the shelter.

"Thank you very much, ma'am." The volunteer smiled up at her.

"Thank *you* for the work you do." Sara stepped away and grinned at Raphael. "And thank *you* for helping me face my fear."

He glanced down at her as he pushed the cart toward her Jeep. "Whatever you need. I am here to help you."

That enigmatic response again. Did she hear an underlying message, or was she imagining things?

·3·

"THIS IS FOR YOU." SARA OFFERED THE WRAPPED package to Raphael after breakfast Monday morning.

The grand opening was less than an hour away. Giving Raphael his gift now helped distract her from her nearly suffocating anxiety.

Sara gazed around her store. The red vinyl booths. The peach, lilac, and white doilies scattered around the dining area. The display case with the pastries and cakes she'd baked that morning.

Suppose no one came?

Raphael took the box from her. "What is it?"

Sara chuckled at his surprise. "Open it and find out."

He carefully unwrapped the box. "Now we both have received gifts."

Sara glanced at the six white roses to which Raphael referred. The arrangement stood in a vase beside the cheerful greeting card. The accompanying note read, *Best wishes for a grand opening. G.* Would she meet the mysterious Mr. G. Archer today?

"These are for me?" His pleased words recaptured Sara's attention.

She smiled at him. "They might be a bit baggy on you. It was hard to judge your size because of the coat."

He reached into the box and unfolded the blue jeans and white jersey. "I need to keep the coat."

"Of course." Sara rushed to reassure him. Had she offended him by purchasing these clothes? "I just thought, perhaps, you'd be more comfortable with newer clothes for the opening."

His dark eyes shone with gratitude. "Thank you."

"You're welcome." Sara sighed with relief.

"I will change in the back room."

She was glad he wanted to put on the outfit so quickly. It proved he didn't resent the gifts. While she waited, Sara cleared the table, tidied the booth, then washed their breakfast dishes.

Less than ten minutes to the grand opening. She took a calming breath. The warm, sweet scent of baked goods lingered in the air. Her nervous hands were looking for something more to occupy them when she heard Raphael return.

She was excited to see how he looked in his new clothes. But it was hard to tell through the coat.

Sara frowned, confused. "I thought, perhaps, you might want to take off the coat for the opening?"

"I need the coat."

Sara pursed her lips. "I see." No, she really didn't. What was it about that coat? He seemed perfectly balanced—mentally healthy—otherwise.

His coat hung open over his new outfit. From what she could see, the jersey and pants fit reasonably well. Sara stepped closer, tempted—but reluctant—to open the coat for a better look. "How do the clothes feel?"

"Very comfortable."

Sara checked her watch again. "Show time." Wiping her sweaty palms on her green jeans, she turned to open her store.

Within minutes, Baked Fresh was packed, and Sara was giddy with success. She also was eternally grateful that Raphael had found his way into her life. She couldn't have handled the past two days—and especially today—without him.

Customer traffic lulled after breakfast. The downtime allowed Sara and Raphael to tidy the dining area, bake more pastries and—best of all—sit.

The lunchtime crowd started early. It took all of Sara's attention to keep up with her customers. As the afternoon grew later, sales slowed. Sara took the opportunity to restore order to the front counter.

"Hello, Sara."

At the familiar sound of the cool, clipped voice, blood drained from Sara's head. She was dizzy and cold. Her ex-husband had found her.

Sara searched the room and saw Raphael watching them. She wasn't alone.

Asa Preston was six feet tall and built like a wall. He was an imposing figure in his dark blue pinstriped suit. Sara considered his round, brown face. The mask of civilization hid the violence well.

"What are you doing here, Asa?"

His dark brown stare pinned her. "You don't sound happy to see me."

It was an effort, but Sara kept her voice steady. "The divorce was final months ago. We don't have anything more to say to each other."

"You cut your hair."

Sara's fingers automatically went to her wavy, shoulder-length locks. She hated that Asa could still get inside her head. She dropped her hand. "I never liked the longer style you preferred."

He looked around her coffee shop. "What do you want with such a tacky hole?"

Asa whittled at her self-image and self-esteem with well-placed cuts. "This is my business, and I'm going to make it a success."

He laughed at her. "What do you know about running a business? You couldn't even balance your checkbook."

Temper flickered beneath her fear. "You wouldn't let me. You wanted me to be dependent on you. Now it's about what I want."

Asa leaned into her space. "You don't know what you want. That's always been one of your faults."

Sara's eyes widened with apprehension. She trembled, re-living the fear she'd known for too many years. She gripped the counter to keep her balance and reminded herself Raphael was only a shout away.

Part of her wanted to give in to Asa, to appease his anger. But experience reminded her his anger could not be soothed that easily.

Her voice shook only a little. "I want to be independent. I want my own identity. And I *don't* want you in my life anymore."

"You need me." Asa stressed the words. "When your mother died, I took care of you. You didn't have anyone else."

Sara stared at him, realization freeing her mind. "No, Asa. *You* need *me* to make yourself feel superior, stronger, and in charge. I'm through with letting you or anyone else control me."

"You're going to regret leaving me." Anger stripped his mask and revealed the brutality just beneath his surface.

She watched Asa stalk off. Rage made his body stiff, his movements jerky. Her gaze shifted to Raphael. He nodded once and Sara relaxed.

"I met Asa six years ago, after my mother died. He was a lawyer in the firm that handled her will." Sara brooded over those memories.

She and Raphael were sharing tea before ending the day. The Closed sign hung in the door, ensuring their privacy.

Sara continued her recounting. "I was so depressed after my mother's death. I just let Asa handle everything—her will, her estate, the sale of her house."

"She was your only family."

Sara nodded. "And my best friend. I felt lost without her. It was easy to depend on Asa. Too easy."

Raphael poured them both more tea from the small porcelain pot Sara had brought to their table. "Did you love him?"

Sara shook her head jerkily. "Not as a woman should love her husband." She met Raphael's gaze. "Looking back, I realize I was grateful to him. But I wasn't in love with him."

"Do you think he loved you?"

Sara thought of Asa's hateful words and violent behavior. "He wants me to believe it's love, but it's not. If you loved someone, you wouldn't hurt them physically, emotionally, or spiritually. You'd want to build them up not break them down."

Raphael nodded as though her answer pleased him. "Is that when you decided to leave him? When you realized he did not love you?"

"I was afraid he'd kill me if I left. After five years of marriage, I realized he'd kill me if I stayed." Sara stared into her teacup. "I always wanted to make my mother proud. She worked so hard for me. When I think about the mess I've made of my life, I'm so ashamed. She'd be so disappointed in me."

Raphael reached across the table and covered her fist with his large palm. "Your mother is proud of you. Do not ever think differently."

Sara frowned. Wiping away tears, she met his dark gaze. "You say that as though you know her."

"If your daughter made a mistake, would you turn your back on her in shame, or would you try to help her?"

"I'd help her."

"I am sure you learned that from your mother." Raphael gave her clenched palm a comforting squeeze. "You are a strong woman, Sara Barber. Somewhere along the path you have forgotten that. I am here to remind you."

Sara shook her head. His words confused her. "How can you say these things? You've only known me three days."

His smile was mysterious. "Some things you can sense in other people."

Sara searched his gaze. He had such patient eyes. Patient and protective. Eyes in which you could lose yourself. Or find yourself.

"I'm talking too much."

"I am here to listen. I want to listen."

It had been years since she'd had someone to confide in. Her ex-husband had made certain of that. She'd been isolated, and he'd become her whole world. She didn't know who she was anymore, but she was trying to find out.

Now a stranger she'd met three days ago spoke as though he'd known her for years. That should frighten her. Instead, he made her feel like the strong, capable woman he said she was.

Sara stood and collected their teacups and saucers. Raphael followed, carrying the small pot.

She spoke over her shoulder as she rinsed the dishes. "I'm a little uncomfortable after seeing Asa today." An understatement. "Would you mind sleeping on my sofa tonight?"

"I give you my word I will not let him hurt you."

* * *

The next morning, Sara was unable to get to her coffee shop. Emergency vehicles blocked the street.

With dread laying like a stone in her gut, she rolled down her window and called to a police officer. "What's going on?"

The tall, young woman approached the Jeep. She glanced at Raphael before answering Sara. "There's a fire at one of the businesses in the strip mall."

"Is it the coffee shop?"

The officer's blue gaze sharpened. She tucked a few strands of blond hair back under her cap. "Are you the owner?"

"Yes, I'm Sara Barber."

The woman continued, her voice softening. "Could you pull your vehicle over there, ma'am?" She pointed across the street. "I'll take you back to the fire investigators."

· 4 ·

SARA PARKED ACROSS THE STREET, THEN SHE AND Raphael returned to the young officer.

The slender woman spoke over her shoulder as they followed her through the crowd. "Captain McLeod, the lead fire investigator, said the damage would've been much worse if the bookstore manager hadn't called it in so quickly."

Sara nodded. Another reason to be grateful to the mysterious Mr. G. Archer.

She glanced up at Raphael. "Thank God you weren't sleeping in the back room."

As they neared her shop, the shock of the damage rocked

Sara back on her heels. Raphael wrapped an arm around her waist and braced her against his side.

The fire had destroyed the right half of the shop next to the alley. Most of the wall was gone and part of the roof. The display windows had shattered.

Tears rushed down her cheeks. "Yesterday we celebrated our grand opening. This morning my dream is destroyed."

Raphael squeezed her waist. "You will repair this."

"Why bother?" a cold, clipped voice spoke beside her.

Sara spun to face Asa, breaking Raphael's hold. "You did this." She jabbed a finger toward the remains of Baked Fresh. "You burned down my business."

Asa's thin lips curved in a sly smile. "Can you prove that?"

"I don't have to prove it. This is typical of you." She shouted the accusation, uncaring of the crowd around her. "You're a spiteful little man. You always have to have your way, and you don't care how you do it."

"You're hysterical."

"I'm enraged." She stepped closer to him. "Yesterday I told you I wanted you out of my life. This morning you set fire to my shop. If you think this is going to convince me to return to you, you've lost your mind."

"You'll come back to me. Without me you're nothing and you have nothing." He speared a finger toward her face. "You think this fire is the end of it? It's only the beginning. You'd better learn your place."

"I wouldn't go back to you if you came crawling to me on your belly like the venomous snake you are."

Asa pulled back his arm as though to hit her.

Sara braced for the blow. But this time, instead of shrinking from him, she held his gaze and squared her shoulders. "Don't be mistaken. I *will* hit you back."

Asa hesitated. His gaze wavered under her direct glare. Sara cocked her chin. Where was his bluster now?

Asa lowered his arm. "What's the point?"

Vicious satisfaction fueled her. "The point is, now that I'm not afraid of you, you don't have any power over me."

A gravelly voice interrupted their exchange. "Ms. Barber?"

Sara turned as a stocky man came to stand beside Asa. He had a shock of red hair and a round freckled face. "Yes?"

"I'm Captain McLeod, lead fire investigator with the Columbus Fire Department. Do you know this man?" McLeod nodded toward Asa.

"He's my *ex*-husband, Asa Preston."

McLeod took hold of Asa's upper arm while the female officer Sara had met earlier slipped handcuffs on her ex-husband's wrists. "Asa Preston, you're under arrest for arson."

Asa gaped. "What? You're making a mistake."

McLeod shook his head. "Sir, we overheard your argument with Ms. Barber in which you confessed to causing the fire."

Despite Asa's shrill protestations, McLeod read him his rights as he led her ex-husband through the crowd.

"I can't believe it." Sara stared in amazement at Asa's retreating back. "Someone has actually stopped him."

Raphael moved to stand in front of her. He caught and held her gaze. "Not just someone. You."

·5·

THE NEXT MORNING THE FIRE DEPARTMENT cleared Sara to return to her coffee shop and arrange the repairs. Working nonstop, except for short meal breaks, it took her and Raphael the entire day to clean what was left of Baked Fresh. She also contacted vendors for estimates on the repairs.

It was late in the evening when she and Raphael relaxed in their favorite booth before closing the store.

Sara poured Raphael's tea and handed the cup to him. "Thank you so much for your help today."

Raphael took a sip then returned his cup to its saucer. "My assignment is complete."

Sara frowned. "What do you mean?"

Raphael watched her with patient eyes. "I was sent to heal you. Now that you have regained your confidence and your courage, I can return home."

Sara's mind spun. Heal her? He has a home? Then why had he slept in her coffee shop? She needed to start at the beginning. "Who sent you?"

"Your mother petitioned God to send me to help you."

"My mother asked for you. Why?"

After five days in almost constant company with him, Sara had thought Raphael was sane. Why did he now sound crazy?

Raphael smiled as though he'd heard her thoughts and found them amusing. "Because I am the archangel of healing, and you needed to be healed."

She heard the metaphorical lightbulb switch on. "You think you're the archangel Raphael."

He chuckled. "I *am* the archangel Raphael."

Raphael stood and started to remove his overcoat. Sara frowned as white fluffs that resembled feathers floated out from under his coat. Raphael let the garment fall to the floor. His coal black gaze locked with hers as he stood in the blue jeans and white jersey she'd bought him.

Then, with a flourish as dramatic as any act of nature—sunrise, sunset, a rainbow after a storm—wings as wide as he was tall sprang up behind him then spread out to his sides.

Wings. Actual wings. Like those of a bird. With feathers blindingly white and thick.

Stunned and a little apprehensive, Sara pressed her back against the bench. She stared at Raphael, who seemed to be standing in a pool of light. "You are so beautiful." Her words emerged on an awed breath.

"Do you believe me now, Sara?"

Her heart felt heavy. "I won't remember this tomorrow, will I?"

He shook his head sadly. "You will remember every act that has occurred these five days, save meeting me."

"Thank you for healing me." She forced the words past the lump in her throat.

"Be at peace." Raphael stepped back, then disappeared.

·6·

SARA STROKED ONE OF THE SIX WHITE ROSES IN THE vase beside her cash register. The card that came with it read, *Welcome back. G.*

It had taken three weeks to repair the fire damage to her store. Each week had felt like an eternity. Asa Preston had better never come anywhere near her again. That is, after he got out of jail. Sara smiled to herself. Justice was sweet.

The chimes above her door heralded the arrival of another customer. Business was brisk this late July morning. Sara glanced toward the entrance.

A tall, lean man walked toward her. He had the loose-limbed grace of a natural athlete. His skin glowed the color of burnt sienna. His eyes were coal black and piercing behind wire-rimmed glasses. His hair was conservatively cut. A neatly trimmed mustache traced a well-shaped upper lip, and a tidy goatee cupped a strong chin.

"Good morning." His deep, lyrical voice captivated her. He seemed familiar, but she couldn't place him.

Sara smiled. "Good morning. What can I get for you?"

He glanced at the flowers between them before returning his attention to her. His dark eyes twinkled, and a slow smile curved his full lips. "I'm Gabriel Archer."

Sara blinked. "G. Archer." She extended her hand and he shook it. His warm, firm touch made her knees weak. "I've waited a long time to meet you."

HANNAH'S CHOICE

KAY STOCKHAM

· 1 ·

"HEY! HEY, DON'T DO THAT! *STOP!*" HANNAH PRUITT didn't take the time to *think*, much less pause and remove her leather sandals or the ridiculously expensive watch she'd splurged on six months ago as an "I am woman, hear me roar" present to herself. Instead she vaulted over the rail of the footbridge crossing the twelve-foot-deep canal that sliced Orchard Park in two, and entered the cold depths with a choking gasp. When a bubble escaped, she belatedly reminded herself that keeping her mouth closed would be a good idea. God knew jumping in hadn't been her brightest one.

The moment her leather-clad toes touched the canal's rocky bottom, she pushed herself to the surface, arms and legs working as she frantically searched for the burlap type sack she'd seen a man toss into the water. Had it gone under? *Where?*

Shaking her head to clear her eyes, she spotted the guy as he shot her a quick glance over his shoulder from his position on the bank before taking off at a dead run into the woods adjacent to the bike paths. Hannah zeroed in on where he'd stood, saw the whitecaps of popping bubbles, and propelled herself through the water with frantic strokes. *No, no, no. Please, no.*

She reached the spot and dove, searching for the bag and trying hard not to think of the past. The water wasn't deep, but since it didn't have a strong current it stayed murky, which made visibility impossible. Unable to find the bag, she surfaced briefly before going down again, praying her blind exploration wouldn't anger a snapping turtle or—*Got it!*

She broke the surface and gasped for air, her lungs burning from strain, and pulled the bag atop her chest. The weight of it nearly put her five-foot-one-inch frame under and she kicked harder, unable to use one arm because she couldn't let go of the sack without the weight of it sliding off into the water.

Just a little farther. Her arms and legs were tiring fast, lead weights that dragged her down. Doubts surfaced about whether she'd make it to shore without releasing the sack, but she pressed on, lifting her arm again and again. She could do this. After what she'd survived, *this* was nothing.

Water splashed over her head from somewhere behind her, and a second later, large masculine hands grabbed hold of her and pulled her up so that her head and shoulders were clear of the water. The bag dragged, heavier than ever, but people didn't toss sacks into the water unless—

Her rescuer gently dumped her on the canal's edge with a disgusted sound. "Lady, there are No Swimming signs posted everywhere."

She shivered despite the warm June sun, her whole body shaking from reaction and cold. In middle school she'd known a girl who'd died jumping off the bridge on a dare. Why hadn't she thought of that before jumping in?

"If you've got a suicide wish there are places you can go, people you can ta—*Hannah?*"

She didn't bother to look up. Now that the adrenaline haze was beginning to fade, she recognized the man's voice. Orchard, Ohio, was no bigger than a thimble, and she'd seen Mitch from afar on several occasions but she hadn't worked up enough nerve to approach him. *But did she have to reconnect with him* now? *Like this?*

Ignoring the fact that Mitch stood over her in a police uniform soaked with canal water, thanks to her, Hannah scrambled to her knees. The knot in the bag was waterlogged and slimy, and she broke Self-Improvement Rule #3 and cursed when it didn't budge.

"You nearly killed yourself jumping in the canal for *that*?"

She ignored Mitch's growling question, her sole focus on the sack and its contents. Maybe it wasn't what she thought it was. Maybe— "Come on, come on, *come on*! Open up you stinkin'—"

Sun-browned hands brushed her fumbling fingers aside and he took over, working the knot back and forth until the burlap released its squishy hold with a rough rasp of cloth. The small crowd gathering behind them pressed closer to see what was inside, but she ignored them all as she snatched the material away from him. "Please, please, please."

It was a litany she'd uttered many times through the years. Please, please, please. No more hitting, no more hurting. No more tossing things in the canal to show her who was boss. *Please, please, please—don't be dead.*

Her father had done this, too. This same monstrous, senseless act. The first time, he'd tossed her dog from the canal bridge, determined to get even with her for some supposed slight he'd taken offense to in a drunken stupor. Ten years later, he'd done it again.

Her mother had claimed her car door wasn't closed properly and when her father sped through the park, it had opened, dumping her onto the asphalt where she rolled and supposedly smashed into a tree. Hannah knew better, but at the hospital her mother had stuck to her story until her last, dying breath, which inherently put a new spin on "till death do we part." That was why she'd left Owen. Why she'd come home. She had to face the past and work toward a future because the cycle of abuse was stopping with her. Her decision, her choice, was made.

Inside the bag, Hannah's searching fingers discovered fur and a dog's hind leg. A sob stuck in her throat, choking her,

spurred on by her nightmarish memories. *How* could someone do this? *Why?*

"I don't know, babe. But I'll find the guy. I'll do my best
to find out who did this."

It took her a moment to realize she'd spoken out loud,
that the strange, strangled noise had come from her. It wasn't
even her dog but— She sucked in a ragged breath and wrapped
her hands around the animal's neck, pulling, straining to lift
its weight. Shifting closer, Mitch helped free the body from
the bag, scowling when it didn't move.

"Come on." She shook the animal hard. "Come on, you
can't let him win. You have to show him. You can do this—
show him. Prove you're tougher, stronger. All you have to do
is *choose.* Get up. Come on, please. Please, please, *please.* Get
up."

·2·

MITCH DONOVAN STARED DOWN AT HANNAH'S
bent head as she pleaded with the dog to move. She
was a small woman to begin with, but toss sopping wet and
shivering into the description, and he found himself grinding
his teeth in an effort to control his anger. Hannah shows up
in town after six years and he can't demand answers to his
many questions because some sick, twisted SOB did *this?*
What would've happened if he hadn't been patrolling the
park? Would she have made it to shore?

He wanted to go after the person who'd done this, wanted
to yell at her for risking her life when— He couldn't do any
of it. Heaven help him, the expression on Hannah's face. He
couldn't give in to the anger eating at his gut, not even after

the pain she'd caused him, not when she looked like she did now.

Mitch determinedly ignored the wet T-shirt clinging to her small curves and watched her shakily lift the dog by the hindquarters so that gravity would take effect. Very little water left the mutt's mouth. Hannah spat out a curse that was more like a sob and wriggled backward, clumsily lifting her knee until it was positioned beneath the animal's belly. Nothing.

"Harder," he murmured, shifting to help balance the dog's weight. "Apply more pressure." He wasn't sure what else to do for the Spaniel-mutt mix, but he knew instinctively Hannah was doing all the right things. Getting the dog's lungs to clear, getting him to breathe, was imperative.

Hannah glanced up, her expression revealing her doubts. He'd heard rumors that she was back in town, but he'd dreaded seeing her again because he wasn't sure how he felt about it. Still . . . "You can do this, Hannah. Press harder," he urged. "If he's dead, it's not going to hurt him, and if he's not, you could save him. You've gone too far to give up now."

Her lashes lowered over her moss green eyes and she swallowed tightly. This time she pressed harder, gently bouncing her knee in the dog's belly. Finally the animal's legs jerked and spasmed and water gushed out of its muzzle. The half-drowned thing lay there draped over her knee a long moment, panting and gagging water, then sneezing and coughing, too weak to do much else.

Hannah's slender hands stroked the dog's curly black fur, and she murmured nonsense in a shaky voice. The dog shifted and huddled against her body, and blinked up at her with big, adoring eyes. Mitch knew the feeling.

Of all the women he'd dated through the years, Hannah was the one who stood out in his mind. The one he'd always thought about, fantasized about. Done the whole "what-if" thing about when it came to the future and picket fences. But they hadn't had a future—she'd seen to that.

A moment more passed, and a long shudder racked the dog's frame before it lifted its head and gave her a sloppy kiss on the chin. Hannah laughed, the sound holding tears and sorrow, way more than Mitch remembered.

Hannah hugged the dog to her chest and rested her cheek on its neck, her shoulder-length brown hair tangled wildly about her head. But even though she tried to hide the tears, he saw them. "Sit tight," he ordered, getting to his feet.

Much as he hated it, some things had to happen first before he could get the answers he wanted. She was back in town and not wearing a ring on her left hand, unlike when she'd left. Mitch held up his hands and gained the crowd's attention. "Anyone see who tossed the bag into the canal?" Everyone but Hannah shook their head. "Well, if you remember something later, call me at the station. The dog's alive, and Hannah and I will take it to Alex to get checked out. Go back to whatever you were doing."

Murmurs of approval and agreement were uttered, but Mitch noticed Hannah didn't budge, not even when an older man roughly patted her on the back a few times. When they were basically alone, Mitch squatted down in front of her once more. "Let me have him. I'll carry him to the truck."

"Why Alex?" she demanded softly, not releasing her hold or looking at him other than to slide him a two-second glance.

"Alex is the vet. Dr. Finn retired right after you left." The words came out more gruffly than he'd intended, but it was the best he could do after dragging her out of the canal and having the reality sink in that she could've easily drowned herself.

The large stones lining the waterway were razor-sharp and dangerous—the reason for the signs she'd ignored—and a long list of people had died or else suffered broken arms, legs, and necks over the years by jumping in. He loved animals as much as the next guy, but Hannah— *Wasn't getting away again.* Not without an explanation.

Mitch scooped the dog into his arms and lifted, amazed that she'd managed to bear the animal's weight. For such a little woman, Hannah was strong. Then again, it was one of the things he'd always admired about her.

Hannah looked dazed as she followed him to his SUV cruiser. She climbed into the passenger seat without comment, and he waited while she strapped herself in before placing the dog on her lap. He hesitated, then palmed her cheek and found himself rubbing his thumb over her soft, full lips. She stared up at him, wide-eyed. "Are you married?" he asked her. His voice emerged husky. She had that effect, though. Always had.

"N-no, not—"

Mitch leaned forward and kissed her, maintaining contact long enough to get her taste to hold on to, because the last time he'd kissed her, he hadn't known it would be the last, hadn't savored it like he should've.

Her lips parted and, despite telling himself to back off and get his answers *first*, the soft sigh she released shot straight to his gut and obliterated common sense. Touching her tongue with his, he eased into her warmth with gentleness when he wanted to lock them away together in some secluded cabin long enough to get her out of his system. Before she took off again and dragged half his heart with her.

Squeezed between the two of them, the dog shifted on her lap, the move nudging them apart. Awareness dawned in Hannah's pretty eyes, and she gasped, turning her head away. Mitch fingered a strand of her wet-slick hair and shook his head at her fiery blush. How sweet was that? "We'll continue this later."

"No, I—"

"I want answers, babe. After all these years I deserve them, don't you think?"

·3·

HANNAH DIDN'T ANSWER. DESERVE THEM HE might, but now that she was face-to-face with Mitch, the gutsy attitude she'd worked so hard to achieve deserted her. How could she tell him the truth? Pride was a sin, but still— She didn't want him looking at her in pity.

Yes, Mitch was part of the reason why she'd come back to Orchard, but she'd grown up in the small Ohio town and felt comfortable here. She couldn't kid herself. Three years was a long time to be on her own and she'd made great strides with her Self-Improvement Plan, but telling Mitch the truth was—*the last step over the threshold into the rest of her life?*

Yeah, that. A part of her had always wondered what had happened to Mitch, whether he'd gotten married, moved on. The kiss he'd just given her stated clearly that he hadn't, because Mitch wasn't the kind of guy to belong to one woman but kiss another. Too bad she was so late in recognizing that fact.

Mitch was a handsome man any woman in her right mind would want. More than handsome, he was a jaw-dropping, heart-fluttering sight. Two years older than her twenty-four, his black hair was cropped close to his head, his shoulders broad, his body big but without an ounce of the post-high-school-sports gut some guys got. No, Mitch was all muscle, with long, lean legs three times as thick as hers. But attractive though he was, nothing could erase the past, and *how* could she ever be sure he wouldn't use his strength against her? Despite the last three years she'd spent rebuilding her self-esteem and coming into her own as a woman, it always boiled down to that overwhelming fear.

Hannah gave Mitch a description of the guy from what she remembered, and he called it into the station. That done, they arrived at Orchard Animal Hospital and Mitch's presence sent Alex's female employees into a tizzy. They were shown to an exam room, the dog was taken for tests, and Mitch was offered everything from a drink to a hug for being a hero and rescuing him. Hannah snorted. That figured, didn't it? Guys always got the credit.

Declining all the offers, Mitch closed the door and paced across the room. Back again. Collecting his thoughts? Preparing his case against her? They had to wait on X-rays and blood work, but no one said they had to wait together.

She watched Mitch cross the speckled tile floors warily, certainly able to understand the women's attraction and interest. He resembled a caged animal, pacing, anxious. *Huge.* Six feet three inches of muscled male who could quite easily pick her up and sling her wherever he wanted like a sack of potatoes or . . . like her ex.

After a lot of hard-core thinking and counseling, she'd thought she was ready for this moment, but now— Would she ever be able to look at a guy without first measuring the size of his fists?

Mitch's gaze abruptly caught hers, and he stopped where he stood. "You're still as stubborn as ever," he murmured dryly. "You're going to fight me on this, aren't you? Refuse to give me answers after all this time?"

Looking down, she fingered her watch with unseeing eyes. Counseling had changed everything. Helped her realize life was made up of choices. Do's and don't's, right and wrong. Decisions only she could make. Getting out of an abusive situation was one of those decisions, but as she worked up the nerve to look at Mitch's above-average-sized body and meaty fists, the doubts resurfaced and multiplied times ten. Not all guys hit, but she was a product of her childhood, of her disastrous marriage.

"Come on, sweetheart. Just tell me," Mitch urged, heading toward her with purposeful strides.

She stiffened and straightened in her seat at the quickness of his approach, fully aware Mitch could take her out with a single blow. Instead he squatted down in front of her and took her hands in his with a gentleness that left her . . . stunned.

"Whatever it is, whatever it *was*, tell me. We had a connection, babe. You can't deny it. I know it frightened you. I get that because it did a number on me, too. We were both young, but if I did something . . . scared you some way, I—"

"You did." She swallowed, the sound audible in the quiet of the room. "You did scare me because y-you . . ." His gaze fastened on hers with frightening intensity, and she faltered.

"What? Tell me *why* you left with Owen. Tell me why you chose him over me."

She heard pain in his voice. After all this time? Surely that was her imagination? She ducked her head, closed her eyes. "I-I'm sorry, but—"

"Sorry? I want more than an apology, Hannah. I want to know *why*. Why did you leave with him instead of giving me a chance to fix whatever it was I did wrong?"

"I did it because . . . because . . ."

"Because?"

"Because you could *hurt* me!" Hannah blinked at him,

unable to believe she'd just blurted it out like that. No sooner had the words left her mouth than the door beside them burst open and Alex, Mitch's older brother, walked through, his brows arching high on his forehead when he spotted Mitch's position.

"The bigger they are, the harder they fall," he murmured. "That was fast, but I'm not surprised. You do realize he's always had a thing for you."

"Not now," Mitch ordered, his voice a tight growl. "Hannah, are you telling me you think I'd—"

Alex snorted. "Yeah, right. Remember when Rachel and I wanted privacy and you said—"

"Not *now*." His gaze narrowed and he leaned toward her, whispering, "*Why* did you think I'd hurt you? Babe, I know I'm a big guy in comparison to you, but if this is about sex—"

·4·

"STOP IT." A HOT FLUSH CRAWLED INTO HER FACE. Hannah glanced up at Alex and saw him suddenly eyeing the ceiling but blatantly listening to every word. She wet her lips, and tugged her hands from Mitch's grasp, pushing him backward so she could stand. Mitch straightened with her, the act reinforcing her doubts. "How's the dog?" she asked Alex, getting back to what had brought them there in the first place. Maybe if she stuck with that, she could give herself time to think. To process things and—

"Fine." Alex's gaze volleyed back and forth between her and Mitch. "He's, uh . . . Would you two like to be alone? I could come back."

"No."

"Yes."

Alex looked at her. "No," she repeated firmly. "How's the dog?"

Alex lifted his shoulder in a what-am-I-supposed-to-do shrug when Mitch glared at him. "Uh . . . no broken bones, and seemingly no permanent damage for all that happened. I'd like to keep him overnight, though, just to be sure pneumonia doesn't develop."

Overnight? "Oh. Okay. Th-that's fine, but about the bill—"

"I'll take care of it." Mitch wrapped an arm around her shoulders. "Send it to me at the station."

Alex tossed aside the file he held and regarded them both with open interest. "Actually, you'll have to get in line. Word's spread and the phone is ringing off the hook with people wanting to donate to his care. We've even received offers from people who want to take him in when he's released."

"But they can't!"

Mitch's older brother frowned down at her. "I thought he wasn't your dog?"

"He's not, but—" She raised her chin. "I saved him so I'm responsible for him now. I'm keeping him."

Alex held up both hands as though in surrender. "Hey, works for me. I wouldn't want him to go back to his owner, and any woman willing to jump off a bridge to save an animal has first dibs on ownership in my book. Agreed?" he asked Mitch.

Mitch nodded. "I don't see a problem with it. I'll help Hannah get him settled when he's released tomorrow."

She fought the sizzle of awareness that spiraled through her at the look Mitch gave her. Why should it matter to her that he approved of her decision? And she was perfectly capable of getting the dog settled on her own. "Shouldn't you be out hunting down the guy who did this?"

Once again a smile tugged at Mitch's mouth. "Nice try, sweetheart, but you won't get rid of me that easily. Not this time. My men are out looking for the guy. I'll take you home to change out of those wet clothes. We'll finish our conversation there."

Hannah took a step away, flustered by the promise she saw in Mitch's face. "Actually, I think I'll stay here. I want to go see the dog. You know, v-visit awhile and get to know him, especially since we're going to be living together tomorrow. I'll walk home when I'm finished here." Biting her lip, she looked up at him, getting a crick in her neck because he stood so close. "You can go now, Mitch. It was good seeing you, but I think we're through."

Mitch grumbled the entire way back to his office. He'd been thoroughly dismissed by Hannah. Short of placing her in handcuffs, he hadn't been able to talk her into letting him drive her home, and something just didn't feel right about forcing her to follow his lead. He knew she felt the same spike of interest he did every time they were together, but why was she so skittish about it? And to say he'd *hurt* her? What kind of garbage was that?

The rest of the day dragged by with agonizing slowness. Questions bounced around the inside of his brain, one after another with no answers in sight. He didn't get any work done, but he did manage to obtain Hannah's phone number. He called, but no one answered, not even a machine picked up. Still at the hospital? Calling Alex to make sure she got home okay wasn't an option. He wasn't in the mood for his brother's ribbing, but at the same time he consoled himself with the knowledge that given everything Hannah had been through today, Alex probably drove her home himself.

Now he turned down Pear Street and checked the numbers on the mailboxes. Hannah had put him off today, and he'd admit that the timing wasn't right, seeing as how they'd been in public settings. But he had a three-day weekend ahead of him, and nothing but time to spend with her sorting things out.

He pulled into the drive of 269 Pear Street and parked behind the Honda he now knew to be hers. Practiced speeches ran through his head, but as he approached the porch they left in a rush. Beyond the screened door Hannah sat curled on her couch, a photo album open on the cushions beside her. She lifted a hand to her face and— *Was she crying?*

Reaching out, he grabbed the button-press latch, and even though it was locked, the fixture was old and opened with a firm *yank*. He'd fix that later.

Hannah's head jerked up. "What are you *doing?*"

"What's wrong? Are you hurt? Sick? Come on," he said, scooping her up into his arms. "I'll take you to the doctor."

"Put me down! Mitch, I don't *need* a doctor!"

He stopped in his tracks and peered at her bare legs and ankles, her hands and arms, looking for cuts or bruises. "Are you sure? Did you hit something when you jumped in the canal?"

"I'm *fine*," she said, sniffling.

Seeing the truth for himself, the air left his lungs in relief. "Then why were you crying?"

Blinking, she stared over her shoulder before looking back at him with a glare. "You broke my door."

"I HAD TO GET TO YOU TO MAKE SURE YOU WERE okay, but I'll fix it later. Good as new. Actually, better than that. Did you see how easily I got in? That's not safe, but I'll fix it up right. First tell me what's wrong. Why were you crying?"

She stiffened in his arms even as her expression softened. "You did that because you . . . you thought I was hurt?"

"Of course. I would've waited for you to open the door, but I had to get to you, to help you. I promise I'll take care of the door, okay? Tell me what's wrong."

Fresh tears appeared in her eyes. "Oh, Mitch. That's very— I wasn't crying," she insisted stubbornly. "It's just . . . everything's gone wrong today and I need a *jeweler.*" She blinked rapidly, the tip of her nose turning bright red because she struggled to hold her tears in check. "And then I came home and realized I moved back to Orchard weeks ago and I've been trying to work up the nerve to t-talk to you, but when I got m-my chance today I just *couldn't.*"

"What's a jeweler got to do with you talking to me?" Confused, Mitch sat down on the couch, Hannah firmly in his lap. Surely he'd misheard her?

She stuck her hand under his nose and waved it. "Can't you *see* it? It's broken! *Ruined!*"

The woman had jumped off a bridge to save a sack when she wasn't sure what was in it and now she cried over a *watch*? His eyes crossed trying to comprehend her thinking. "Your watch is broken?" he repeated dully.

"I just told you it was!"

Hiding a smile, Mitch pulled her to his chest and tucked her head under his chin, spearing his fingers into her freshly washed hair. Unlike this afternoon when he'd pulled her out of the canal, she smelled good. Clean and fresh, like flowers and summer sun. Holding her close, he lifted her arm and the watch attached to her wrist, holding it up for his perusal. Sure enough, it had stopped running, the hands fixed, the face foggy with moisture.

A glance down at the album beside them gave him more information about what she'd been thinking about when he'd arrived. Not good. No wonder she was so overwrought. The photos were of Hannah and her mother. Hannah as a girl with a small dog. Too much after today's events? "I'll buy you a new watch."

"I don't *want* a new watch. I want *this* watch," she muttered angrily, tears choking her and making her voice husky. "Just this one. *Only* this one."

Catching on that there was more to the watch than telling time, he frowned. Since he was older, he hadn't really known her until his family had moved from the outskirts of town into his grandfather's house near Hannah's, but he didn't remember her having a dog. Mitch pressed a kiss to her forehead, his unease growing. He'd heard some nasty rumors and gossip about Hannah's father through the years, but everyone knew to believe half of what they saw and none of what they heard. That was especially true in small towns. If anything had been going on at home while she was growing up, Hannah had never let on. "Okay, I get it, but why that one?" He stared down into her beautiful face, noting the way she bit her lower lip. Clearing his throat, he fought the urge to soothe the ache. "Sweetheart, why that one?"

A fiery red blush crawled up her neck. "Because it reminds me," she whispered, her gaze avoiding his.

"Of the time? Any watch can do that."

She shook her head slowly back and forth, inhaling a ragged breath. "No, not . . . not time, per se, but . . ." She sat up, giving him an unamused look when he didn't let her slide off his lap. Stretching backward, she grabbed the album off the cushion beside them and shoved it at him. "Here."

"What's this?"

She took another fortifying breath. Whatever she had to tell him, he obviously wasn't going to like it.

"This is *why*. It's why I jumped into the canal today a-and why I bought this watch. I used to have a dog, but my father—he did the same thing to Coco when I was eight. He put her in a sack and tossed her off the canal bridge and . . . she didn't make it. I knew what that guy was doing t-today because I'd seen my father do that. That's why I jumped in." Hannah sniffled, then flipped through the pages until she jabbed a finger at a picture of her father, and one of Owen, disdain etched on her face. "The watch reminds me of when I *finally* figured out who I am away from the men who . . . a-abused me. That's why it's so important."

A volcano erupted inside him, spewing anger and red-hot fury so intense he was afraid to try to set her aside on the couch because if he so much as moved, he'd leave to hunt down the men and— "Men? As in plural?" He swore long and loud. "Owen, too? That little SOB—he *hurt* you?"

Head down, she nodded. "I let him. Just like my mom let my dad hurt her."

"Yeah, I can just see you asking them to *hurt* you. Dammit, Hannah, no woman asks for that." He swore again, the images in his head angering him to no end. "Why would you say something like that?"

"Because . . . my father knocked both my mom and me

around when I was growing up," she whispered. "And he always said we deserved it or needed it or . . . *something*. When Owen started doing the same thing, I thought . . . for a while I thought maybe my dad was right." A world-weary smile touched her lips before she lifted her chin. "I know now they were wrong, but back then I felt like I was completely alone in the world, scared of my own shadow."

Jaw tight, he tried not to think about getting his hands on Owen or her father. Best to concentrate on Hannah. "But you're not alone. And you're obviously not scared anymore. No one scared of their own shadow would do what you did today." How many children grow up and follow the example set by their parents? Abusive to children, *pets*?

Hannah had proven herself to be stronger than that—stronger than her past. Remembering her words to the dog today, the final puzzle pieces fell into place. She'd *chosen* to be stronger, to put the past behind her. Which is why she'd just told him the secrets she'd kept for so long. "That took courage, babe, and a lot of it. I'm very, very proud of you. Just don't ever do it again. I thought I'd have a heart attack when I realized it was you I'd dragged out of that canal."

A smile teased her lips up. "It was pretty gutsy, wasn't it?"

"No doubt about it." Mitch tugged on a lock of her hair. "That dog didn't stand a chance without you." He tucked her hair behind her ear, fingering the small shell shape. "Hannah . . . you left town with Owen the day after I told you I loved you. Why?"

6

SHE DIDN'T LOOK AT HIM. "I THOUGHT I WAS DOING the right thing. My mom had just d-died and I couldn't go h-home. Owen—we worked the same hours at the Stop 'n' Shop and we got to know each other there. Sometimes he'd say things but . . . he could be suave, even charming when he wanted to." She snorted. "He always said he worried about me dating you. He knew you didn't like him."

"Got that right. The guy was a class A—"

"Yeah, well, I agree, but at the time I actually appreciated his concern because I thought it was sweet." She made a face. "I thought he was okay. A friend, you know? Then you said you loved me right when everything was happening with the police questioning my dad and I freaked because it was just too much. Owen really seemed to care and he said . . . he said you saying you loved me then was just a control thing. Like my dad with my mom. He said he loved me, too, and he didn't want to see me get hurt because he knew how guys like you operated. That you were possessive and jealous, and that it would only get worse."

Mitch swore silently. "I was jealous of him because he got to spend so much time with you. But, honey, he played you."

She nodded. "I know that. Now, anyway. But Owen and I grew up the same way, the hitting and stuff. He said he wanted to stop and not be like our dads, but he chose not to. Less than a month after we l-left town, he smacked me. Then it got worse."

Mitch was silent a long moment at her words, unable to

speak because of the images in his head. Men who abused women were cowards, every last one of them. "You could've talked to me about this. Told me these things. You didn't have to leave. And you could've come home before now."

Her smile was shaky, cynical. "I had to make the decision on my own. Choose. Fear or strength. Abuse or life. I'm sorry, Mitch. I'm so sorry. I was scared and grieving and angry at what my father had done to my mom. Scared enough that I listened when Owen said big guys like you and my dad liked to take things out on their women." Her hands gripped his chest. "I should've known better. I should've seen through his lies." She sniffled but held his gaze. "It's just . . . with everything going on with my parents, and then h-her accident, it got to a point where every time you looked at me— I didn't want to end up like my mom."

"Sweetheart, I looked at you because I couldn't help myself." He framed her face with his hands, cradling it gently, raising it so she'd see him and not the monsters in her head, in her past. "I look at you because you're beautiful."

"You make me feel that way." A rough laugh escaped her. "And that scares me, too, because now you probably hate me and think I'm nuts."

Mitch ran his hands over her arms in soothing strokes. "None of those. I understand now. I don't like it that you believed the lies and didn't come to me, but at least I get *why* you did it."

Hannah looked down at the watch on her wrist, a wry twist to her lips. "It's taken me awhile to work up to telling you this, but I am because I'm choosing to move on, Mitch. I'm ready." She met his gaze. "I'm finally ready and I came home hoping maybe you'd forgive me and . . . choose me one more time."

The last part of his heart holding out against letting her hurt him again opened. Knowing what she'd been through didn't make the past any easier to accept, but at least now he understood her decisions, her thinking. "Sweetheart, of course I—"

She pressed her lips to his, cutting off his words. Settling himself more comfortably on the couch, Mitch let her kiss him at her leisure, keeping himself well under control by thinking of her watch and who he could contact to get it repaired.

Lifting her head, she frowned at him. "You're holding back."

"I don't want to scare you," he murmured huskily. "I've loved you for so long, I don't want to scare you away again." He cradled her face in his palms, conscious that the flat of one hand could cover her delicate features and then some. Large or small, how could men hurt something so precious?

"Mitch, I want to know what I've been missing all these years. I want . . . I want you. A future. I want it all. I'm sorry I made the wrong choice before, but now I know what I want—who I want. And that's you."

He tilted his head to the side, refusing to consider the time they'd lost or the heartache she'd carried alone, deciding then and there that the past was the past. He couldn't hold the decisions she'd made back then against her now. "I want you, too, sweetheart. So, how about—"

A knock sounded at the door, followed by a male voice clearing his throat loudly. "Am I interrupting?"

Mitch glared at his brother's face on the other side of the screen. "Yes. Go away."

Hannah scrambled off his lap, blushing furiously. "No! Alex, it's . . . uh, it's fine. Come in. Is something wrong with the dog?"

7

ALEX OPENED THE DAMAGED SCREEN DOOR AND stepped through. "Yeah. He's fine, but his owner came to see him. His real owner. Turns out the guy Mitch is looking for is her estranged husband. She heard what happened today, and went home to find her dog missing and her rental trashed. The guy told her if she left him, he'd drown the dog and do worse to her." Alex looked at Mitch. "I already called the station. Your men took a statement from the woman and got a few ideas on where the guy might be. I saw a couple of them handcuffing a guy over on Deemer on my way here. Based on the description, it's probably him. Anyway, I just wanted to let Hannah know that while she—you," he corrected, looking at her and smiling, "won't be bringing home the dog you saved, there are several at the hospital that could use a good home. That is, if you're still interested in having a pet."

Mitch kissed the top of her head and gave her a gentle squeeze. "I'd be glad to help out if you decide you want one."

"Yeah, well, I just wanted to let you know," Alex said. "I'll be going now."

"Thank you, Alex." Hannah smiled, but she was sad at the thought of losing her temporary pet. "I'll think about it and let you know. I appreciate your help today, too. I'll wash the scrubs and bring them back to you."

"Don't go yet." Mitch waved his brother close. "I want you to do something for me. For us."

Alex nodded. "I'll try."

Mitch looked down at her, love in his eyes, his expression heartbreakingly tender. "If Hannah ever comes to you and says she needs help because I've—"

She inhaled sharply. "*Mitch.*"

"—hurt her or scared her in some way, *you* are to beat the crap out of me," he ordered his brother, "and protect her at all costs. Understood? She's leery of the differences in our sizes, and justifiably so. *But,*" he said more softly, sliding a hand into her hair and tugging her close for another kiss, "she's brave enough to trust me now. She knows I'll never intentionally hurt her and that I love her enough to take things slow."

"You love me?" She stared up at him, incredulous.

"I, uh—*ahem.* I definitely interrupted. On that note I think I'll go. But I'll do it," Alex promised with a laugh. "Hannah, I heard what he said, okay? You ever feel the need, you come to me. Day or night, got it? I'll be glad to take him out for you," he added with a good-natured grin. "So, uh . . . yeah. Why don't I lock up on my way out?"

"Do that," Mitch ordered, lowering his head, but stopping a breath away from contact. "Yeah, I love you. I have for a long, *long* time."

Hannah watched as Mitch slowly closed the distance between them, his lips brushing hers. The door shut, and she smiled against Mitch's mouth.

"I'll never hurt you, sweetheart. Your watch might've stopped today, but it's a good thing."

She pulled away, indignant. "No, it's not. I bought it to celebrate my independence, as a symbol of my freedom and my strength as a person."

Mitch gave her another sexy smile. "And it stopped—just when you achieved it. Check the time."

Hannah looked down and blinked. She'd jumped into the canal a little after noon, but her watch hadn't stopped until almost one—around the time when Mitch had told her that he could handle whatever it was keeping them apart and she'd blurted it out. "I think I see what you mean."

"Good."

"But there's one little thing."

"What's that?"

"Do we have to take things slow?"

Mitch paused mere seconds before he slid his hands down to her rump and lifted, sliding her up his body and allowing her to feel his rapidly growing arousal. Gasping, laughing, she parted her legs and wrapped them around his hips.

"Yeah, we do. But you'll like slow," he promised, his voice a husky, seductive growl of want and need and love. He carried her across the floor, every step rubbing her against his hard length, back to the couch where he sat with her straddling his lap. She moaned at the delicious pressure and feel of him beneath her. Slow would drive her insane.

Mitch's big hands slid over her waist, spanning the circumference, his calloused fingers rough against her skin. Excitement flooded her while she watched his fingers slide beneath her T-shirt and up, over her ribs. He cupped and squeezed her breasts, driving her nuts because she wanted more, wanted him not to hold back because she'd seen the bulk of him and not the man beneath the skin and bone. She hadn't seen his heart then, but she did now. Hadn't chosen him then, but she did now.

Hannah placed her hands over his and pressed, loving the heat that burned in his eyes, the firm line of his lips as they parted to draw in more air. He leaned forward on the couch, one hand sliding behind her to support her back while he pushed her bra and shirt out of the way and took her nipple into his mouth. *"Oh."* She tightened her legs around him and snuggled her hips deeper into the cradle of his, wanting to rub, to feel, to—

"Slow, sweetheart," he murmured against her skin, a smile in his voice. "My size comes with other aspects you might not have considered."

She pulled away. "You mean—"

"This will take awhile," he informed her with a sexy grin. "Before I make love to you I want to make sure you're very, *very* ready for me."

"I am."

Mitch slid his hand beneath the wide leg of her shorts and up her thigh toward the heat of her. "I'm still possessive and jealous," he murmured. "And I am going to put a ring on your finger as soon as you're ready. You probably should take that into consideration."

She smiled. "I'd like that. Oh—I like *that*," she moaned as he stroked her. So close. So very, very close.

Opening her eyes proved to be a monumental effort, but she managed just in time for another teasing stroke. His knuckle ran the length of her and brought her to the edge, back and forth until she went flying over, climaxing there on his lap and still fully clothed. Head back and gasping for air, she heard his growl of approval, his declaration of love. She shuddered as she collapsed against his chest in an indelicate sprawl.

Mitch was right. Moving beyond her past might take awhile, but time had stopped—so she could make the right choice for her future. And no doubt about it. She chose Mitch.

THE MOUSE
WHO ROARED

J. C. WILDER

·1·

"YOU REALIZE YOU'RE TAKING ADVANTAGE OF AMY," a deep masculine voice rumbled. "She's a nice woman and a hard worker who deserves better than that."

Amy stood outside her boss's office with a stack of invoices in one hand and the other hung in midair, poised to knock on the door. Slowly she lowered her arm, and the skin on the back of her neck prickled.

"She's a good worker because I pay her to be," Eve replied.

"Isn't that how it normally works?" The male voice was aggravatingly familiar but Amy couldn't immediately place it. "Someone works long hours for you and in return they receive a paycheck. It's the basis of a capitalist society."

"You're so not funny," Eve said.

"Yeah, well, that's what my last ex-wife said."

Clutching the papers to her chest, Amy eased forward to peer through the crack afforded by the partially open door.

Eve, her boss, was seated at her fussy French Provincial desk. She'd removed her designer jacket to reveal a cream colored, lace-trimmed camisole. As usual, every ice-blond hair was in place and she looked as perfect as a model on a magazine cover. Her gaze was focused on the man sitting in the chair on the opposite side of the desk.

Amy gulped when she saw one of their clothing vendors, Dan James, a man Amy had once harbored a secret crush for several years ago. That is, until she found out the very-married Dan was having an affair with the very-unmarried Eve Maxwell, her usually abrasive boss.

He was pleasant enough, but underneath his polished snake-oil-salesman veneer, he was a complete pig. The man had women all over town. She couldn't help but wonder if Eve knew about his other lady friends.

Amy retreated until her back touched the wall. Her stomach was already in a knot when her mother's voice sounded in her mind.

You're just like a ladle, always dipping into someone else's business.

Nervous giggles bubbled up and she slapped a hand over her mouth. The urge to laugh aloud was so strong she was forced to bite her tongue until the desire subsided.

"This weekend is going to be utter heaven," Eve was saying. "With the Mouse in charge of the shop, I can leave everything in her calloused, unpolished hands. Lord knows I could use the break."

Calloused?

Amy looked down at her smooth hands and neatly trimmed nails. Not likely.

"Don't you think you're taking advantage of Amy's loyalty?" Dan asked.

"Do I care?" Her laugh was careless. "She gets a check every week, and besides, I really need to take a break."

"Come on, Eve. You hardly pay her what she's worth." His tone was dry. "She practically runs your store and does any outrageous errand you request of her. If I worked here and you tried that with me, my career would be short-lived."

"Then I'm lucky you don't work for me," Eve purred.

Amy peered into the office again just in time to see the other woman smile at Dan. With her lethal, red-tipped nails, she reached for his hand.

Amy rolled her eyes. The desire to make loud gagging noises was almost irresistible. She couldn't imagine how many erstwhile lovers Eve had shredded with those ghastly she-devil nails.

"Eve, the woman has a degree in business administration," Dan said.

"She wears support hose, for heaven's sake. A woman wearing support hose in a designer clothing store—"

"And a good sense of merchandising . . ."

"Nursing shoes," Eve sneered.

"You said yourself that within six months of her starting here she'd more than doubled your sales."

"Her hair is a train wreck."

"A gifted salesperson."

"And her glasses are *so* eighties . . ."

"She's dependable . . ."

"Tedious . . ."

"Honest . . ."

"Dull as hell."

"Trustworthy."

"You make her sound like a lapdog for some little old lady." Eve laughed.

Lapdog?

"She's hardly a—"

"Oh, for heaven's sake, Dan." Eve sat back with a bemused expression. "You almost sound as if you like the girl."

"I do. She's warm, friendly, intelligent—"

"And she doesn't have a life outside of this shop," Eve snapped. "She works ten- to twelve-hour days even though I only pay her for eight. She spends her lunch hours dreaming about opening a bookstore . . . *A bookstore!* Can you imagine anything more dull? The Mouse has no imagination, no drive. If she did open a bookstore, she'd go under within six months without me to guide her."

Amy's teeth slammed together and her fingers crinkled the edges of the invoices. It took all of her strength not to march into the office and tell both Eve and Dan where to get off.

"Who in the world would want to open a bookstore, for crying out loud? She has no imagination whatsoever."

"Because you haven't read a book since high school, it might come as a shock to you to learn that many people do read." His tone was dry. "Not to mention that Haven doesn't have a decent bookstore. This is a college town; she'd make a fortune selling textbooks at reasonable prices."

"I had no idea you were such a bore, Dan. Maybe I should've made more of an attempt to listen to you after we'd had se—"

"Eve." His tone held a warning.

She tried to soften the blow with a breathy giggle that made Amy want to vomit.

"Listen, baby, I look at it this way. At least by working here she has a chance to meet wealthy men and cultivate some sort of social life. The poor thing wouldn't even have that much if she didn't work here."

"Eve, the patron saint of the socially challenged saleswoman," his tone was sarcastic. "Amy meets men who come into your store to buy lingerie for their wives *and* their girlfriends. That is hardly the type of man she should be getting involved with."

"You mean a man like you?" Eve sneered.

"Exactly." His tone was tight. "She deserves better than someone like me."

Well, at least someone was sticking up for her, even if it was in a backhanded, slightly insulting manner.

"Between you and I," Eve spoke in a loud whisper, "I don't think she's ever had a real date. In the years she's worked here I've never heard her talk about a man."

"And that means she doesn't date?"

"Well, last week I overheard her talking to Carla, and it

seems the Mouse has developed a crush on someone we both know."

"Good for her."

"It's Jack O'Reilly, the fire chief." Eve cackled. "Can you imagine Mouse with a hunk like him?"

"He's a nice guy—"

"Who would never look twice at a woman who dresses like she does." Eve's voice dripped with disdain. "He's gorgeous and can get any woman in town. Why would he want a hag?"

"You're being a bitch, Eve." Dan's tone was sharp.

"You used to like that side of my personality," she purred.

"I was dropped on my head as a child."

"Funny."

"Amy Mouse is a very nice woman, and yes, her wardrobe might be a little out of date, but she has some incredible talents. Any man in Haven would be pleased to walk into a room with her on his arm."

"Humph."

"She's good company in a quiet, understated way, and she has a lovely smile."

"Since when did you ever notice her smile?" Eve sounded perturbed.

Not wanting to hear any more, Amy crept away from the office. She felt as if Eve had stuck a knife in her back. The urge to vomit returned, stronger than before.

Carla stood behind the register with the phone tucked into her shoulder. For the first time Amy paid attention to her sleek figure and stylish clothing. The other woman was dressed in a trendy pink skirt and a V-neck shirt with sparkly lettering across her generous breasts.

WHAT ARE YOU LOOKING AT?

Exactly.

Stepping behind the desk, she tossed the crumpled invoices

into the cubby marked Arrivals. Grabbing her purse from its hiding place, she stalked toward the front door.

"I'm taking an early lunch, Carla."

The other woman held up one finger, indicating she wanted Amy to wait for a moment, but Amy was having none of that. Slinging her purse over one shoulder, she stomped out the wide front door, for once eschewing the employee entrance in the back.

"That horrible, horrible . . . wretch," she muttered.

With determined strides, Amy set off down the busy sidewalk toward the town square with the vague idea of indulging in a giant chocolate milkshake to soothe her battered feelings.

At the best of times Eve was a tolerable boss, especially when she was out running errands or lunching with vendors.

At the worst of times she was incredibly selfish and overbearing. Long ago Amy had lost count of how many lunch hours she'd sacrificed to Eve's manicures, pedicures, or massages. Other than ensuring the store was a financial success, her one goal in life was to look perfect at all times.

Amy's jaw clenched. Who knew Eve's beautiful face and keen business sense would hide such a mean, self-absorbed interior?

Who are you kidding?

With her gaze fixed on the sidewalk, her pace increased. She'd known since day one that Eve was self-centered, but Amy never imagined the woman would spread vicious gossip about her employees to a vendor. Then again, her younger sister always said Amy was naïve because she preferred to see the best in people rather than—

Someone slammed into her shoulder causing her to rock back in her sensible shoes.

"Get out of the way, lady."

Stumbling into the doorway of a bridal shop, she scowled after two youths toting skateboards.

"Well, fiddle!"

Other pedestrians walked past, though none looked in her direction. There were times when Amy felt as if she didn't exist.

Out of the corner of her eye she caught her reflection in the store window. Her long brown hair was pulled back into its customary ponytail and her thick, round glasses with dark frames did remind her of a popular cartoon character. Her lips twisted. How could one woman be born so *plain*?

Her gaze dropped to her sturdy, well-supported walking shoes.

Damn, Eve was right. She was a hag.

Disturbed, Amy resumed her walk, this time at a much slower pace.

It was true she spent her lunch hours dreaming of opening her own bookstore. Books were a passion from her childhood and she'd always had a desire to own her own place, though lately she'd despaired of her dream ever coming to fruition. In six months she'd turn thirty years old, and she was still working for Eve.

How depressing.

Amy wasn't bothered by the years moving past. Her anxiety stemmed from feeling as if her life had been in a holding pattern ever since college. She'd taken an internship with Eve her senior year and then accepted a full-time position after graduation. Let's face it, with a pile of student loans weighing her down, what other choice did she have?

Her original plan was to work at the store for two to four years, saving money and gaining business experience to open her own place. Now, eight years later, what was she doing?

Still working at Eve's Closet.

Her stomach sank. Just last week her best friend asked her if she was afraid to go into business alone. Last year Renee had taken the plunge and bought her own hair salon on the square. According to Renee it was an uphill battle but nothing could beat working for herself.

So what was stopping her?

It certainly wasn't the fear of making a mistake, as she'd made quite a few of those so far. Her grandmother was fond of saying, "Life is full of mistakes, it is the wise woman who pays attention and learns from them." Granny Nell called Amy a serious, cautious young woman. A late bloomer as it were.

So when would she bloom?

It wasn't as if she sat around doing nothing toward achieving her goal. Six months ago she made the terrifying decision to call a Realtor and begin searching for the perfect place to open her store. Jennifer had located three possible buildings, and while they all had promise, there was one that was perfect for her.

The storefront occupied a corner right in the heart of uptown. With huge windows that guaranteed sunlight for the bulk of the day and the original wooden floors and tin ceiling, the space screamed bookstore to her.

Next door was a popular coffee shop, and the college was only a few blocks away. Given the location, combined with the heavy foot traffic, there was no way she could fail.

In her mind's eye, she could see her store as vividly as if it really existed. Plush, cozy chairs and couches grouped in the nooks and crannies provided by the bookshelves, which would be custom-made of course.

She'd stock not only the latest and greatest titles, but familiar favorites like Hemingway and Burroughs. There'd be a separate room for college textbooks, a bright colorful children's area, and some desks for customers to use.

It would have a lazy, comfortable atmosphere where students could kick back in the afternoons, and there would be social events in the evenings. Poetry readings, chats with authors and artists, maybe a roundtable or two.

Maybe the coffee shop would agree to an interior door

between the two stores where customers could get some snacks before browsing the shelves. The store would become a social hub for the town, a peaceful getaway from the inevitable stresses of daily life.

Paradise.

Up until this morning, she'd thought her life to be a little dull but pleasing nonetheless. No, she didn't date much, though contrary to what Eve believed, she'd dated a few men in the past year. But she'd yet to find anyone who captured her attention. It wasn't as if she were waiting for the perfect man to sweep her off her feet, for crying out loud!

Her lips twisted.

Unfortunately, Eve had been correct in one respect: She didn't do much with her time other than work and dream about her store.

Amy came to a halt. What if it never happened?

A vise squeezed her gut and her palms went icy cold. It felt as if all of her adult life had come down to this moment. Ugly and painful, yes, but for the first time ever, Amy could see her life from the outside in.

Dull.

Boring.

Unfulfilled.

Just what the devil are you waiting on, girl?

The shriek of tires and the loud, insistent blare of a horn jolted her back to reality. The bumper of a bright yellow cab was mere inches from her right leg. She blinked. What the heck?

With a start she realized she stood in the center of an intersection, the busiest in Haven.

Not twenty yards away was the storefront, the place she'd always dreamed of. But what if she never made her move? What if tomorrow she were struck dead and she'd done nothing to halt her slide into mediocrity.

Was she destined to die an unfulfilled woman?

It was risky, very risky, but she'd been scrimping and saving for most of her adult life, so money wasn't the issue.

What was?

Fear.

Her breath caught and she slowly turned toward the cab, her gaze coming to rest on the red-faced cab driver who was yelling at her.

She was terrified of failing, of losing the one dream she'd harbored all of her life. If she failed, that dream would fizzle like snow in the sunshine. And then where would she be?

The blare of a horn jerked her back into reality. Staggered by the sudden realization of what was holding her back, her knees went wobbly. Somehow, while she'd been soul searching, she'd managed to create a one-woman traffic jam. Car horns blared, people stared openly while one or two others yelled at her as if she were crazy.

"Lady, are you deaf or something? Get the hell out of my way," the cab driver bellowed.

"No!"

Amy didn't realize she was screaming at the man until her voice echoed off the surrounding buildings. Many of the horns went silent and people began edging away as if she were a dangerous animal.

Haven't these people ever seen a woman have a complete breakdown in an intersection?

"No, I'm not deaf. I'm someone!" she shrieked at the cabbie. "I am going to stand here until this whole dratted town sits up and acknowledges me, Amy Mouse, soon-to-be bookstore owner!"

The cab driver went silent.

Someone in the crowd shouted, "You tell him, girl!"

"Yeah, lady, you're someone all right." The cab driver rolled his eyes clearly believing she was crazy. "Everyone sees you standing in the middle of the street. Now, can you get out of the way? My wife is holding lunch for me."

Looking around, Amy saw the cab driver was right. Everyone within earshot had stopped what they were doing to watch her.

Amy Mouse.

Stunned and more than slightly embarrassed, she clutched her purse and wove her way through the stopped cars until she reached the sidewalk. A few people clapped while most returned to whatever they were doing before she had lost her mind in the middle of the intersection.

Her cheeks burned but she refused to duck her head; not anymore. She was Amy Mouse, a force to be reckoned with in Haven, Ohio.

Digging for her cell phone in the depths of her purse, she hit the speed dial for her Realtor. Her hands were shaking so badly she almost dropped the phone.

"Brooks Real Estate, Jennifer speaking."

"Jen, it's Amy."

"Amy, funny you should call." Paper rustled. "The owner of the storefront on the square just dropped her price by ten thousand—"

"I'll take it."

Silence.

"Are you still there?" Amy asked.

"Wow, that was a quick decision. We've been looking at properties for a few months now—"

"Doesn't matter, I want that one," Amy's gaze landed on the wide windows and the dusty interior. "Make it happen."

"Uh, okay." Jennifer paused. "Can I ask what made you change your mind so abruptly?"

"Fear."

"Fear?"

"I can't explain it right now." A nervous giggle threatened to escape Amy and she had to tamp down the impulse. "Look, I'll come by on Monday to sign the papers, just get me the best deal you can. I'll bring danish and explain everything."

"You've got it." Jen laughed. "I just want you to know that whatever you're on, I want it, too."

Amy laughed then disconnected. Overhead, the sun seemed brighter than before and excitement bubbled just under her skin. She had the strangest desire to break into a song in the middle of the sidewalk.

"Hey, Amy!"

A familiar pickup truck turned the corner and the driver was none other than Jack O'Reilly, the man of her most fevered daydreams.

"When are you going to stop by and see me?" His handsome face sported a wide smile and he waved.

Her stomach tingled. "Soon, very soon." A huge grin nearly cracked her face and she took off with a special destination in mind. "Maybe sooner than you think."

·2·

"HEY, JACK," SEAN, ONE OF THE PARAMEDICS called out. "Where do you want the barbecue setup?"

"Outside the sally port door." Jack circled the truck to open the tailgate. "It might rain and we can use the garage for shelter."

Hefting several twenty-pound plastic bags of ice, he headed for a line of open coolers.

The department was getting ready for the annual Fourth of July cookout with their families. Heading into the holiday weekend, the guys who were stuck on duty wouldn't be able to spend much time with their loved ones, and the barbecue was a fun way for the kids to spend time with their parents and enjoy an early holiday.

The image of Amy standing on the corner flashed into his mind's eye and he grinned.

He did that a lot lately when he thought of her. Though they'd gone to high school together, Jack had to admit he hadn't noticed her. She'd been very shy and he'd been young and full of himself. Back then he thought his life's goal was to date every cheerleader in town.

Luckily for him he'd outgrown those impulses.

Jack headed for the truck.

Over the past year he'd had numerous interactions with Amy, and her quiet smile and wicked sense of humor had grown on him. They'd worked on the city planning committee for the Fourth of July parade on Sunday, and during those months he'd become more aware of her as a woman. Her soft, floral perfume was enough to set his nervous system on high alert and her laugh was enough to send him over the edge.

When he was talking to her he found it difficult to concentrate on her words when all he could think about was kissing her.

He grabbed several more bags of ice.

After the committee meetings he'd asked her out for coffee many times. She'd accept only if other people were coming as well. While he didn't want to share her attention with anyone else, it had been enough to sit beside her and enjoy her relaxed company.

He sounded like a love-struck schoolboy!

Last week he'd asked her out on a date and at first she'd looked terrified, then acted as if he were kidding. Her response was if he wanted to pick up a nice lady, maybe he should join a church.

Jack dumped the bags into the coolers. That was the problem—he didn't want some random woman; he wanted Amy Mouse.

"Do it."

Amy was sweaty and out of breath when she burst through the door of Renee's salon. Throwing her voluminous purse into the chair, she tore off her tan sweater.

"Are you kidding?" Renee sat in the nail tech chair with a glossy fashion magazine in one hand and a can of soda in the other.

"Do I look like I'm kidding?"

"Well, no . . ."

Amy glared at the sweater in her hands. Why was everything in her life beige?

"So what brought this on?" Renee flicked the magazine shut and put it back in the display rack. "Were you hit over the head recently or did the fashion police finally catch up with you?"

"Neither."

Amy tossed the offending sweater into the trash can. For a moment she debated removing her boring sage green dress and tossing it into the bin, though she didn't think the salon would be impressed with her parading around in her serviceable white underwear.

Grabbing her purse, she slung it onto the counter before sitting down and promptly bursting into tears.

"Oh, so that's how it goes." Renee presented her with a box of tissues then hurried off.

Amy knew the other ladies in the salon had scented a drama and were holding their breath to see what would happen next. At this point she couldn't care less. Right now she couldn't have stopped herself from crying any more than she could've prevented the sun from setting.

She blew her nose.

Renee returned with a cape, a towel, and a frozen bar of chocolate, which she shoved into Amy's hands.

"I've far surpassed best friend status because I'm sacrificing my chocolate stash for your breakdown." Renee's gaze met Amy's in the mirror. "Now spill."

"I-I-I overheard Eve at work."

Renee made a rude noise. "What did that she-devil have to say? Nothing pleasant, I'm sure." She removed the ponytail holder, then began combing Amy's hair. "That woman is poison, pure poison."

"She said . . . said . . ." Amy felt the tears threaten again and she tore at the candy wrapper. ". . . I was a hag!"

The last was said around a mouthful of chocolate. Tears spilled over and she began to chew, barely tasting the rich Swiss chocolate.

"She called you a hag? That woman is older than dirt and the only reason she doesn't look like a raisin in the sun is because she and Dr. DeMarco, the cosmetic surgeon over on Oak, are having an affair." Renee shook her dark head. "I swear that woman goes out to lunch then pops over to his office and has her meal sucked out through her ass."

Amy choked, then began to laugh, tears still streaming down her cheeks. Renee always seemed to know what to say to put a smile back on her face.

"I didn't know that Eve had cosmetic surgery."

"Girl! Are you blind?" Renee picked up a pair of sharp scissors.

"I guess so," Amy sniffed.

Renee gathered Amy's long brown hair into a ponytail and their gazes met in the mirror once more.

"Speak now or forever hold your peace," Renee warned. "Once I do this, there is no going back."

"I don't want to go back, not now."

The other woman's smile was broad. "I was hoping you would say that."

Amy felt a slight pressure on her head, then seconds later it was gone—along with eight inches of hair. Her stomach clenched.

"So that's it? The beast-who-shall-not-be-named called you a hag and that was enough for you to go into breakdown, full-out-panic mode?"

"No." Amy's shoulders slumped. Suddenly she felt weary to the bone. "I was going to her office to turn in the invoices when I overheard Eve and Dan—"

"That dishy salesman you had a crush on a while back?"

"That's the one. They were talking about how Eve was taking advantage of me because she suckered me into working this weekend."

"Hey now, you're supposed to go with me—"

Amy held up her hand and Renee fell silent.

"Then she laughed and told him I didn't have a life anyway." She looked up into her friend's deep green eyes. "Please tell me she was lying."

"Truth time?" Renee's brow rose.

Amy's nod was jerky.

"Look." Renee pushed her head forward until her chin touched her chest. "You do have a life, just not a very exciting one to most people."

"But I'm happy."

"No, you're complacent." Renee's tone was matter-of-fact. "You're like most anyone else who gets comfortable with their life and you become lazy. Making changes is a challenge because you feel safe with your life just as it is."

"What's wrong with safe?"

"Nothing if you're a toddler." Renee snorted. "But you're not a child, Amy. Think back to high school."

An image of her teenage face with pimples and metal braces came to mind.

"No, thanks."

"Come on, girl." She tugged on Amy's hair to get her attention. "It's time to move outside your comfort zone. What happened to the girl who was going to turn this white-bread town on its ear with the coolest, hippest bookstore on the planet?"

Amy couldn't help but smile. Her dream of owning a bookstore started very early in life. Many of their free hours had been devoted to planning out their parallel futures to the nth degree.

"I called my Realtor and told her to make a move on the Main and State property."

"Shut up!"

Renee gripped the arms of the chair and flung Amy around so hard the crumpled remains of the chocolate bar flew from her hand.

"Yeah, I did."

Her friend gave a loud squeal. The next thing Amy knew, they were dancing around the salon, shouting with joy. "I'm so proud of you, girl," Renee crowed. "And to think all it took was Eve calling you names." She laughed. "If I'd known that would do the trick I would've been talking trash about you years ago."

Amy laughed. "Well, it took more than that."

"Whatever it took, I'm so happy for you." Renee hustled her back into the chair. "Now, let's make you look like a million dollars."

"Good, that's exactly what I want."

Amy's cell phone began to ring and she ignored it. The custom ring tone told her it was Eve and she'd just bet the other woman wasn't too happy with her right now.

·3·

IT WAS LATE AFTERNOON BY THE TIME AMY RETURNED to the store. With the exception of a wide-eyed Carla still at the desk, the store was deserted. That's what they got for being open on the Friday before a long holiday weekend.

"She's been looking for you—" Carla started.

"I'll bet." Amy stashed her purse in a drawer. "Where is she?"

"Office supply store. She had to run out and pick up more register paper. Boy was she mad." Carla laughed then stopped abruptly. "Wow, check out your hair."

"I know." Amy turned to admire her new haircut in the mirrored wall behind them. "What do you think?"

"Y-you look fabulous," Carla stuttered.

"Thanks. Renee is an amazing hairdresser, isn't she?"

"I'll say."

Somehow her best friend had transformed her normally out-of-control hair into a crop of wide, loopy curls. With her new blond highlights, her hair seemed to have a life of its own. It was spunky, curly, and very different from what she was used to. It was the hair style of a confident woman, not a mouse.

"Did Ellen make it in yet?"

"Ah, yeah, she got here a few minutes ago."

"Good. Call her up to the front, as I'm going to need your assistance."

"Okay." Carla, like most cashiers, was always happy to escape the register.

Eve's Closet was one of Haven's most upscale clothing

stores, carrying anything from Armani suits to designer jeans. It was *the* place to shop, and Amy was about to take full advantage of her employee discount.

Bypassing the expensive suits, she headed for the summer clothing. Skinny little dresses, short shorts, and minuscule T-shirts abounded in this area, and most of them were far more expensive than she'd ever think of paying for any single item of clothing.

But right now, that just didn't seem to matter.

"Okay." Carla literally skipped toward her. "What do you need help with?"

"What do you think?" Amy snatched a babydoll dress from one of the racks. "Red or yellow?"

"You're shopping?" Carla looked astounded. "But you never buy your clothes here."

"Then it's time for a change, isn't it?"

Amy held the dress in front of her, then wrinkled her nose. It would make her look pregnant, which was definitely *not* what she was going for.

"No." Carla snatched the dress from Amy's hands. "It's so not you. You have great legs, girl. Let's look at some shorts."

Carla took her arm and Amy let her lead the way. The other woman was a gifted fashion stylist and Amy knew she wouldn't lead her astray.

After trying on what felt like hundreds of outfits, Amy knew the moment she'd struck fashion gold.

The image in the mirror was so different from her everyday self that she hardly recognized the woman staring back at her. Long gone was the untidy hair and oversized clothing, and in its place was a younger, hipper creature.

Pale rose capri pants accented her shapely legs and silently she gave thanks to the owners of her apartment building, as more often than not the elevator was on the blink and she had to run up four flights of stairs to her apartment.

Her shirt was a simple crop top with narrow spaghetti straps that made wearing a bra impossible. On the clearance rack Carla had found a sheer white blouse and the hem had given way on one side. Amy tied the shirt around her waist, both concealing the lack of hem while leaving her not feeling quite so exposed.

Carla threw back the curtain to the dressing room and gave a loud whistle. "Girl, you're a hottie with a naughty body. Who knew all that loveliness was under those hideous clothes?"

"Yeah, who knew?" Amy's voice was faint.

"All we need now are some shoes." Carla was staring at Amy's feet. "White sandals with something sparkly. Wait, I have the perfect pair." She headed out of the dressing room again.

Even with the mirror in front of her, she could barely comprehend what she was seeing. With her new hair style and modern clothing she was looking pretty good. She twisted in the mirror to check her backside. FLIRT in silver thread and a rhinestone heart occupied the left pants pocket. She grinned.

Flirt, indeed.

What would Jack say when he saw her? Would he be shocked?

She bit her lower lip. He'd asked her out on a date, though at the time she didn't dare believe he'd been serious. Just the thought of sitting alone in a restaurant with Jack O'Reilly was enough to give her hives. What would she say to him?

He seemed to date quite a bit, though lately she hadn't heard his name linked with anyone else. Maybe he was taking a break?

Maybe he'd found that someone special . . .

Her heart gave a painful twinge. She didn't want to think about that possibility. She was going to keep her head up, march into that fire station and—

"Found them!"

A breathless Carla ran into the dressing room. "One pair left in your size." She opened the glossy box and inside were a pair of simple white sandals with silver rhinestones in the center of the leather strap across the foot.

"Those are perfect," she breathed.

Amy was giddy when she slipped them on. The tiny heel added about a half inch to her short stature, and she'd take any extra height she could get. Jack was at least six inches taller than she was.

"You're all set, girl," Carla said. "I don't know what you're up to but I hope he appreciates it."

"Who said there's a he involved?" Amy couldn't wipe the smile off her face.

"Because you're beaming. That kind of smile usually has a man behind it."

Amy laughed. "Not quite. I will say one thing, though. If you want to put a big smile on your face, go out and tell Eve you quit. If that doesn't make you happy, then nothing will."

"Where in the hell is everyone?" a voice bellowed from the direction of the front desk.

"She's back." The two women looked at each other then dissolved into laughter.

"You'd better head up front," Amy said. "I'll be right behind you."

"Got it."

Carla slipped from the tiny dressing room, leaving Amy to pick up the clothing she'd picked out. Careful to keep the items she wanted on top, she heaped the rejected clothing and hangers into her arms then headed to the front.

Eve stood near the desk, her normally immaculate hair wind-blown and her cheeks bright with anger.

"Will someone tell me where in the hell Amy is?" she shouted at Ellen and Carla.

"Right here." Amy dropped the pile of clothing on the counter.

"Where the—"

Eve caught sight of her and Amy thought for a moment the other woman's eyes were in danger of popping out of her head.

"W-what . . . w-where . . . what the hell have you done with yourself?" the other woman sputtered.

"I had my hair done. Do you like?" Amy reached up and twisted a fat curl around one finger. "It remains to be seen if I can keep it looking like this, but I'm going to give it a good try."

"All you need is a good curling iron." Carla popped her gum. "And a little styling gel. It's really no big deal—"

"I do *not* want to hear about Amy's hair care regime," Eve interrupted. "Where have you been all afternoon? I don't remember giving you time off."

"I don't remember asking." Amy shrugged. "I figured since you take off all the time I was entitled to a few hours as well." Her gaze met Eve's. "Seeing as I'm working this weekend so you can go to the spa."

Eve blinked. "Well—"

"Not that I mind working. I just wish you hadn't lied to me about it."

Amy began putting the rejected clothing on the hangers to be put back on the racks. That was one thing she'd miss about not working here—she adored eyeing the scrumptious fabrics and checking out the latest styles.

"Lied?" Eve's laugh was high and forced. "Who ever said I lied? I told you I was going home to see my parents—"

"And you lied." Amy continued working. "I overheard you talking to Dan in your office earlier."

"What? You were listening in on my private conversation?" she blustered.

"If your conversation was meant to be confidential then you should've shut your door."

Eve slapped a plastic shopping bag on the counter, almost hitting Carla. Her gaze was sharp.

"What else did you hear?" she hissed.

Amy looked her boss straight in the eye. "Everything." Taking the last hanger, she put it on the rack at the end of the counter. "I never realized you disliked me quite as much as you do."

Eve's skin flushed.

Busted!

"I don't dislike you, Amy," she twittered. "How can you even think that?"

"Come clean, Eve. We've worked together for the past eight years and I know you. You're rude to your employees; you constantly try to scheme your way through life, never realizing that people will gladly help you out if you'd treat them with respect and a little compassion." Amy pulled her bag out from its drawer. "Not everyone is out to get you, you know."

"Of course not. What a silly notion." Her tone was stiff.

"Here are your clothes, Ms. Mouse." Ellen handed her a stuffed shopping bag. "I've used your employee discount; shall we put this on your account?"

"No, Carla, you can take the balance due from my final check." Amy shouldered the bag. "Now, if you ladies will excuse me—"

"Oh, no you don't." Eve moved between her and the front door. "You can't have the rest of the day off, too—"

"I don't need the rest of the day off, Eve." Amy smiled wide and the other woman looked momentarily relieved. "Because I quit."

Eve blinked and Carla began to laugh.

"You what?!"

"Quit." Amy walked toward the front door.

"But you can't quit. I have reservations!"

"You'll have to change them. That happens from time to time."

"But where will you go?" Eve snapped. "No one will hire you and I won't give you a decent reference."

"I don't need your reference, Eve." Amy shot back. "I'm opening my bookstore within six months and I'd be happy to send you an invite to the opening, but you don't read, do you?"

Carla laughed even louder while Ellen looked both horrified and stunned. Amy waved at the two girls behind the counter.

"And, ladies, if you ever need a job, please don't hesitate to stop by and give me a holler."

"You've got it," Carla said.

Ellen looked as if she were going to faint. The poor girl had never dealt with Eve one-on-one. Boy, was she in for an experience.

Amy exited the store while behind her all hell broke loose. She smiled as Eve began screaming at the top of her lungs.

·4·

"HEY, CHIEF, SOMEONE HERE TO SEE YOU!" FRED Raines, one of the new firefighters, came jogging over. "She's waiting in your office."

"Thanks, Probbie. Why don't you man the grill until I get back?" He handed the spatula to the firefighter.

"Gee, thanks." His grin was wide. "I don't know who she is, but she's hot."

"Hot?" Jack grabbed his uniform shirt, wincing when he put it on over his sweaty T-shirt. "Boy, at your age you think anything with breasts is hot."

Raines chuckled. "You have a point, but this lady, she's really hot. A four-alarm fire, if you ask me."

"I didn't ask, but thanks anyway, son. Now flip some burgers."

"Yes, sir."

Jack headed for the station door. The back lot and garage were packed full of people, tables, and tents. The adults seemed to be enjoying themselves, while the kids played any number of games.

The station was blissfully cool and quiet when the door shut behind him. Raines said his visitor was hot, though Jack didn't care much about that. He'd give up a hundred good-looking visitors if Amy would show up at the cookout.

His office door was propped open and a woman leaned against the edge of his desk. Raines had been right about one thing—she was hot.

From the tips of her dainty sandals to her tousled, curly

hair, she was lovely. Her wide, terrified hazel gaze met his and a shock jolted his system.

It was Amy, and it would appear his wish was about to come true.

She was ready to bolt by the time Jack filled the doorway, or at least she hoped it was him, as without her glasses she couldn't see a darned thing. Her palms were damp and her knees were incapable of supporting her. If it wasn't for the desk she'd be on the floor in a split second.

Not exactly the way she wanted this moment to play out.

"Amy?"

His voice was low and the sound sent shivers down her spine. Seeing that her tongue was suddenly glued to the roof of her mouth, she couldn't trust herself to speak, so she nodded instead.

"Wow, look at you."

He walked toward her and she didn't have to see his eyes to know he was scrutinizing her new look. The heat of his gaze warmed her skin.

"You look amazing. I mean, you looked good before—"

"Thank you, Jack."

"I'm speechless."

"That's a first."

She stepped closer and inhaled the scent of burning wood, barbecue, and sunshine. "Are you surprised to see me? I mean, you did ask me to stop by."

"That I did." His grin grew. "So you stopped by for some barbecue and fireworks?"

Her legs were shaky but she forced them to take her closer to him.

"Is that the agenda for the evening?"

Up close she could finally see his expression was a mixture

of admiration and pleasure. A slow tingle awoke in her belly.

"It is." His gaze fixed on her mouth and he licked his lips. "Unless you have something else in mind?"

"That depends on your flexibility." She stood close enough to him that every nerve was on high alert. "I'm the kind of woman who enjoys the unexpected."

"Is that so?"

"It is." She laid her hand on his arm: the muscles contracted beneath her palm. "May I escort you to dinner?"

"You have no idea how long I've waited to hear that from you." Jack's big hand landed over hers and that sexy smile grew wide. "It would be my pleasure."

Anticipation hummed through her veins when he tucked her hand into the crook of his arm. She, Amy Mouse, was going to spend the evening with the man of her dreams.

They walked out into the hot sunshine and the scent of grilled meat and the laughter of children assailed her. It had been a long and simply amazing day, and Amy knew the only thing that could possibly make it better would be a long, soulful kiss from the man who held her hand.

COPYRIGHT NOTICES

ABOUT THE CONTRIBUTORS

Lori Foster first published with Harlequin in January 1996. Since those early days, Lori has routinely had six to ten releases a year. She's a Waldenbooks, *USA Today*, *Publishers Weekly*, and *New York Times* bestselling author with more than sixty titles published through a variety of houses, including Berkley/Jove, Kensington, St. Martins, Harlequin, and Silhouette. Lori visits daily with readers as part of the "Running with Quills" blog at www.runningwithquills.com and at her message board featured on her website www.LoriFoster.com.

Toni Blake wanted to be a writer from the time she was ten years old. Early in her career, Toni was a recipient of the Kentucky Women Writers Fellowship and a nominee for the prestigious Pushcart Prize for literary fiction, as well as having more than forty short stories and articles published. Since 1998, Toni has written romance novels for NAL, Kensington, Harlequin, and Warner Books, and is currently writing sexy romances for Avon.

Dianne Castell gained a love for the romance genre when her daughter tossed her a dog-eared, clinch-cover Harlequin. She said it was "great," then confessed it had been passed around the eighth-grade class as a "supplement" to their sex ed class. Dianne was instantly hooked on Harlequins, and it wasn't long before she started writing stories of her own. She lives with her husband and four kids in Milford, Ohio, and writes humorous, sexy stories set in small-town USA because there's nothing more fun than falling in love.

Karen Kelley became adept at how things work in the publishing world. You write a book, mail it off, get rejected, and write another book. She did this for six years until one day she talked her husband into mailing her manuscript for her. She couldn't take one more look of pity from the postal workers. Being the loving husband that he is, he mailed *Bachelor Party* to Hilary Sares at Kensington for the Precious Gem line on a Tuesday. On Friday that same week, Hilary called to offer Karen a contract. Currently Karen writes for Brava with Kensington Publishing and has the fabulous Kate Duffy for an editor.

Rosemary Laurey is a *USA Today* bestselling author, an expatriate Brit, a retired special ed teacher, and a grandmother, who now lives in Ohio and has a wonderful time writing stories of vampires and shape-shifting pumas.

Janice Maynard, who lives in east Tennessee, writes sweet and funny romances with super hot love scenes for NAL's Signet Eclipse imprint. She has been happily married for many years and has two grown daughters who make her proud. Please visit her at www.janicemaynard.com.

Erin McCarthy sold her first book to Kensington Brava through author Lori Foster's website contest in 2002, much to her continued amazement. Twenty-four books later, Erin is entertaining both Brava and Berkley readers with her sassy, sexy tales of contemporary and paranormal romance. Her Las Vegas Vampires series debuted in August 2006, with *High Stakes* hitting number one on the Barnes and Noble trade romance list. Erin has also sold two paranormal young adult novels under the name Erin Lynn.

LuAnn McLane writes for Signet Eclipse, an imprint of New American Library. Although she enjoys penning sensual contemporary romances, she now also writes romantic comedy, including *Dark Roots and Cowboy Boots*, an August 2006 release followed by *Dancing Shoes and Honky Tonk Blues* in May 2007. *Love, Lust and Pixie Dust,* her current release, is a sexy, whimsical comedy with a touch of paranormal elements set in Nashville, her favorite city to visit. She lives in Florence, Kentucky, just outside of Cincinnati, Ohio, and when taking breaks from writing, she enjoys long walks, watching chick flicks with her daughter, and trying to keep track of her three active sons. She loves to hear from her readers. You can reach her at luann@luannmclane.com.

Lucy Monroe sold her first book in September of 2002. Since then she has sold more than thirty books to three publishers and hit national bestsellers lists in the United States and England. She's a passionate devotee to the romance genre and her highly charged, sensual stories touch on the realities of life while giving the reader a fantasy story not easily forgotten. Whether it's a passionate Harlequin Presents, a sexy single title for Kensington or a steamy historical or paranormal for Berkley, Lucy's books transport her readers to a special place where the heart rules and love conquers all.

Patricia Sargeant mixes sensual romances with suspenseful plots as a backdrop for her strong, engaging characters. In addition to the national Romance Writers of America (RWA), Patricia is a member of two RWA chapters, the Central Ohio Fiction Writers, and the Futuristic, Fantasy & Paranormal chapters. She's also a member of Shades of Romance.

Kay Stockham sold her seventh completed manuscript to Harlequin Superromance in February 2005, and hit the Waldenbooks Bestseller List at number seven eight months later. In little more than a year and a half, she's sold an additional six novels to Superromance, three of which were on the shelves in 2007 featuring a single mom struggling with a secret-ridden Goth teen, a breast cancer survivor and an amnesiac soldier. For more information on Kay and her books, check out www.kaystockham.com.

J. C. Wilder left the world of big business to carry on conversations with the people who live in her mind—fictional characters that is. She has worked as a software tester, traveled with an alternative rock band, and currently volunteers for her local police department as a photographer. She lives in Central Ohio with six thousand books and an impressive collection of dust bunnies. The award-winning author also writes as Dominique Adair and you can visit her website at http://www.jcwilder.com or email her at wilder@jcwilder.com.